A Chorus
OF
Detectives

Also by Barbara Paul

A Chorus
OF
Detectives

BARBARA PAUL

St. Martin's Press
New York

This novel contains the names of real people, but it is in no way intended to represent their true characters or opinions.

Design by Paolo Pepe

Library of Congress Cataloging in Publication Data

Paul, Barbara, 1931–
    A chorus of detectives.
    I. Title.
PS3566.A82615C4   1987   813'.54   87-4394
ISBN 0-312-00576-8

First Edition

10 9 8 7 6 5 4 3 2 1

A Chorus
OF
Detectives

1   Giulio Gatti-Casazza, general manager of the Metropolitan Opera, was not in the habit of taking orders from scrub-ladies. But this time he thought he'd better make an exception.

"You come!" The woman was wild-eyed and distraught, motioning with both arms to compensate for her imperfect grasp of the English language. "Evil thing. Come now!"

Evil thing? Gatti-Casazza gestured to her to lead the way. A big, lumbering man now with gray in his beard, Gatti did not normally move quickly; he had to exert himself to keep up with the woman.

The scrublady led him to the chorus dressing room on the fourth floor but stopped at the doorway. "Inside. You go!" she commanded imperiously, and refused to budge.

With a shrug Gatti stepped into the dressing room—and gasped. There, dangling from an overhead water pipe, the body of a man rotated slowly back and forth, his eyes bulging in death. Gatti covered his own eyes with one hand; the poor man had hanged himself with his own suspenders.

Evil thing. When Gatti could stand to look again, he recognized the dead man as one of the tenors in the chorus. A new man, hadn't been with the Met long. With heavy step Gatti moved over to stop the obscene rotation of the body. The corpse was still warm.

The general manager edged back out into the hallway and closed the door behind him. He hurried downstairs and rounded up three stagehands to take down the body. After explaining their unpleasant chore, he swore them to secrecy. "The other choristers, they must not know of their comrade's sad end until after the performance tonight," he insisted. "It is hard enough even then!"

The stagehands gave their word. "But won't they miss him?" one of them asked.

Gatti pulled nervously at his beard. "Perhaps they think he is ill. I myself tell them afterward." He took out his watch and checked the time. "Please! The others, they start to arrive any moment now. You must make haste."

Without another word the stagehands hurried up the stairs. That evening's opera was *Mefistofele,* a work that kept the chorus fairly busy; perhaps they would not have time to worry about the missing tenor. Belatedly, Gatti remembered the scrublady and looked around for her.

She had disappeared.

"The poor man," soprano Geraldine Farrar said the next day. "What could have gone so wrong in his life that he'd do such a thing? He wasn't very old, was he?"

"A mere boy," Antonio Scotti replied, "only twenty-nine, Gatti says." He adjusted the limousine's lap rug. "Are you warm enough, *cara mia*?"

"I'm fine," she murmured absently. "That's two members of the chorus who've died—and within four days of each other."

"Ah, but the young soprano—she does not kill herself, remember. An accident, *cara* Gerry."

And such a bizarre one, Gerry thought. Right before the final scene of last Friday's performance of *Samson and Delilah,* an ornamental urn had toppled from its pedestal on to the head of the chorister unlucky enough to be standing beneath it. Fortunately the curtain had not yet opened and the audience was spared the sight of a member of the Metropolitan Opera chorus dying on stage. "It wasn't even a real urn," Gerry said. "It was only a stage prop."

"But heavy enough to crush the skull," Scotti remarked. "The opera stage—it can be dangerous place, no?"

"So can the street," Gerry gasped as the limousine unexpectedly swerved to avoid hitting a crowd of people. "What is it, Albert?"

"Don't know, Miss Farrar," the chauffeur said. "Buncha men carrying signs. Couldn't see what they said."

"Veterans, probably. Could you read the signs, Toto?"

Scotti shook his head. "Anarchists," he muttered darkly. "They are everywhere."

Gerry peered through the tiny back window of the limousine. "No, I think they're veterans. Several of them are on crutches. What a sad sight."

The war had ended two years earlier, but the peace that followed had proved an uneasy one. Nothing could go back to what it had been, but the discontent that muttered and throbbed and threatened constantly to erupt into violence was in its own way as frightening as the war itself had been. The Allies' long-awaited triumph over the Central Powers had not restored harmony to the world, as everyone had been so sure it would do.

That lack of political harmony was nowhere more evident than at the Metropolitan Opera, where the international make-up of the company was a source of constant friction. During the war, singers, conductors, managers, members of the orchestra, valets, maids, and backstage workers had all divided into antagonistic camps, each individual loyal to his or her home country. Gatti-Casazza had responded to the American audiences' patriotic fervor and let all the German soloists go, vowing that the Metropolitan would be at least half American. Wagner was dropped from the repertoire.

The wound left by the war was deep and only now beginning to heal over. In the fall of 1920, Gatti-Casazza had nervously restored Wagner to the repertoire—but Wagner sung in English; the German language was still anathema to most of America. The first postwar performance of *Tristan and Isolde* had gone off without incident, however, and the opera company began to breathe a little more easily. But now a few weeks later, in December, resentments and bad feeling still lingered; it would be a while yet before any 'family' atmosphere returned to the Metropolitan Opera.

. The limousine carrying two of the Met's most lustrous stars turned on to Park Avenue just south of Grand Central Station and came to a stop in front of the Vanderbilt Hotel. Enrico Caruso and his wife had moved into the penthouse apartment only a few months earlier and had been 'warming the house', as the tenor put it, ever since. Gerry Farrar had missed one of the Carusos' lavish dinner parties the evening before because of a prior engagement, so both Enrico and Dorothy Caruso had insisted she come to lunch to make up for it.

"You eat the left-behinds, yes?" the tenor had said, his face a study of guilelessness.

It was a joke; Caruso would slit his wrists before he'd allow leftovers to be served at his table. So Gerry had come to the Vanderbilt for her compensatory luncheon; Scotti, who had been at the dinner party, came along because he always came along.

"*Cara* Gerry! Toto!" Caruso greeted first the soprano and then the baritone with a warm embrace. Dorothy Caruso smiled and extended her hands in a less Italianate welcome.

"Rico!" Scotti exclaimed in mild alarm. "Something you eat— it does not agree with you?"

The tenor spread both hands and placed them on his expansive waist. "Everything I eat agrees with me! Why you ask?"

"You do not look well."

Caruso waved one arm dismissively. *"È niente."*

"His color is not good," Gerry said to Dorothy, low. "Has he seen a doctor lately?"

"Several," Dorothy answered with a delicate grimace. "But I do not trust them. Besides, Rico thinks it's a sign of weakness to give in to illness."

Italian men, Gerry thought glumly.

Lunch was light—broiled chicken; Dorothy had finally convinced her dangerously overweight husband that it wasn't necessary to eat pasta at every meal. Halfway through the luncheon Caruso sighed and said, apropos of nothing, "I miss you, Gerry."

The other three at the table knew what he meant. No one had seen the names of Enrico Caruso and Geraldine Farrar on the same printed program since opening night of the preceding season. The two stars sold out the house every time either one of them sang, so Gatti-Casazza had figured he was losing money by scheduling them in the same production. It had been over a year now since they'd sung together. "Maybe Gatti will change his mind," Gerry said to Caruso, not really believing it.

Talk inevitably turned to the man who'd hanged himself in the chorus dressing room. There was some speculation as to why he'd done it, but no one knew the man well enough to suggest a reason with any certainty. Then someone mentioned the young chorus woman who'd died on Friday.

"I see it!" Caruso exclaimed, bug-eyed. "I stand in the wings and look straight out to the stage and I see it happen!"

"Try not to think of it, dear," Dorothy said in her genteel voice.

As a matter of fact, Caruso had been flirting with one of the dancers in the ballet at the time of the accident, but by now he was thoroughly convinced he'd witnessed the whole thing. The last scene of *Samson and Delilah* takes place in the temple that the hairless hero ultimately brings down; with the soloists, the chorus members, and the corps de ballet all on at the same time, the stage did get a bit crowded. It was understandable how someone might jar the pedestal and dislodge the lethal urn.

"Perhaps she did it herself," Gerry suggested. "Bumped against the pedestal, I mean. What a horrible way to die! I'd just assumed all those urns and pedestals and things were anchored in place."

"They are supposed to be," Scotti said.

"No, no, she touches nothing!" Caruso insisted. "She just stands there, and—*crash!* The urn, it falls on her head! *Per dio!* We are none of us safe, no?" The tenor shuddered as intimations of his own mortality touched him.

"A lot of people are on stage for that scene," Gerry commented. "I suppose vibrations from the stage floor could have started the urn wobbling."

"That stage, it is not safe!" Caruso exclaimed.

"Nowhere is safe," Scotti contributed somberly. "On our way here, we see anarchists rioting in streets, Gerry and I!"

"Oh, Toto!" Gerry laughed in exasperation. "That was no riot. And they weren't anarchists, they were veterans. Don't exaggerate."

"Veterans can be anarchists too," the baritone proclaimed earnestly. "These anarchists, they are everywhere. And those two in Massachusetts—they want to set them free!" Of the entire Italian community at the Metropolitan Opera, Scotti was the only one who thought Sacco and Vanzetti were guilty.

"Let's not talk politics," Dorothy murmured quickly as she saw her husband starting to turn red. "Tell me, Gerry—when do you sing your first *Butterfly* this season?"

The soprano acknowledged that a change of subject might be wise. "Not for another few weeks. On Christmas Eve."

"But. . . ?" Dorothy cast a puzzled look toward her husband. "I thought you were singing *La Juive* Christmas Eve, Rico."

"*Sì*, Doro—*La Juive.*"

"*Butterfly* is the matinee performance," Gerry explained.

"Ah. Then, Toto, you must be singing the matinee with Gerry."

"*Ma certo,*" Scotti said, lifting Gerry's hand to his lips with a smile. "Always."

Gerry sighed; it was a little scene she should be used to by now. Scotti was perpetually announcing to the world that he was head over heels in love with Geraldine Farrar.

Again.

Gatti-Casazza sat in his office at the Seventh Avenue and Thirty-ninth Street corner of the Metropolitan Opera House. Although the steam heat was on full, he was wearing overcoat, muffler, and gloves. Even after twelve years, Gatti had never gotten used to New York winters.

Less than a month into the new season, he was worried. Caruso was not in the best of health. Baritone Pasquale Amato had cancelled a performance, unusual for him. Soprano Emmy Destinn was not herself—had not been, in fact, ever since her return to the Met after the war's end. And it had been a mistake to let Geraldine Farrar sing Marguérite in *Faust*. Her top notes, alas, were gone— and not only her top notes. Since her throat operation a couple of years ago, Gerry's voice had lost something. The operation, coming as it did in the midst of the trauma of an ugly divorce, had taken its toll; the voice had never quite returned to form.

Not that it made any difference to the singer's popularity;

Geraldine Farrar was still the public's *beniamina,* the pet child who could do no wrong. She was the only Carmen the Met audiences wanted. Her *Zazà,* now in its second year of production, was a *succès de scandale.* A Farrar performance still filled every seat in the house, and every year the soprano attracted new gerryflappers—those hordes of teen-aged girls who jumped up and down and squealed every time their idol opened her mouth. But the role of Marguérite in *Faust* was too high for Gerry now; letting her sing it had been a mistake.

All of which was why Gatti-Casazza was thinking now in terms of back-up singers and eventual replacements. Young Rosa Ponselle had enchanted New York audiences from the moment she first set foot on the stage—but she was still learning; she had a long way to go yet. Not so with Maria Jeritza, the Viennese soprano Gatti was bringing to the Metropolitan the following year. Jeritza was an established star, and a glamour girl in the tradition of Farrar. New York would love her. Geraldine Farrar would not.

But that wasn't all. Sad as the thought was, Gatti mused, Caruso couldn't go on forever; eventually he, too, would have to give way to a younger singer. No one could ever replace Caruso, of course, but the world was full of young tenors eager to try. Gatti had taken a chance on one of them, and on November 26, 1920, newcomer Beniamino Gigli had made his Metropolitan Opera début. The audience had responded warmly to the bright-voiced new tenor; if their enthusiasm continued unabated through the rest of the season, the transition to the next generation of singers might go a little easier when the time came.

Gatti's assistant, a man named Edward Ziegler, walked briskly into the office, the very picture of no-nonsense efficiency. With his silver hair parted in the middle and wearing rimless pince-nez, Ziegler looked more like an investment banker than an opera impresario's assistant. His presence had its usual effect of making Gatti straighten his shoulders. "Quaglia and Setti have agreed on the new chorus tenor," Ziegler said. "I'll make out a pay sheet."

The general manager grunted. "They agree? Unusual."

"Actually, the man is Quaglia's choice," Ziegler said. "Setti gave in just to keep the peace. He doesn't have the appetite for controversy the Maestro does."

Alessandro Quaglia was a conductor now in his second season at the Metropolitan. An imperious and inflexible man, Quaglia was not the one to yield when differences of opinion arose. Giulio Setti, on the other hand, was usually tactful and persuasive enough to get what he wanted without having the matter come to a confrontation. Something must have gone wrong this time. Setti was the Met's chorus master; he'd come to New York from Milan with Gatti-Casazza . . . and with Toscanini. When that temperamental conductor had eventually departed the Metropolitan in a huff, Setti had stayed. Gatti trusted him and valued his opinion.

"Eh, it is good to have this unpleasant business done with," Gatti murmured, more to himself than to Ziegler. The singer just hired was the replacement for the unfortunate man who'd hanged himself. The Metropolitan had a pool of available singers to draw upon when the need arose, both choristers and soloists alike. The replacement of the dead man should have been a simple matter; but Quaglia, it sometimes seemed to Gatti, enjoyed complicating things. Probably it was only a way of asserting his authority; any conductor living in the shadow of the great Toscanini was bound to feel diminished by comparison now and then.

Ziegler interrupted his thoughts. "We may have a problem, Mr. Gatti. Emmy Destinn is now saying she doesn't want to sing on Christmas Day."

Gatti-Casazza muttered one word: "Contract."

"Oh, she's read her contract. She's saying she may wake up ill Christmas morning. We have a *Tristan* scheduled for the Wednesday after Christmas—I suppose we could switch." His tone of voice made it clear he thought little of his own suggestion. A rather frosty man by nature, Ziegler had scant patience with singers' whims. "Shall I make the change?"

"No." Gatti got up from his desk. "*Aïda* is scheduled for Christmas Day and *Aïda* it will be. I talk to Emmy."

"Do you think it will do any good?" Ziegler asked. "Nothing seems to please her anymore."

Gatti shrugged and changed the subject. "The new man—Setti coaches him now?" At Ziegler's nod he walked out of the office; he wanted to make sure the chorus master was satisfied with Quaglia's choice.

As Gatti cut through the foyer, he had to detour around a woman down on her knees wringing water out of a rag over a scrub bucket. He looked again and saw it was the woman who'd led him to the dead man in the chorus dressing room.

"Excuse me," he said to her, "I do not have chance to thank you for . . ." Gatti trailed off when he realized she didn't understand what he was saying. He tried Italian. *"Le sono molto tenuto. . . ."* But she just gazed at him uncomprehendingly. Gatti raised his voice and tried again. "What is your name?"

At the word *name* the woman's face lit up. "Mee-zhus Bukaitis. Bukaitis." She jabbed a forefinger against her chest three or four times to make sure he understood.

Gatti smiled. "Mrs. Bukaitis, I want to thank you for your help. I know it is upsetting for you. . . ." She was scowling. Gatti ended up doing a pantomime of a hanging man.

Mrs. Bukaitis slapped both hands over her eyes and let loose a stream of words in a language the general manager didn't know. The scrubwoman shook her head vigorously and went back to her job of cleaning the lobby floor, apparently not knowing she'd just been thanked.

Gatti sighed and continued on his search for Setti and the new chorus tenor. He found them in a small rehearsal room; the chorus master was seated at a piano, playing with his left hand and conducting with his right. Setti was a small man and getting on in years; he looked like a gnome hunched over the keyboard. The new tenor had a good voice, one with an unusual quality to it. Gatti stood in the doorway until the chorus master noticed him. Setti told the singer to wait and stepped out into the hall.

"You are satisfied?" Gatti asked. "You do not take someone you do not want?"

"No, no—a good singer, this one," Setti reassured him, his head tilted back to gaze up at the much taller man. "My only concern is—his voice, does it blend with the others in the chorus? You notice the distinctive sound?''

"*Sì*, I notice."

"Well, we find out tomorrow night. In *Pagliacci.*"

"You start him so soon?"

"He knows the music. *Pagliacci* tomorrow night, and *Carmen* Thursday. *Parsifal* he does not know—in English, that is. So he does not sing Friday. But by then we know if he blends with the other choristers or not."

Gatti nodded. "Eh, that is all right, then."

"Perhaps." Setti scowled. "The other choristers—they may make trouble for him."

"*Cielo*—why?"

The chorus master shrugged, a gesture involving arms, shoulders, and back. "Who knows why? Always they fight—they *look* for things to fight about. The Italian singers hate the Austrians, the Austrians hate the French, the French hate the Germans, the Germans hate the Americans, and the Americans hate everybody. Squabble, squabble, squabble! And when they fight among themselves, they do not listen to *me.*" His eyes twinkled. "Sometimes I think I fire them all and start over from scratch."

"Oh, you cannot do that!" Gatti was aghast, taking him literally. "To train an entirely new chorus . . . in midseason? Unthinkable!"

Setti grinned. "Eh, perhaps I fire only part of them. The German part, yes?"

Gatti understood he was joking and gave him a weak smile. "In time, the squabbling stops. The war is over. They cannot go on fighting forever. It is against human nature."

The chorus master grimaced. "I wish I share your view of human nature." He nodded to Gatti and went back into the rehearsal room, to give the new tenor as much instruction as he could before Wednesday night's *Pagliacci.*

Emmy Destinn stared coldly at Gatti-Casazza's assistant, who was trying to persuade her to come speak to the conductor.

"Bitte, kommen Sie mit," Edward Ziegler entreated from the doorway of her dressing room. *"Herr Quaglia erwartet . . ."*

"I do not speak *that* language," Emmy said with enough ice in her voice to freeze over the sun. "Furthermore, I do not permit it to be spoken to me."

"La prego di dispensarmene," Ziegler switched immediately. "Signor Quaglia—"

"If Quaglia wishes to speak to me, he knows where the star dressing room is." She dismissed Ziegler with a wave of her hand. The nerve of the man—speaking *German* to her!

Emmy had known the language most of her life and had sung it hundreds of times. But that was before the war; now she refused to let one word of German pass her lips, and everyone at the Metropolitan knew it. In spite of his last name, Ziegler was American-born; German was not his native tongue. His addressing her in the language he knew she loathed had to be a calculated insult.

Emmy was singing Nedda in *Pagliacci,* a role she normally enjoyed even though the tenor invariably stole the show—especially when that tenor was Enrico Caruso. But tonight she wasn't looking forward to it much, nor to the upcoming *Aïda.* Somehow, the joy was gone.

"We do the hair now?" her maid asked.

Wordlessly the soprano sat down at her dressing table and let the maid arrange her hair. For the first time in her life, Emmy Destinn found herself envying Geraldine Farrar. Gerry's voice was going, but she could still give a performance that left audiences standing and cheering. You could tell just from the way she made her first entrance how much she loved what she was doing; Emmy envied her that. Her own voice had never been better, but more and more Emmy was having to force herself to walk out on the stage and sing.

An impatient *rat-a-tat* sounded; the maid opened the door to admit Alessandro Quaglia, who had the profile of a Roman statue and the overmuscled body of a prizefighter. Emmy sniffed irritably. The conductor had an annoying habit of always passing on some new bit of instruction just minutes before the curtain. She dismissed the maid.

"Since the star will not come to me," Quaglia said with sarcastic overpoliteness, "you see I come to the star." He stood like a soldier at attention, stretching out his six-feet-two in an attempt to intimidate her.

"I had not finished dressing," Emmy answered indifferently. "I knew you would not want me running up and down stairs and arriving on stage out of breath."

Quaglia's eyes traveled slowly from the top of her head down to her toes, and then slowly all the way back up again. He said nothing, but his meaning couldn't be clearer: *If you'd lose forty pounds, you wouldn't get out of breath climbing stairs.*

"What is it you want?" she asked sharply.

Quaglia smiled, knowing he'd scored. "About the *Stridono lassù*—"

"You change tempo too quickly," Emmy snapped. "It should be gradual."*Stridono lassù* was her only aria in *Pagliacci,* and she didn't want to the orchestra playing tricks with the tempi.

"Tonight we do it your way. Gradual change."

"What?"

"I think the gradual change is wrong, as you know," Quaglia said earnestly, "but it is better that we are wrong together rather than you sing one tempo while orchestra plays another. Tonight, I follow you."

"Thank you," Emmy said numbly.

Quaglia bowed stiffly and left the dressing room. Emmy shook her head. What a strange man! Nasty one minute, understanding and helpful the next. God, how she missed Toscanini! With that hot-tempered man, you always knew where you stood. He made sure of that.

She finished warming up. It was still a little early, but Emmy made her way down the stairs to the stage level and was surprised to hear herself happily humming her entrance music. Well, well. Maybe some of the old spark was left after all.

At the bottom of the stairs stood baritone Pasquale Amato, who was singing the role of Tonio that night; he'd been waiting for her. "Quaglia," he said, "he comes to you with last-minute instruction?"

"In a way," Emmy answered. "He says he will follow my tempo in the *Stridono lassù*."

The baritone nodded. "It is same for Rico and me. Always something! Quaglia, he is always tinkering, is he not? Right up until curtain time."

Emmy shrugged. "He wants everything to be right."

"As do we all, *non è vero*?" Amato exclaimed. "But this one, he never stops! You will see, he comes backstage during intermission with even more instructions, *può credermi*. Always the fussing!"

She stared at him curiously. "Pasquale, you've never been a complainer—what's wrong?"

Both of Amato's eyebrows climbed high at this totally unexpected suggestion that something might be wrong with *him*. "You think I imagine things?"

"No, Quaglia does fuss a lot. But you don't usually let things like that bother you. Is something wrong?"

He scowled as he thought about it. "No, nothing is wrong. But Quaglia, he does . . . bother me."

Emmy smiled. "Just another of life's burdens, Pasquale."

"Eh, you laugh." Suddenly Amato smiled too. "Perhaps you are right, Emmy. I do not let him bother me anymore." He walked away, repeating his last sentence under his breath.

The various members of the chorus were drifting out on to the stage to take their places before the curtain opened. The chorus master was talking to a good-looking man in costume that Emmy had never seen before; Setti seemed to be trying to reassure him. It must be the new chorister, Emmy thought, the dead man's replacement. Just then the new man looked up and caught Emmy's eye; she smiled at him. He looked pleased and flustered, the way a minor singer is supposed to look when noticed by a major star.

She was still smiling when she caught sight of Caruso, deep into his usual pre-performance panic. He was surrounded by well-wishers, all trying to soothe and calm him. The tenor had been singing professionally for twenty-five years, but he still went to pieces at the thought of facing an audience. His suffering was real, but it was more comic than pathetic—since everyone knew that the moment he set foot on the stage, his jitters would vanish like magic.

Caruso spotted her and rushed over. "Emmy! Tonight is disaster! I cannot sing!"

"Now, Rico—"

"The voice, it is gone! The hands shake, I have a hurt in the side, the mouth is dry—my spray! Where is my throat spray? Mario!" His valet rushed up with an atomizer bottle. Caruso sprayed his throat and tried a note; it came out thin and wobbly. "I cannot sing!"

"Of course you can sing," Emmy murmured automatically. "When the rest of us are dead and buried, you'll still be here singing. Try to relax, Rico."

"Disaster! Tonight is disaster!" He hurried away, not listening.

Emmy left him to his private terrors while she concentrated on heaving her considerable bulk into the donkey cart in which she made her entrance. Then came the word *Quiet, please,* and Pasquale Amato was out in front of the curtain singing the prologue.

The curtain opened; on stage, the chorus was busy setting the scene. Then Emmy was gripping the sides of the donkey cart, holding on for dear life, as Caruso grasped the donkey's bridle and led on the small troupe of actors they were playing that night. Caruso's first notes were strong and clear as a bell; no one would have known that only minutes earlier he'd been on the verge of collapse.

When the time came for Emmy's aria, Quaglia kept his word and followed her tempo. At the aria's conclusion, Emmy felt a small glimmer of the old satisfaction that used to follow every job of good singing, but the opera didn't give her time to enjoy it. She was plunged immediately into a quarrel with Pasquale Amato, followed by a love duet with the *other* baritone in the piece—which still felt odd to Emmy, as many times as she'd sung it; love duets were supposed to be sung with the tenor. Then followed a scene with Caruso, and at last she was off the stage.

Caruso was on stage alone, leading into the opera's big aria, *Vesti la giubba.* Normally at that point Emmy would be hurrying up the stairs to her dressing room to change into her Columbine costume for the second act. But tonight she lingered, wanting to feel the old Caruso magic working on her, hoping to rekindle the spark. Therefore she was backstage when the unthinkable happened.

Caruso's voice broke.

There was a stunned silence backstage. Singers and stagehands alike exchanged uneasy glances, each of them wondering, *Did I really hear what I think I heard?* The trouble had come at the climactic moment of *Vesti la giubba,* when the melodic line soared up to a high A. The A had proved Caruso's undoing, and the golden voice had cracked. It was a sound no one in the world had ever heard before.

Caruso finished the aria, and the first-act curtain closed to the sound of applause mixed with murmurs of surprise. "Disaster!" the tenor shouted as he rushed off the stage. "I know tonight is disaster!" He pushed his way up the stairs to his dressing room, muttering to himself.

Exclamations of dismay bounded back and forth. In any other singer, a break in the voice would be either glossed over or snickered at, depending on one's personal feelings toward the singer. But *Caruso!* Quaglia appeared backstage, his whole body quivering with alarm. "Where is he?" he demanded. A dozen fingers pointed, and the conductor dashed up the stairs to the dressing-room level. Soon Gatti-Casazza appeared, followed by his assistant, Edward Ziegler; Caruso's dressing room would be crowded.

Eventually enough order was restored that the second act could be started. In Act II, the troupe of traveling actors put on a little play for an audience of townspeople, enacted by the chorus. Caruso didn't enter immediately; the others sang away, all the while worrying about their tenor. No one worried about the trap door in the stage floor.

The trap was located in the exact center of the stage. When it was open, a pneumatic platform could be elevated thirty feet from the substage floor. It was especially effective for raising devils from Hell and the like, but it was not needed at all in *I Pagliacci*. No one on stage or off was even thinking about the trap door.

By the time Caruso made his entrance, even the Metropolitan's real audience was as keyed up as the make-believe audience on the stage. A small platform stage had been erected stage left, and it was there Caruso stood with Emmy Destinn and Pasquale Amato and sang. And he sang with an intensity and vigor that showed he was determined to make up for the flaw that had marred *Vesti la giubba*. The chorus filled up the rest of the stage to the right of the platform stage. Some were sitting, some were standing in various casual postures. None were expecting disaster.

Then, without even a sound to give warning, the trap door fell open. Three men of the chorus who'd been standing on the trap dropped out of sight through the hole in the stage floor. Shouts of alarm interrupted the music; Amato jumped down from the platform stage and elbowed his way to the open trap. In the orchestra pit, Quaglia made the cut-off sign with his baton. Caruso and Emmy, still on the platform stage, were craning their necks and trying to see what was happening.

One of the falling men had managed to grab the edge of the stage and there he hung precariously, screaming for help. Amato and three of the chorus men caught hold of his arms and hauled him to safety. Thirty feet below the open trap, on the pneumatic platform that had not been raised because it was not needed, lay the other two choristers. The leg of one was twisted awkwardly under him; the other's neck was broken.

The dead man was the new tenor.

□ 2 □

Two baritones sat in Delmonico's Restaurant on Fifth Avenue, nibbling at appetizers while they waited.

Pasquale Amato gazed around the interior of what was once the most famous restaurant in New York. "Delmonico's," he said, "do you think they really tear it down?"

"*Sì,*" Antonio Scotti answered without hesitation. "Its day of hay is over. All the good old places, they tear them down. Me, I must find new place to live. Next year the Knickerbocker becomes a place of commerce." He made a face. "Offices instead of homes."

"So much progress," Amato said wryly.

Scotti changed the subject. "When Rico gets here, we must not mention last night at all. He is not well and must not excite himself. We do not talk about it. You agree?"

"I agree. But how do we keep *Rico* from talking about it?"

"We interrupt with much rudeness and talk of something else. You know how superstitious he is. He will look back and see the break in the voice as an omen. His voice, it never breaks before, ever. Then when it does, a man dies."

The two baritones were silent, thinking of this latest tragedy to befall the Metropolitan Opera chorus. Only a catastrophe as great as that could overshadow the lesser tragedy of the great Caruso voice's having cracked on a high note.

Finally Amato stirred. "He sings too often. He should slow down—perhaps stop altogether for a while."

Scott threw up both hands. "*You* tell him that! Perhaps he listens to you. He does not listen to me, he does not listen to Dorothy, he does not listen to the doctors—"

Just then the object of their concern came bustling in, looking and sounding like the old Caruso they knew so well. "*Scusa, scusa* . . . I am late! The time, it goes so fast! You do not start without me? Eh, let us order without delay."

With Caruso's arrival, three waiters quickly materialized around the table. The singers ordered their lunch; Caruso tried to heed his wife's warnings and eat only a steak, but at the last moment he yielded to temptation and asked for a side dish of pasta.

When the waiters were gone, Caruso blurted out, "Pasquale, Toto—do you know the chorister who dies last night is new man?"

Scotti cleared his throat. "Rico, do you think we have snow tomorrow?"

"It is his first time on the Metropolitan stage," Caruso rushed on, unheeding. "His first and his last!"

"I think we go to Belasco Theatre tomorrow night," Scotti persisted, "if we do not have snow."

"Poor man." Caruso shook his head. "Poor, poor man."

"Rico, listen to me," Scotti insisted. "I have problem you help me with, yes? I do not know what Christmas present to give to Gerry. You suggest something?"

"*Sì, sì*—tomorrow. Why does the trap door fall open? It never happens before!"

Amato tried to help. "I, too, have problems with Christmas presents—"

"Christmas, Christmas!" the tenor cried. "Christmas is two weeks away! Why all this talk of Christmas? Something terrible happens last night—and you do not talk about it!"

Amato smiled ruefully at Scotti. "It is hopeless, Toto." Scotti nodded in resignation. Then Amato asked Caruso, "Do you know the new man, Rico?"

Caruso said he'd never spoken to the dead man. The other man who had fallen through the trap had suffered a hip injury as well as multiple fractures of the leg. "He is gone the rest of the season," the tenor said mournfully. "That is still two more chorus singers that must be found!"

"How do you know this?" Scotti asked.

"Mr. Gatti tells me. You understand what all this means?" Caruso laid one finger alongside his nose. "*Una maledizione!*"

"Oh, Rico!" Amato exclaimed in amused exasperation. "There is no curse! Do not say such things."

Caruso nodded wisely. "The chorus of the Metropolitan Opera—it is cursed! How else do you explain what happens? First the young soprano in *Samson and Delilah*. Then the poor man who hangs himself. Then last night . . . eh, I *feel* disaster in the air, even before we start! And I say so—ask Emmy! Then the voice breaks, and I think *that* is the disaster! But no, it is merely sign of worse things to come. A trap door that never mal-, mal . . . never misbehaves before—wide open it drops! One more death, and another man seriously hurt. That makes one injury, two fatal accidents, and a suicide, all within a week. Do you ever know so much misfortune to come so close together before? There is only one explanation. *Una maledizione.*"

All the time Caruso was talking, the waiters had been putting food on the table while listening openly to what the tenor was saying. Both Scotti and Amato had made shushing gestures to Caruso, who either did not or would not see. When the waiters had gone, Scotti burst out, "Now all of New York will be saying the Metropolitan chorus is under a curse! You should have waited until they are gone, Rico."

"Who?"

"The waiters," Amato said. "They drink in every word you say."

Caruso waved a fork in dismissal. "Is not important! *La maledizione,* that is important! Think, my friends—what starts in the chorus, can it not spread to us as well? Pasquale, you are there last night, you hear! Do you not understand?" He put down his fork and grasped his throat dramatically. "The voice, it is the next to go!"

"Rico, you are foolish man," Amato remonstrated. "Your voice, it breaks because you sing too often. You need to rest it more."

"He is right," Scotti added. "I tell you many times, not so much singing! You do not listen, and see what happens? Right in most important part of *Vesti la giubba*—"

"It is not too much singing," Caruso insisted stubbornly. "It is a curse. Only on the chorus right now, but—"

"And who places this curse on the chorus?" Amato asked patiently. "Who has the power? Who hates the chorus so much?"

"I do not know. Perhaps we find out?"

"Perhaps we forget this nonsense and finish our lunch. Your pasta grows cold."

"It is not nonsense!" the tenor protested. "Tell me true—are you comfortable when you go in opera house now?"

He had them there; the two baritones acknowledged the point. "Always, backstage there are accidents," Scotti said, "but so many? And so close together? No, I am not comfortable."

"And it does not end," Caruso said in a whisper, beginning to take a perverse enjoyment in his role of forecaster of doom. "There will be more accidents, more suicides. You will see! The curse has not yet run its course. Something else happens—perhaps tonight!"

Amato frowned; Geraldine Farrar was singing *Carmen* that evening. "Rico, you do not say this to Gerry, do you?"

The tenor was indignant. "What you think? You think I want to frighten her? No, I say nothing."

"Good," Amato smiled. "She is perhaps already nervous—no need to make it worse. Do you think she is nervous?"

Scotti sighed. "I call her on the telephone this morning. She screams at me to leave her alone and slams down the receiver, crash!"

"She is nervous," Amato nodded.

"We go tonight," Caruso decided. "We keep close watch, yes?"

The others agreed. Although all three men had sung in *Carmen* in the past, none of them was scheduled to sing that evening. Scotti had only recently added the role of the toreador to his repertoire; he'd sat down to learn the part the minute he heard Geraldine Farrar was divorcing her husband. Now that she was free again . . .

"*Per dio!*" Caruso cried, jumping up from the table.

Scotti slowly became aware of something hot and wet on his chest. Amato was angrily wiping at one sleeve with a napkin. The frightened-looking waiter stood paralyzed, the coffee pot he'd just dropped still lying in the middle of the table.

Caruso stared down at the big brown stain on his green vest. *"Una maledizione,"* he muttered gloomily.

"There it is, Mr. Gatti," said the stagehand. "I dint touch a thing, just like you said."

Gatti-Casazza and Edward Ziegler stood on the pneumatic platform thirty feet below the stage, looking up at the trap door hanging open over their heads. "Take us up, please," Gatti said to the stagehand. Slowly the platform lifted until the general manager and his assistant were almost at eye level with the stage. "Stop."

"Look at that," Ziegler said immediately. "The middle one's pulled loose."

The trap door was hinged at the back and normally fastened into place at the front by means of three heavy bolts, one at each corner and one in the middle. In addition, a heavy crossbar had been installed to run the width of the trap door, providing reinforcement. But the crossbar was not in place, and the middle bolt was wearing its holder, which had been wrenched free from its bracing crossbeam.

Gatti peered closely. "These other two bolts . . ."

Ziegler made a clucking sound. "Somebody forgot to shoot the bolts!"

From below, the stagehand called out, "Thass not my job!"

"So instead of three bolts and a crossbar," Ziegler went on, "the trap was supported by only one bolt—which eventually pulled loose. I'm surprised it didn't fall open sooner than it did, what with the chorus tramping back and forth over it for an entire act."

Gatti thought back. "Monday night. The trap door is used Monday, in *Mefistofele*." *Mefistofele* was performed on Monday, Tuesday the opera house was dark, and Wednesday the trap door had broken open during the final minutes of *Pagliacci*. "Only a little longer," Gatti lamented. "If the bolt holds just a little longer, maybe someone notices—and corrects the error, yes? And nobody dies." He motioned to the stagehand to take them back down.

As they were being lowered to the substage floor, Ziegler said thoughtfully, "Mr. Gatti, why would anyone bother riding this platform up to the trap—and then shoot only one of the bolts?"

The general manager shrugged. "Haste? Absent-mindedness?"

Ziegler turned to the stagehand. "Is there any way one person could operate this platform by himself—and ride it up to the stage, too?"

"He could get hisself up there," the stagehand answered, "but he couldn't get hisself back down. You need somebody down here to pull the lever."

"So there's no way for one person to get up there alone?"

"Well, you could climb a scaffold."

"We have one that tall?"

"Sure we do. Right over there." He pointed.

Gatti stared curiously at his assistant. "You think it is deliberate?"

Ziegler looked perplexed. "Well, considering the other things that have happened . . . I think this platform must be kept raised all the time from now on. We don't want to chance its happening again."

Gatti turned to the stagehand. "Whose job is it to see the trap door is properly bolted?"

The stagehand scratched his head. "Don't rightly know. Depends on who was crewin' Monday night. You'd hafta ask the stage manager."

Gatti nodded. "Ziegler, I want you to find out from the stage manager who it is and have him dismissed. Even if trap door is deliberately unbolted by someone else, it is responsibility of backstage workers to check everything, yes? If you—"

Abruptly, the sound of a piano being played on the stage above their heads interrupted him. The music had an incongruous sound in the opera house; someone was pounding out a sassy ragtime tune.

Ziegler adjusted his pince-nez. "Our Rosa is here. I'll leave her to you." He hurried off to find the stage manager.

Gatti sighed heavily and told the stagehand to raise the platform one more time. He'd told her and he'd told her—the Metropolitan Opera was not the proper place for a performance of Mr. Joplin's ditties, no matter how impromptu.

On the stage, a bright-eyed young woman broke off her playing and burst into laughter at the sight of the Metropolitan's general manager rising majestically through a hole in the floor. "Oh, Mr. Gatti—now that's what I call making an entrance!"

"Rosa, please," Gatti said with a pained expression. "I ask you many times not to play the jazz here."

"And I tell you many times," she mimicked in a friendly way, "you're making a mistake keeping American music out of the Met."

"But jazz? Ragtime? Not all Americans are so enamored of its sound as you are. Our audiences would be unhappy—you know they would."

"I s'pose," she acknowledged. "I guess I just spent too much time on the circuit." Young Rosa Ponselle had gone straight from vaudeville to leading roles at the Metropolitan Opera, the only singer ever to make such a leap.

"Rosa, why are you here? You do not sing this week."

"Costume fitting. I had to have a new *Forza* costume made, since the old one got ruined."

Gatti knew better than to ask how the old costume 'got ruined', all by itself. "When do you finish?"

"I'm finished now. It took only a few minutes."

"Then go home." He wagged a finger at her in a fatherly manner. "A man dies here last night. Now is no time to play—"

"You're right." She sobered instantly. "I'm sorry, I didn't think." She left the piano and went over to the side of the stage where she started pushing among the teaser curtains, releasing clouds of dust that made her sneeze. "By the way, I think Mr. Setti could use some help. The chorus sounds as if they're in re-

volt.'' She finally found what she was looking for and wheeled out
her bicycle.

Gatti made a sound of exasperation. "Rosa, how many times do
I tell you? *Do not ride the bicycle in traffic!*"

She threw a sheepish grin over her shoulder and hurried away.
American girls! Gatti thought in annoyance. Always they did what
they wanted to do and rarely what they *ought* to do. Sometimes he
thought young Rosa needed a good spanking.

Not that anyone would ever give her one; she was too special.
Rosa had a voice that could hypnotize audiences, and her musicianship was as impeccable as it was instinctive. But Rosa Ponselle had grown to young womanhood without having ever studied
opera. Gatti-Casazza had been stunned the first time he heard her
sing, at an audition Caruso had asked him to grant the young
vaudeville performer. That had been two years earlier; the general
manager had signed her to a contract even though at the time she
hadn't known even one operatic role. Everything she sang had to
be taught to her, slowly and laboriously. She knew three roles
now, and was learning a fourth. No one had ever before made a
career of opera in quite so slapdash a fashion. But then, Rosa was
Rosa.

What had she said about Setti's needing help? Gatti made his
way upstairs to the rehearsal room where the chorus master was
holding forth. From behind closed doors came the sound of angry
shouting. The door burst open and a scowling man shouldered his
way past the general manager. "What. . . ?" Gatti started to ask,
but the man stomped down the stairs without looking back.

Inside, Giulio Setti was pleading with the rest of the chorus. "I
know all that is possible is being done to ensure your safety! Do
you think last night's accident passes unnoticed? I am certain the
backstage workers take extra precautions now to—"

"Three deaths and one injury," a tall, thin man interrupted,
towering ominously over the chorus master. "All within one
week. I tell you, it's too much! Something has to be done."

"One of those deaths—it is suicide," Setti said quickly. "Two
accidents only, one in *Samson* and—"

"That's two more than there should be!" a contralto shouted. Murmurs of agreement ran through the group.

A small dark man cleared his throat importantly. "Do you notice? These accidents, they never happen to the Germans, no?"

Setti was appalled. "What do you say?"

"Perhaps they are not accidents after all?"

An impossibly blond older man stared down his nose at the small dark man. "You accuse us? You accuse *me*?"

"That is absurd!" the chorus master exclaimed. "I will hear no such accusations!"

"Why do you always take the Germans' side?" a woman shrieked at him. "Do you forget you are Italian?"

"The war is over!" Setti bellowed. "Now we must work together!"

The blond man sneered. "He never takes the Germans' side! He is too *Italian*." He made the word sound like an obscenity. Immediately three Italians stepped up to him and spat on the floor. Polyglot curses flew back and forth, accompanied by some energetic pushing and shoving and interrupted now and then when a disgruntled chorister would stop to shake his fist in the direction of the chorus master.

Gatti-Casazza waited until Setti had restored order and then went in. The general manager explained to the chorus that the cause of last night's tragedy was a bolt holder that had worked its way loose from its moorings. He explained that the man responsible for checking the trap door was even then in the process of being dismissed. He explained that all backstage workers were being instructed to doublecheck everything before the curtain opened each night.

"You see!" Setti cried triumphantly. "I tell you all is well!"

The various members of the chorus muttered under their breath and eyed the chorus master suspiciously, but their internecine squabbling eased off for the time being. Setti told them to warm up, that they would begin rehearsal in five minutes. He motioned Gatti-Gasazza out into the hallway.

"You are having trouble finding the two replacements?" Gatti asked him when they were alone.

"Five replacements," Setti corrected. "Three resign today—two sopranos and one bass-baritone. If there are more accidents, we may not have a chorus."

The general manager pulled nervously at his beard. "There are no more accidents."

"You guarantee it?"

More beard-pulling. "No."

Setti threw up his hands. "I say once I like to get rid of entire chorus and start over—but not this way!"

"How can I make guarantees? Do I hire guards?"

Setti's face crinkled into a gnomish smile. "Not so bad an idea, my friend!"

Gatti shook his head. "Too much fuss! We have one week of misfortune, yes—but it does not last forever. Discourage talk of the accidents, Setti. Everyone calms down in time."

"You think?"

"*Sì*," Gatti nodded emphatically. "All we need is few performances where nothing happens. They forget—you will see."

"I hope you are right. Pray for a *Carmen* with no accidents tonight. Now I must rehearse. They do not sing together as they should, do you notice?"

Gatti had noticed. So had the soloists, the orchestra, the audiences, and the critics. "*Buona fortuna*," he said to Setti.

Geraldine Farrar was doing her warm-up exercises as she applied her Carmen make-up. Antonio Scotti sat in his usual chair beside her make-up table, humming along.

Rosa Ponselle leaned on the back of Gerry's chair, carefully watching the older soprano's making-up process. "Do you s'pose I'll ever sing *Carmen*?" she asked.

"Not while I'm still here." Gerry laughed.

"The voice must darken first, little one," Scotti said.

Rosa looked around Gerry's private dressing room. "Isn't it

awfully warm in here? I find I sing better if I keep the dressing room a bit cool.''

Gerry smiled. ''A bit cool? Emmy Destinn says you always leave the star dressing room feeling like an icebox.''

Rosa made a face. ''Oh, she complains about everything. Nothing pleases *her*.''

Gerry and Scotti exchanged a look but said nothing. The Emmy Destinn who'd come back after the war was not the same Emmy they'd known for twenty years; but they weren't going to talk about their old acquaintance in front of this knowing young woman. Gerry finished warming up.

''Are you through?'' Rosa asked, surprised. ''It takes me a lot longer.''

Scotti sat up straight in his chair and said, ''Rosa, my charming child—as always, your presence is a joy and a delight, but please go away now. I want to ask this woman to marry me again.''

Rosa's face was all innocence. ''Marry you *again*?''

''*Ask* her again. Now go. *Parti*. Scout.''

''Scoot,'' Gerry corrected.

Rosa heaved a big sigh and headed for the door. ''I don't know why you bother. You know she's just going to say no.'' She left.

''Are you?'' Scotti asked. ''Going to say no?''

''Of course I am,'' Gerry said. ''I've had enough of marriage, Toto.''

''You do not have any marriage with *me*,'' he said indignantly. ''Do not judge me by that, that *actor* you marry with!''

She leaned over and gave him a kiss. ''I wouldn't dream of comparing you, Toto,'' she said, secretly doing just that—to Scotti's advantage, if he'd only known. The attack of nerves that had pestered her all day was gone; just being in familiar surroundings and preparing to do something she loved doing was enough to restore her equanimity.

But when Gerry and Scotti went downstairs to the stage level, they ran into a tension that had nothing to do with pre-curtain jitters. It was a toss-up as to who was more on edge, the choristers or the backstage workers who'd been threatened with mass unemployment if even one more accident occurred. "Cross your fingers," Gerry said to Scotti. "This isn't going to be an easy one tonight."

"It is better once the music starts," he said reassuringly. "When they see *you* are not affected by what happens, they grow calm again."

"You're right. It's up to me to set an example . . . oh God, there's Emmy."

Emmy Destinn sailed toward them like a battleship at top speed. Before the war she'd come to Gerry's performances of *Carmen* simply because she liked them; now she came because she knew it annoyed Gerry. "You must wear this tonight," she said without preamble, holding out a chain with a pendant dangling from it.

Gerry took the chain. The pendant was a cross, ornately decorated in the Czechoslovakian manner. "It's beautiful, Emmy—but I don't think it goes with a Spanish costume."

"It is a good-luck charm. The chain is long—the cross will hang down inside your dress. But you must wear it."

Surprised and rather touched, Gerry slipped the chain over her head. She had no faith in charms and talismans and such, but this was the first friendly gesture the other soprano had made since her return. "Thank you, Emmy."

Emmy nodded curtly. "I want this accident nonsense settled and everything back to normal. Before I sing again." She sailed away without another word.

"I should have known," Gerry said wryly. "Toto—is that Pasquale?"

Scotti glanced over to the other side of the stage where he caught a glimpse of Pasquale Amato making his way cautiously through the wings. "Pasquale and Rico and I," Scotti explained, "we watch from backstage tonight."

"Why?" she asked suspiciously.

The baritone was saved from explaining further by the arrival of the man who would conduct that evening's performance. Quaglia looked angry, his boxer's body twitching in annoyance.

"Maestro Quaglia," Gerry smiled brightly, artificially. "I do hope you haven't come with any last-minute changes."

"No, dear lady, not tonight." Quaglia matched her artificial smile. "I have one or two things—but they must wait until we have full chorus again. Do you know three of the choristers quit today?"

"No!"

"Yes. Setti brings one elderly chorister out of retirement to help fill in for the time being . . . but if there is another accident, more will quit." Quaglia suddenly gave vent to the anger he'd been suppressing. "They think they are soloists, these chorus singers! I must adjust to *them*! I never have so much trouble with a chorus before in my life!"

Scotti started to say that wasn't precisely true but then decided that wouldn't be too diplomatic. "You can not blame them for worrying," he said instead. "They are afraid."

"Pah!" Quaglia exclaimed, his face turning red. "Spineless nobodies! *I* am not afraid!"

"*You* do not sing in the chorus," Scotti said gently.

"Why do they think they are singled out for such special attention? Some of them are claiming these accidents are no accidents—they say everything that's happened is deliberate."

"*Ridicolo.*"

"Of course it's ridiculous." Quaglia made a visible effort to calm down. "I've told Mr. Gatti, either Setti whips that chorus into line immediately or I will delete the chorus numbers from all the operas I conduct the rest of the season."

Gerry half-gasped, half-laughed. "Surely you're not serious! You can't just eliminate the chorus from opera!"

"I am thoroughly convinced that I can." The conductor pulled out a handkerchief and patted his forehead. "Ah, it is time." He grasped Gerry's hand, gave it a perfunctory kiss, and hurried away to take his place in the orchestra pit.

The soprano watched him go. "Sometimes I believe that man thinks he's Toscanini."

Scotti nodded solemnly. "All of the temperament, but . . ."

"But little of the artistry," she finished. The sound of polite applause from the auditorium told them Quaglia was making his way to the podium. Scotti gave her an encouraging squeeze of the hand and slipped away.

The opera started.

Gerry listened carefully to the chorus; their attack was ragged and one or two voices stood out over the others. Not good. The tempo was too fast, for one thing, faster than what they'd rehearsed. She put the chorus out of her mind and concentrated on her own role. Enter . . . *now*.

"Quand je vous aimérai?" She sang her first line with all the authority she could muster. *When will I love you?* Who knows. She deliberately slowed down the tempo of the *Habanera* and ignored Quaglia's attempts to get her to pick up the speed. The first half of the aria was ruined by a conflict of the two tempi; but when Quaglia saw she wasn't going to follow his beat, he glowered at her and slowed the orchestra to match the pace she was setting. She rewarded him with a smile, all the while thinking that Toscanini would never have allowed her to get away with *that*.

She finished the *Habanera* to enthusiastic applause—and to the sound of a few voices chanting *Ger-ee, Ger-ee!* from the back of the auditorium. *Not yet, girls,* Gerry thought as she sashayed off the stage; *musmt cheer yourselves out before the final curtain.* Every year new gerryflappers appeared in the audience, fresh-faced young girls eager to join the army of females who worshipped the ground Geraldine Farrar walked on. The ones who'd been around a while knew just when to start the chanting—not too early, not too late.

Gerry's maid was waiting offstage with a towel and make-up so she wouldn't have to run up the stairs to her dressing room and right back down again; she had to go back on again as soon as the tenor finished singing his duet with the *second* lady of the opera. Gerry took the towel and started patting dry the light film of perspiration on her face.

"I hold the mirror, yes?" a familiar voice asked.

"What are you doing, Rico?" Gerry asked, powdering down. "You and Toto and Pasquale—what are you up to?"

"We watch," he said importantly. "We watch and make certain no more accidents bedevil us."

"Hold it a little lower—there. How can watching stop an accident?"

"Oh, we are very busy," Caruso announced. "We check stage ropes and props and scenery—hey, *scugnizz',*" he broke off, "what do you do here?"

Rosa Ponselle came over for a hug from her favorite tenor. "Everybody else was staying backstage—I didn't want to miss anything. Gerry, that was a great *half* a *Habanera.*"

"Mm, yes, it took Quaglia a while to catch on. Hold the mirror still, Rico."

"I think Mr. Gatti and Ziegler are both on the verge of nervous breakdowns," Rosa remarked. "They're both fussing around like old mother hens."

"We all check," Caruso explained. "We make sure no more accidents."

"I've got to go on," Gerry said, patting her hair. "Everybody go away."

They left her alone and once again she directed all her concentration toward her role. In the next scene she got into a fight with one of the chorus women. She'd always liked that part.

Yelling and screaming—all musical, all rehearsed. Women pouring on to the stage, filling the stage, taking over the stage. Geraldine Farrar in the middle of it all, pulling free from the soldier who was trying to restrain her, turning to strike at the chorus woman . . .

. . . who wasn't there.

Without hesitating, Gerry lashed out at a different woman of the chorus—who looked shocked at first but then caught on and played out the incident. It wasn't art, but it got done.

Eventually everyone left the stage except Gerry and the tenor, the seduction of whom she was to complete in exactly one aria.

Halfway through the *Seguidilla,* she became aware of raised voices backstage. Angry, she started singing louder, causing Maestro Quaglia to raise an eyebrow at her. But the backstage voices didn't stop, and she could even hear someone running. The *idiots*—creating a disturbance while a performance was in progress!

Then it hit her. There'd been another accident.

Her fears were confirmed when she glanced off into the wings and saw Scotti standing there watching her worriedly. When next she happened to look off the other side of the stage, there stood Caruso, wringing his hands, anxiety written all over his face. The tenor she was singing the scene with missed a cue, also aware that something was wrong.

Gerry finished the *Seguidilla* on automatic and rushed off the stage toward Scotti, who immediately wrapped both arms around her and started making comforting noises. "Don't *soothe* me, Toto," she ordered, "tell me what's happened. There's been another accident, hasn't there? How many this time? And how serious? Who is it?"

"Only one, but it is as serious as it can be. She is dead."

She knew it, she knew it! "Who, Toto?"

"The chorus woman you are supposed to fight with," Scotti said. "She is not onstage tonight because she is lying dead behind one of the roller curtains."

"My God." Gerry was silent for a moment, shaken. "What kind of accident was it this time? Did the roller curtain fall on her?"

"No." Scotti's face was full of pain. "This time is no accident. Someone stabs her, Gerry! There is long knife in her heart. This time it is murder."

Gerry drew in a deep breath. *Murder.*

"And," Scotti finished anxiously, "this time we are supposed to know it is murder. The killer, he wants us to know—he wants us to know he is here."

□ **3** □ In 1918, the city of New York had done away with the corrupt and inefficient coroner's office that had been the scandal of city government for so long. And now, two years later, the Metropolitan Opera was seeing the new medical examiner's office in action. Pathologists and technicians descended on the opera house along with the police; they examined the body and estimated the time of death to be between four and seven o'clock, since rigor mortis was just beginning to set in.

The murdered woman's name was Teresa Leone. She was a mezzo-soprano from Baltimore who'd been singing in the Metropolitan Opera chorus for four years. Teresa had shared rooms on Bleecker Street with another chorister, who hadn't seen her roommate since noon. It seemed that Teresa always had voice lessons scheduled for late Thursday afternoons; so instead of making the trip downtown to her rooms and back up again, she was in the habit of going straight from her voice teacher's studio to the opera house. Pending the voice teacher's confirmation of the time Teresa had left the studio, the police then set the time of death at around six o'clock.

Teresa Leone had been engaged to marry a publisher of catalogues and Bibles, a prosperous man who'd been in Cleveland for the past three days on business. She had no obvious enemies among the other choristers; Giulio Setti told the police she was one of the least contentious singers in the chorus. Teresa's roommate said nothing had been troubling her lately; Teresa was, in fact, happily looking forward to meeting the rest of her fiancé's family at Christmastime.

Every member of the chorus volunteered the information that Teresa's death was simply the most recent of a series of malevolent acts directed against the chorus; Gatti-Casazza volunteered the opinion that the choristers were understandably upset and were jumping to conclusions. The body had been found by Edward Ziegler, during his ongoing accident-prevention patrol. The two or three choristers who'd missed Teresa while they were getting into costume and makeup, including her roommate, had simply assumed Teresa had dressed early and was waiting in the greenroom. There was precedent for such an assumption.

The police were faced with the problem of finding out whether Teresa Leone's murder was connected to the earlier 'accidents' or whether it was an isolated event. Also, the ostensible suicide of the man found hanging in the chorus dressing room would have to be looked into more closely. There was much to be considered.

Sixteen more choristers resigned.

"Una maledizione," Caruso croaked. "I say so—do I not say so, Pasquale?"

"Yes, Rico, you say so." Amato sighed tiredly. "It is still foolishness what you say."

"Not so foolish. I say something more happens, and I am right."

They had gathered the next day in Geraldine Farrar's apartment on West Seventy-fourth Street—Caruso, Amato, Scotti, and Gatti-Casazza. Emmy Destinn had arrived shortly thereafter, demanding her good-luck pendant back from Gerry. "I sing before you do again," she explained. "We will take turns wearing it."

Gerry gave her her pendant back. "You don't really think this will protect you, do you, Emmy?"

"I think we need all the help we can get." She plumped herself down in an armchair. "Are you serving anything?"

Since it was still morning, the refreshments the maid brought in were coffee and tea and little dainties to go with them. When Caruso had consumed about four thousand calories, he tried to press his 'curse' theory again. "Suicide, accident, murder," he said. "Things such as these, they do not happen unless there is curse behind them."

"Only in opera," Gerry said grimly. "In real life, there has to be a human hand behind such goings-on."

Scotti raised an eyebrow. "You think they are all murder?"

"I think we'd be fools not to consider it. I only hope the police are thinking the same way."

"The police say very little," Gatti-Casazza remarked. "Only that the knife, it is of a kind that can be purchased anywhere."

"Not much help," Emmy grunted.

"Mr. Ziegler finds the body," Scotti mused. "Why is he the only one who looks behind roller curtain? Perhaps he knows the dead lady is waiting there?"

"Non lo credo," Caruso objected. "Finding her does not mean he kills her. Me, I also find dead body once! Ten years ago—remember?"

"Besides," Amato smiled, "it is Mr. Gatti who finds the man hanging in chorus dressing room. Do you also suspect Mr. Gatti, Toto?"

"Cielo! No!" Scotti was horrified.

"Eh, I am only second one to see him," Gatti said. "One of the scrubwomen, she finds him."

"Oh?" Emmy said. "I didn't know that. How did she happen to find him? What is her name?"

"Her name is Mrs. Bukaitis, and I imagine she finds him when she goes into chorus dressing room to clean. I do not know."

"Didn't you talk to her about it? Ask her questions?"

"I try to talk to her next day, but she has little English and no Italian. I think she comes from one of those new countries, the ones that used to belong to Poland or Russia?"

"Estonia?" Gerry suggested. "Latvia? Lithuania?"

"Sì, Lithuania. I think."

"Un momento," Amato said. "Why does this Mrs. . . . ?"

"Bukaitis."

"This Mrs. Bukaitis, why does she go into chorus dressing room to clean so near to curtain time? Surely this must be done earlier in day—before the choristers start to arrive?"

"That is good point, Pasquale," Scotti said. "We must find someone who speaks Lithuanian and ask her."

"Ziegler did something else besides discover a body," Emmy said unexpectedly. "He insulted me."

"Emmy!" Caruso exclaimed. "How?"

"He spoke German to me."

Gatti spread his hands. "A slip of the memory—"

"No, wait," Emmy said. "Why German? Everyone speaks Italian backstage. If Ziegler didn't want to speak Italian for some reason, he would have spoken in his own language—English. Why did he choose German? He knows I do not permit that language to be spoken to me. It was a deliberate insult.''

Nobody had an explanation, and nobody else thought it particularly important. Caruso made a few sympathetic cooing sounds in Emmy's direction and turned the subject back to the murder. "Why does somebody hate the chorus? What has the chorus done to deserve such treatment?''

"Perhaps it is anarchists,'' Scotti said gloomily.

"Oh, Toto,'' Gerry sighed. "You've got anarchists on the brain. Would you kindly explain to me why *anarchists* would want to harm the chorus of an opera company?''

Scotti threw up both hands. "Who knows why anarchists do the things they do? *Nessun lo sa.* All I know is they destroy things.''

"I think it is one murder,'' Gatti said ponderously. "One murder, and the other incidents are precisely what they appear to be—one suicide and two accidents. I think we are making mountain out of, uh. . . ?''

"Molehill,'' Gerry said. "I hope you're right.''

Caruso burst out coughing. It was so bad that Scotti rushed to his side, concerned. "Rico? What is it?''

"Cigarettes,'' Gatti muttered.

Caruso had recovered from his coughing fit. He wiped his lips with a handkerchief and said, "I do not have one cigarette yet today.''

"Yet.''

"Two each day, that is all now.''

"Really?'' Gerry said. "Good for you, Rico.''

"Perhaps Mr. Gatti is right,'' Amato said suddenly. "Perhaps there is only one murder—one important murder, that is.''

"*Important* murder?'' Emmy echoed disbelievingly.

"Important to the killer,'' Amato explained. "Perhaps all these other 'accidents' are arranged to, eh, to lay down the screen of smoke?''

"That is possible,'' Scotti nodded.

"And almost impossible to prove," Emmy commented. "How could we ever know if only one of the killings is significant?"

"We will know," Amato said thoughtfully, "if they stop."

The Metropolitan Opera generally held auditions in the afternoons during the regular season; always, a horde of singers could be found pounding eagerly at the doors, unknowns who thought they were good enough to sing at the Met—and sometimes they were. Young Rosa Ponselle had joined the company in just that way, but it had taken her three auditions to do it. At one of them she'd been so nervous she had fainted.

But now the need was for chorus singers. Most of the defecting choristers had been replaced from the pool of standby singers the Met maintained; but there were still a few openings to be filled, and the standby pool itself needed replenishing. The day after Teresa Leone's murder, Gatti-Casazza was busy practicing his specialty, that of keeping the press at bay without actually granting an interview. That left Edward Ziegler to take his place at the auditions. Ziegler, who attended every audition anyway, was joined in the auditorium by Alessandro Quaglia and Giulio Setti. They'd just dismissed a thin-voiced soprano from the stage with a courteous expression of thanks and were now listening to a young tenor wobbling all over the scale. The Met-employed piano accompanist couldn't stop himself from making faces.

When the wobbling tenor had finished and the next singer had not yet appeared on the stage, Ziegler said, "I've had an outrageous thought. Do you suppose someone could be killing off choristers just to create an opening? Could our killer be a frustrated singer?"

Quaglia laughed humorlessly. "Then why does he kill both men and women? Your frustrated singer would have to have most unusual voice to sing both men's and women's parts."

"Oh dear, that's right," Ziegler winced. "Not too brilliant a suggestion—please forget I said anything."

Setti smiled ruefully. "Besides, the chorus is what they wish to escape from, no? It is only a stepping stone—at least for *this* chorus. They all think of themselves as soloists who have been denied their rightful place center stage.''

Quaglia grunted agreement; that was one matter on which he and the chorus master were in accord. The chorus had degenerated abysmally from its halcyon pre-war days; now they sang competitively instead of *ensemble*. No one seemed to know what to do about it. Quaglia blamed Setti; he thought the chorus master should exercise stronger control.

All three men put the recent series of events out of their minds when the next auditioning singer stepped out on the stage. He was a handsome bass-baritone who turned out to have just the kind of voice they were looking for. Unfortunately, the bass-baritone was Greek and didn't speak a word of English; he'd brought a young boy with him to act as his interpreter. The boy's English, recently acquired, was not quite the aid to communication it was meant to be; it remained uncertain just how much chorus music the bass-baritone knew. Ziegler suggested they put him on standby until they could determine the extent of his knowledge. The other two agreed.

By the time the day's auditions were finished, they'd hired two sopranos and chosen three other singers for standby, including the unintelligible Greek bass-baritone, in decisions made more hastily than usual. Not wasting any time, Setti hustled the two sopranos off to a rehearsal room. Ziegler said to Quaglia, ''I've scheduled a special audition session for Sunday afternoon, Maestro.''

Quaglia nodded curtly. ''I will be here.'' Of all the conductors at the Metropolitan, Quaglia was the only one who concerned himself with the hiring and firing of choristers, claiming he'd had too many performances ruined for him in the past by unruly or inept choruses.

''I do hope the police don't dally in their hunt for the killer,'' Ziegler said as he stood to go. ''Conditions will never return to normal here until they find him. The chorus will undoubtedly use the murder as a bargaining point when next they ask for more money—they're not overly burdened with ethical considerations, I've found.''

Quaglia looked startled. "Do they not just get new contract?"

"That won't stop them," Ziegler said sourly. "I had to give them the sun and the moon this time—next time they'll want the stars as well. I'm sure they'll ask me to renegotiate this last contract, as soon as one of them thinks of it."

"Mmm. The longer these incidents continue . . ."

"The more intractable they become. Well, perhaps the killer is finished now—let's see what happens during *Parsifal*."

Nothing happened during *Parsifal*. The lengthy Wagnerian opus went off without a hitch; there were no accidents, no suicides, no murders. Even the normal backstage problems that plagued every opera production were less troublesome than usual. But any hope that this uneventful production would help allay the choristers' fears was soon dispelled; most of them were quick to point out that this was a *German* opera that had escaped being sabotaged. To the non-German segment of the chorus, that was further proof that the German singers at the Met were exempt from and possibly responsible for the unsettling series of incidents that had been taking place. The chorus remained as divided as ever.

Pasquale Amato was not thinking of the chorus; he was thinking of what an incredibly lucky man Antonio Scotti was. They'd both been singing for over a quarter of a century, but Amato had never had a beautiful soprano buy *him* a fur coat for Christmas.

"Turn around," Geraldine Farrar commanded.

He turned slowly, letting her examine every inch of the expensive mink coat he was modeling. "It is loose in the shoulders," he complained.

"That's all right, Toto is bigger through the shoulders than you are." She flashed him a smile to let him know she wasn't being critical. "What do you think, Pasquale? Do you think he would like this one?"

Amato stroked the fur lapel sensuously. "He is fool not to like it, Gerry. It is lovely present."

"Mmm." She didn't look convinced. They were at Revillon Frères on Fifth Avenue; Gerry had warned Amato that she expected him to devote all of Saturday afternoon to helping her find just the right coat for Scotti's Christmas present. "I wonder if the belted style is right for him? He *is* getting a bit thick around the middle, you know."

"Toto loathes the coats that hang straight down."

"I know. Perhaps one of those with the indented waistline but without the belt?" She motioned to one of the three clerks hovering nearby. "You know the ones I mean?"

The clerk assured her he did indeed know the ones she meant. He disappeared momentarily and came back carrying three coats. Gerry selected one and Amato slipped it on. "I think I like this one best," he volunteered. He was getting a little tired of modeling.

Gerry squinted her eyes, trying to visualize what Scotti would look like in the coat. Another clerk came forward expectantly, holding out a chestnut-colored coat. Gerry waved him away. "Wrong color. It has to be black."

"*This* one is black," Amato said pointedly, holding out both arms to illustrate.

She laughed. "Another minute." The baritone and the three clerks all kept quiet while she tried to make up her mind. "I just don't know," she finally said. The four men sighed.

Gerry asked the clerks to put the coat aside for a few days, just long enough for her to think about it. The two singers left and paused for a moment outside. Fifth Avenue's wide sidewalks seemed more crowded than usual. The air was crisp and smelled good; the afternoon light was beginning to fail and the electric streetlights would be coming on soon. Reluctant to call it a day just yet, Gerry took Amato's arm and started to stroll unhurriedly up the avenue.

They looked in store windows that displayed their wares among carefully arranged wreaths of holly and big red bow ribbons and cornucopias spilling out oranges and pears and walnuts. One store window had a mannequin of Saint Nicholas, complete with long-stemmed pipe and cape, standing beside an open burlap bag bursting with toys—a puppet, a toy drum, a bright yellow wooden horse. Two boys pressed up against the window, their noses flattened against the glass.

Amato made a *tsk*ing sound. "The Christmas shopping—every year, it starts a little earlier."

Gerry smiled. "It can't start early enough for me. I love Christmas."

"I must buy new *galosce,*" he muttered. Overshoes. "Before the New York snow starts to cover us up."

"Oh, good heavens!" Gerry stopped in her tracks. "You've just reminded me, Pasquale. I left my new boots in my dressing room." She looked up at the darkening sky. "Do you think it will snow this weekend?"

"*Senza dubbio,*" he said fatalistically. "Always it snows when one leaves the boots in the dressing room."

"That settles it, then. We'll have to stop by and pick them up."

"Can you not send the maid?"

"*Nobody* gets the key to my dressing room." Geraldine Farrar was the only singer at the Metropolitan with her own private dressing room; she'd guarded the only key jealously for over ten years now. "I wonder if the matinee performance is over yet."

Amato had to unbutton his overcoat to get to the watch in his vest pocket. "I think so. They all go home by now. The smart ones, they go home at end of first act." That Saturday afternoon's opera was *Oberon,* not one of Amato's favorites.

Gerry's chauffeur and limousine were waiting for them on East Thirty-fourth Street by Altman's. They drove west past the Waldorf-Astoria to Herald Square and turned up Broadway the few remaining blocks to the Metropolitan Opera. The two singers slipped in quietly through the Fortieth Street entrance, in case any of the audience were still lingering out front.

The backstage hustle and bustle that normally characterized the changing of stage sets between matinee and evening performances were missing; that evening's performance was being staged at the Brooklyn Academy of Music, one of several so scheduled during the season. The opera was *L'Elisir d'Amore,* one of Caruso's vehicles—not one of his best, some of his friends thought. The unusual late afternoon quiet gave the Metropolitan's backstage area an eerie quality—so both Gerry and Amato jumped when two policemen stepped out of the shadows and blocked their way.

Gerry gasped. "Good Lord—something else has happened?"

The Met's doorkeeper hastened to assure her that the afternoon's performance had been uneventful, and that the policemen were there to make sure no more 'accidents' took place. The doorkeeper identified both singers for the police, who memorized their faces and then nodded.

"Locking the barn door after the horse is stolen," Gerry muttered as the policemen moved aside to let her pass. Amato busied himself asking them questions while Gerry hurried up to her dressing room.

She found her boots and was on her way back when she heard a light hissing sound. She stopped; so did the sound. She started walking; she heard it again. Only this time the hissing said her name.

"Pssst! Gerry!" Rosa Ponselle was peeking around a corner of the corridor.

"Rosa! What are you doing . . . *lurking* there like that?"

"Are they gone?"

"Are who gone? There's no one downstairs except Pasquale and the doorkeeper. And the police."

A big sigh of relief. "I s'pose it's all right, then." She joined Gerry at the top of the stairs. "I wanted to make sure they'd all left before I came out."

"Make sure *who* had left? What are you talking about, Rosa?"

"The chorus. Our wonderful, professional, warmhearted, and helpful chorus."

Gerry looked at her sympathetically. "They did it again?"

"Did they ever. The audience had to keep consulting their programs to find out who was singing the female lead today—they certainly couldn't tell by looking at the stage. The chorus blocked me out every chance they got."

"Oh, Rosa—I'm sorry. Really, Setti must not allow this to continue."

"Setti can't control them. Gerry, today one of them tried to trip me! They hate me."

"Oh, that's inexcusable! Do you know which one? You can have him dismissed . . . or 'her'?"

"That's just the problem—I don't know which one it was! And it's happened before . . . I couldn't be sure then, but there was no mistaking it this time. They really hate me. They're even spreading rumors about me now—they're saying I'm having an affair with Caruso!"

Gerry had heard that nasty little story. "You must go over Setti's head. See Gatti."

"I've already done that. All he did was sit me down and give me a lot of fatherly advice I didn't want." Rosa was angry. "Don't you see, Gerry? Mr. Gatti doesn't dare crack the whip now, not with all these terrible things happening to them. He's afraid more of them will quit. And they know that. They're just going to keep on and on until one day they pick me up and throw me into the orchestra pit and I end up in the bassoon player's lap." Rosa made a face. "Look at me! *Hiding* from the chorus! I sang the lead role at the Metropolitan Opera this afternoon! Why should *I* have to hide from a bunch of second-rank musicians who're so jealous they can't see straight?"

"Ger-ee!" a baritone voice floated up from below. "Do you stay up there until Christmas?"

"Coming!" she sang back. "Rosa, listen. It's not just you. The chorus has been nothing but trouble this entire season. They're doing the same thing to the new tenor—"

"Oh, they're just needling Gigli because he thinks he's the next Caruso. They'd do that to anybody who wanted to take Rico's place." Rosa's anger had died away. "Besides, what they do to him isn't nearly as *nasty* as what they do to me. Gigli's paid his dues, you see. He came to the Met the way you're supposed to come . . . from other opera houses, from working his way up—not from vaudeville, the way I came. They resent me, Gerry. They resent me because I didn't go through all the lessons and training

and work they went through. Gerry, did you know I'd seen only
two operas in my *life* before I made my début?''

"No . . . only two? Ever?'' Gerry knew Rosa didn't have the
background the rest of them had, but to have seen only two operas
in her entire life . . . Gerry thought what that meant. To have
stepped out on that huge Metropolitan stage, to have faced that
glittering audience that had heard every great voice of the times—
what courage that must have taken! "I didn't realize,'' she said
faintly.

"Do you know what the first one I saw was?'' Rosa mused.
"*Tosca.* You and Caruso and Scotti were singing. Gerry, it was as
if I'd been sleeping all my life up to that night. Then sometime
during the second act I woke up to the fact that it was *that* kind of
singing I ought to be doing. I became an opera singer because of
you, Gerry.''

That came as a shock. Gerry knew she should feel flattered and
did manage to murmur something by way of gracious acknowledgment. But she felt history was repeating itself; and this time
around, it hurt. She too had decided to become a singer because of
the first performance of an opera she'd attended as a girl, in her
case, Emma Calvé's *Carmen.* And now here was . . . *the next
generation* telling her *she* had been a similar source of inspiration.
Gerry suddenly felt a hundred years old.

"Ger-*ee!*'' Amato called. "Perhaps I come help you down the
stairs?''

Not quite yet, she thought, straightening her shoulders. "We'll
be right there!''

"'We'?''

Gerry had invited Amato to dinner; the cook could stretch it to
include one more. "Rosa, come dine with Pasquale and me. Unless you have plans?''

"No plans. Thanks, Gerry—I really don't want to go home.''

Gerry had thought not. "Let's go before Pasquale has a fit. My
limousine is on Fortieth. You didn't ride your bicycle to a performance, did you?'' The younger woman shook her head. "Come
along, then.''

Amato's face broke into a broad smile when he saw he would have the company of *two* beautiful sopranos at dinner that evening.

Mrs. Bukaitis had turned in her mop and pail early, collected her day's pay, and left. The fancy folks wouldn't be using their opera house that night.

She headed east on Thirty-ninth Street, taking no pleasure from the store window displays she passed. These Americans, how they wasted money! They had no sense of proportion. And there was no making them understand the war was not really over.

A man with a red mustache tried to sell her a roasted chestnut from his cart; she ignored him, in spite of being tempted by the smell. That was the trouble with New York City: too many temptations. How easy it would be, to give in to capitalistic self-pampering and forget about those at home. Mrs. Bukaitis was disgusted with herself.

The Third Avenue line had recently added an express track to its elevated train; Mrs. Bukaitis boarded and took a seat among a crowd of talkative and laughing passengers. She hadn't completely gotten over her nervousness at riding the el. It wasn't the noise and the speed—that was something you adjusted to quickly in New York. But it just didn't seem natural to be riding in a train way up there above street level. But then, nothing about this country was what you would call *natural*.

She stared out of the window, trying to shut out the loud voices around her as well as the *clang-rattle-screech-thunk* of the train itself. Mrs. Bukaitis let herself slip into a favorite fantasy: What if an elevated train ran right through the center of Vilnius? How startled and amazed everyone would be! It might even scare those accursed Poles right out of the city.

This would be Mrs. Bukaitis' third Christmas away from Lithuania's capital city. Mrs. Bukaitis and her husband had had to leave first the city and then the country, only a few steps ahead of their pursuers all the way. Mr. Bukaitis had openly opposed the foreign occupation of Vilnius, derailing trains and raiding arsenals and doing anything else he could think of to make clear his disapproval. Then someone in their little band of saboteurs had betrayed them, and the Bukaitises had had to flee for their lives. Their second day in America, Mr. Bukaitis had fallen off the roof of their tenement building and broken his neck. It was sheer carelessness; he had leaned out too far, trying to see all of New York at once.

The farther downtown the el traveled, the less English Mrs. Bukaitis heard spoken around her. Now the voices were talking in Russian and Polish and Italian and Yiddish. The train screeched to a halt at the station built in the middle of the Bowery at the corner of Canal Street. Mrs. Bukaitis got off and walked back uptown one block to Hester Street, then west one more block to Elizabeth.

She passed the corner saloon (now closed) and the Elizabeth Street Pawnshop and entered the third building. Up five flights . . . not easy after a day spent on the knees scrubbing floors. Mrs. Bukaitis was short of breath, but not just from climbing the stairs. She was excited. She was excited because Antanas had promised the man would be there to talk to them this time.

She knocked four times, waited, knocked once more. Antanas quietly opened the door. His face was as serious as always, but Mrs. Bukaitis was quick to notice his eyes were dancing. The man had come! After disappointing them twice, this time he had come!

There were nine people in Antanas's room. Eight of them Mrs. Bukaitis knew; a few nodded to her, but no one spoke. The ninth person was a man she'd never seen before. He was leaning against the far wall, a small table covered with unfamiliar objects in front of him. The room's two chairs were taken; Mrs. Bukaitis sat on the floor and wrapped her arms around her knees. The poorly lighted room was chilly and damp; someone was coughing.

They waited without speaking until two more people had joined them. Then Antanas announced it was time to begin. The silence in the room was tense as the stranger stepped up to the small table and began to demonstrate how to build a bomb.

Emmy Destinn waved a hand impatiently through the cloud of cigarette smoke that drifted over from the next table and tried to concentrate on what Antonio Scotti was saying. It was difficult;

he'd more or less been saying the same thing for the past fifteen years.

"She has new lover!" Scotti moaned. "She does not tell me, but I know it! Why does she do this to me?"

"Toto, you're being silly. She probably just had something to do today."

"Oh yes, she has something to do today! She has to see *him* instead of me!"

"You can't expect Gerry to spend every free minute with you," Emmy pointed out, bored to death with the subject. "Be reasonable."

But Scotti didn't hear, caught up as he was in his perennial lament. He enjoyed his role of persistent suitor, Emmy thought, and he played it to the hilt. Emmy suddenly found herself thinking about another man. He was a man from whom she'd parted after a years-long affair, and the parting had not been amicable. Scotti knew about the affair, but it hadn't seemed to occur to him that his lament about his own romantic misfortunes might be a source of pain to her. He would have done better to choose a different confidante.

Scotti was off on a nostalgic journey now, remembering all the good times. Emmy tired of hearing of the perpetual wonderfulness of Geraldine Farrar and let her attention wander. They were in a large basement room. Someone had hung a few pictures on the brick walls and placed several overly optimistic potted ferns here and there about the place. The small tables and their uncomfortable chairs were shoved close together; at one end of the room was a Lilliputian bandstand, little more than a low platform. The place was only half full; it was early yet.

Emmy was not comfortable there. She objected to having to break the law to get a drink; but ever since last year, when the United States of America in its infinite wisdom decided to make the consumption of alcoholic beverages illegal, these semi-hidden little speakeasies were the only answer. On a Saturday night the place would be packed. In a few hours three or four musicians would squeeze on to the tiny bandstand and start playing that rag-

time or Dixieland or whatever they called it. Emmy could enjoy
that kind of music for about ten minutes before she started getting
bored; she couldn't understand Rosa Ponselle's enthusiasm for it.
But then Rosa liked being different. Oh, yes. Rosa *worked* at
being different.

"All through her marriage I wait for her," Scotti was complaining. "I marry no one! I wait for Gerry." He broke off long enough
to admire the shortness of the skirt a young woman was wearing.
"She knows I am waiting." He managed to establish eye contact
with the young woman. "But does it make any difference to her?
No!" A husky young man stepped in front of the woman and
glared darkly at Scotti, who turned smoothly back to Emmy. "She
has no heart, that woman."

"And yet you managed to survive somehow," Emmy remarked
dryly.

"Eh, we must all bear our burdens as best we can," he said
with a long-suffering air. "But I grow no younger. And Gerry, she
is no longer the early chicken."

"Early chicken? Do you mean early bird?"

Scotti frowned in concentration. "*Spring* chicken, that is what I
mean. It means no longer young, does it not?"

"She's not forty yet."

"Ah, but the day comes soon. It is time to settle down. For both
of us."

Emmy consulted the lapel-pin watch she wore. "I must leave,
Toto. I want to go to Brooklyn to hear Rico tonight." That wasn't
true; Emmy was one of those who thought *Elisir* was not one of
Caruso's better operas, but she'd listened to Scotti's complaints
about Gerry as long as she could without becoming rude. "I must
go home and change."

"And I," Scotti said with sudden resolution, "I go to Gerry's
place and I wait. I meet this new lover face to face! I confront
him!"

And make a fool of yourself, no doubt, Emmy thought. The
speakeasy was beginning to grow crowded; the two singers worked
their way among the tables to the door. Outside, it had turned

dark. Scotti's limousine was less than a block away; he told the chauffeur to take Emmy home first and then drive him to West Seventy-fourth Street.

A fine time to get a coughing fit, Enrico Caruso thought, *fifteen minutes before curtain time.* If only his side didn't hurt so!

"Let me call the doctor," Dorothy begged. "You're in no condition to go on!"

He shook his head *no* and sprayed his throat generously, leaving enough liquid there for a good gargle. But even he became alarmed when he saw blood stains in the washbasin.

"That does it," Dorothy said firmly. "I'm calling the doctor!"

"No, Doro, I cannot wait for doctor! Now is time to start! You go take your seat now—you do not wish to miss curtain!"

Dorothy protested, but found herself gently shooed out of the Brooklyn Academy star dressing room. It was time to sing.

Caruso's throat hurt him. His side hurt. He was sweating. He got halfway through the first act of *L'Elisir d'Amore* without having to cough, but then when he did he looked down at scarlet flecks all over the front of his costume. He kept on singing, but he could feel the blood coming out of his mouth. He could see the first few rows of the audience staring at him, horrified.

A movement offstage right caught his eye; someone was standing there waving a white towel. He sang his way over to the side, snatched the towel, and wiped his mouth. He kept the towel with him as he went on with his role, patting at his mouth in between phrases. Before long, the towel was thoroughly soaked and useless.

Part of the scenery for *Elisir* was a well, placed in the exact center of the stage; that's where Caruso decided to deposit his bloody towel. Unfortunately, the audience saw him do it. Unfortunately, he was still slobbering blood.

A chorister nudged him and passed him a fresh towel. The chorus kept relaying towels to him all through the rest of the act.

* * *

Scotti was surprised to find Gerry about to sit down to dinner with Pasquale Amato and Rosa Ponselle. What was this? The new lover was not here? "Where is he?" Scotti demanded.

"Where is who?" Gerry asked.

"Where is this man you spend the afternoon with?"

"I am right here," Amato said, puzzled.

"You, Pasquale?"

"He was helping me do some Christmas shopping," Gerry said. "What *are* you carrying on about?"

"Why you take Pasquale shopping and not me?"

"Do not be *stupido,* Toto," Amato whispered behind his hand.

"Non capisco," Scotti muttered. "What do you say?"

Rosa was laughing. "I'd guess he's telling you they were shopping for your present, Toto."

"Oh, do let's change the subject." Gerry sighed. "Toto, have you had your dinner?"

Finally he caught on. *"Cara mia!"* he cried, and swept her up in a bear hug. "I think such terrible things! Can you forgive me? I am desolate! Forgive, forgive! No, I do not have dinner yet. You invite me?"

Laughing, Gerry disengaged herself from his embrace. "I think I may invite us all to go out to dine." She summoned the maid. "Will you ask the cook if she could possibly feed one more? I don't suppose she can."

"Oh, there's plenty of food," the maid answered easily—and then blushed. "I made a mistake. I told her Mr. Caruso was coming tonight."

Gerry laughed again and asked her to set another place. The four singers sat down and actually managed to forget the troubles at the Metropolitan Opera for a while—until Rosa started talking about what the chorus had done to her that afternoon. Only this time she told it wonderingly instead of angrily, as if amazed at the depth of the mean-spiritedness the chorus had shown her.

"They are changed," Amato said, shaking his head. "They are

not really a chorus anymore. They are many angry people who happen to be on the stage singing at same time.''

"Anarchists," Scotti muttered.

"Oh, now the *choristers* are anarchists?" Gerry asked, amused. "But Pasquale is right. The chorus has changed."

"The Metropolitan itself is changed," Scotti added sadly. "And Emmy—perhaps Emmy most of all. She is not *simpatica* as before.''

"Try spending a war virtually locked up in your own house with armed Austrians watching every move you make and see how *simpatico* you are when it's over," Gerry said. "No wonder she's changed—" She broke off suddenly, catching sight of Rosa drinking it all in, hoping for some gossip. "Besides," Gerry finished, "can you name something in the world that has *not* changed?"

The evening was well advanced by the time they'd finished dining, but no one seemed inclined to leave. Rosa tried to turn the talk back to Emmy Destinn. "I know she's had an unhappy love affair and she had a hard time during the war—"

"Do you think it snows before morning?" Amato pointedly asked Scotti.

"*Sì*, I think so," he answered, wishing he'd never brought up Emmy's name. She was still a friend. He walked over to a window. "Eh—it starts already! It snows now."

The maid came into the room. "Miss Farrar, telephone. It's Mr. Gatti." As Gerry passed her she whispered, "He sounds upset."

Dear God, not another 'accident'. Gerry hurried away to the phone.

"Why won't you people talk about Emmy Destinn when I'm in the room?" Rosa complained crossly to the two men. "Is there some big dark secret about her?"

"No, no secret, little one," Scotti said kindly. "But Emmy, she does not have easy life during the war, and she does not wish to talk about it."

"But she's not here, is she? Why won't *you* talk about it?"

Amato spoke up. "Because Emmy is lady we know for longer than you are alive, young Rosa."

Rosa made a self-mocking face. "None of my business, hm?"

The two baritones smiled at her. Scotti glanced up to see Gerry standing frozen in the doorway. "*Cielo!* Do you see ghost, *cara mia?*"

White-faced, Gerry stammered, "That, that was Gatti. *Elisir* . . . in Brooklyn—oh, it's Rico! He started hemorrhaging. He was coughing up blood on the stage. It got so bad they had to stop the performance."

□ **4** □ Of all of Caruso's friends, it was Scotti who was most visibly shaken by what had happened in Brooklyn. The others were stunned into a kind of paralysis; Scotti had burst into tears.

According to what Gatti-Casazza told them the next day, Caruso had managed to finish the first act while filling up the stage well with bloody towels. Dorothy Caruso had called his doctor, whom she herself did not trust; he was waiting for the tenor in the dressing room by the time the act was finished. The physician who had cared for Caruso's throat for most of his career was recently deceased; Dorothy did not believe his replacement was either conscientious enough or skilled enough to care for her husband properly.

Her distrust was quickly justified. After a cursory examination, the doctor glibly announced that all the blood had come from a tiny burst vein in the tip of Caruso's tongue—even though the tenor was so hoarse he could barely speak. The doctor pronounced him fit to continue singing; Caruso believed him and started getting ready for the second act.

At that point the house manager took matters into his own hands. He went before the curtain and told the anxious audience that Caruso was ill but he was willing to continue if they wished him to. *NO!* they roared back, many of them in tears. Caruso had accepted their decision with relief. The rest of the performance was cancelled.

The Sunday following the aborted *Elisir* performance the tenor spent resting his throat, not even speaking, pointing and waving his arms when he wanted something. Dorothy Caruso said, *Please, no visitors;* and the tenor's worried friends honored her request. Caruso reclined in regal splendor on a chaise longue, surrounded by baskets of flowers, reading messages from well-wishers, eating ice cream.

The next day he was ready to conquer the world.

"I sing!" he told Gatti-Casazza over the phone. "You listen." Caruso demonstrated he hadn't lost any of his high notes.

Gatti admitted the tenor sounded as good as ever. "What does the doctor say?"

"Pah! What does he know? Doro is right, he is not good doctor. I tell you I sing now. *Intendete?*"

"I hear. Do you find new doctor?"

"I have many doctors, Mr. Gatti. Do not worry so."

"Still, more rest might be wise." Gatti was torn; he wanted to get the tenor back on the stage as soon as possible—but not at the risk of losing him for the rest of the season. "Stay home, rest. Do not exert yourself."

"Stay home?" Caruso sounded insulted. "No, no, Mr. Gatti—I feel too good to stay home all the time! No, tonight I go hear the new tenor!"

"Enrico—"

"Everyone, they say I am afraid of him! They say that is why I do not go to his performances! So tonight I prove them wrong, yes?"

Gatti argued with him for a while, but it was a lost cause. Caruso was determined to bounce back, and all the words of caution in the world weren't going to stop him. He didn't *want* to be sick, and that was that.

It can be a mite disconcerting to see the man you're trying to supplant stand up and applaud your efforts.

Face frozen into a smile, Beniamino Gigli bowed as graciously as he could toward the artists' box, where Enrico Caruso was pounding his hands together with enthusiasm. Everyone in the audience knew Caruso had risen from his sickbed to come hear Gigli sing, and most of them seemed to be paying more attention to the artists' box than they were to the stage. Gigli felt his face would crack if he had to smile much longer.

At last the applause began to die, and Gigli was able to escape. One more act.

Backstage, a couple of the choristers sniggered as he hurried by; they thought it was funny, how Caruso had stolen his thunder without singing a note. Gigli sensed his face turning red as he rushed up the stairs to the star dressing room. He'd been haunted by the Neapolitan tenor throughout his whole career; even when the critics raved about his singing, they said things like *Only Caruso could have sung it better.* Caruso! To have to compete with his presence when he had a performance to concentrate on . . . it was too much. Besides, the big toe of his right foot hurt; one of the chorus singers had stepped on him.

"Roberto!" he called. "Make haste!" Gigli's valet had his fourth-act costume ready for him. Two costumes, actually. A simple black cloak was the first; it would cover the second, a fifteenth-century knight's costume. Remove the cloak, and *voilà!* A costume change. The opera was Boïto's *Mefistofele,* which had served as Gigli's début vehicle at the Met only a few weeks earlier. Gigli had been quite happy with that choice until he learned that Gounod's *Faust* would also be in the Metropolitan's repertoire that season. *Two* operas about bargaining with the devil? *Ridicolo.* And all because that Farrar woman insisted on one role each year that she hadn't sung the year before; *Faust* had been this year's choice. If that was a fair example of the way Gatti-Casazza ran his opera house, there was going to be trouble ahead. Eh, well—the Viennese beauty Maria Jeritza would be joining the Metropolitan next year; they'd see how high and mighty la Farrar was then.

The valet dressed the tenor without speaking; Roberto knew storm clouds when he saw them. Gigli was thinking ahead to the fourth act. The chorus would play a prominent part, but it was a women's chorus. They might cross the stage while he was singing or do something else to distract the audience, but at least they wouldn't be stepping on his toes. The corps de ballet would be on for part of the act, but the dancers never made trouble for him. Nor did the soloists. Nor the conductors. Nor the orchestra. Nor the stagehands.

Only the chorus.

Gigli exploded into a fit of cursing and looked around for something to break. Roberto quickly moved a flower-filled Limoges vase out of the way and handed the tenor a cherub-ornamented clock that was a pain to dust. Gigli hurled the clock against the dressing-room wall, where it shattered satisfyingly into a thousand pieces. But the tenor was still fuming. Here he was, after years of living in the shadow of Enrico Caruso, singing at the Metropolitan Opera at last—and he was spending all his time worrying about the *chorus*! *Incredible.*

Time for Act IV.

The first part of the act passed without incident. The chorus did nothing at all out of the ordinary; the women had evidently decided to leave him alone for the time being. Gigli forgot about them and poured his heart and soul into his performance. For the first time that evening, he felt like singing.

Then, during a duet with the soprano singing Helen of Troy, the woman looked over his shoulder, widened her eyes, and screamed.

Gigli whirled to see a scenery flat come crashing down from the flies. Warned by the soprano's scream, four of the chorus women jumped out of the way just in time. The orchestra couldn't cover the sound of ripping canvas and splintering wood and a cry went up from the audience. Somebody was yelling. Somebody else closed the curtain.

"Are you hurt, Mr. Gigli?" a voice asked.

"No, no," he said dismissively, already over his shock and beginning to grow angry.

No one was hurt, as it turned out; the flat had come close but had not actually hit anyone. Within five minutes the debris of the shattered flat had been removed and a stagehand was sweeping splinters and nails from the stage floor. What little pleasure Gigli had been able to derive from that evening's work was now gone forever. He gritted his teeth and determined to get through the rest of it somehow.

He finished the fourth act and dashed off the stage. He donned a beard, a white wig, and a cloak to hide his knight's costume. He went back on the stage. He sang the Epilogue. He bowed to the audience. He left the stage. He went up to his dressing room. He kicked a chair and broke it.

And started his toe hurting again, the one the lead-footed chorister had stepped on. Deliberately. Gigli sat down on the dressing room's remaining unbroken chair and philosophized about that for a while. What does it signify that a man should work all his life toward a single prize, and just as his fingers close around it—somebody steps on his toe?

It was too much for him. He could understand the chorus's badgering of Rosa Ponselle, in a way. She had not earned her starring-role status; she'd had it handed to her on a platter. She'd not spent her life learning languages, memorizing scores, practicing scales three hundred sixty-five days a year. She'd not experienced the rejections and the small humiliations that were part of every singer's life. She had not *suffered*. The chorus was wrong to badger her—Ponselle had the true gift, after all—but he could understand why they did it.

What he couldn't understand was why the chorus was treating him the same way. He'd expected *some* resistance from the Caruso-lovers, but not to this extent! It was inexcusable. To think that a soloist at one of the major opera houses of the world should be subject to harassment by a gang of nameless musical thugs! And he could do nothing! He'd complained to the conductors, he'd complained to the chorus master, he'd complained to Gatti-Casazza, he'd complained to Gatti's assistant.

A thought struck him. About the only ones he'd not complained to were the choristers themselves. Lead singers did not normally involve themselves in the concerns of the chorus, but in circumstances as extraordinary as these—

"Magnifico!" a world-famous voice boomed out. *"Stupendo! Eminente!"*

Gigli groaned inwardly as Caruso burst into his dressing room, followed by his Nordic American wife. *Smile. Show him a rival who is self-confident and relaxed.*

"A great *Mefistofele* tonight!" Caruso cried. "You make great Faust, eh?"

"We both enjoyed your performance immensely, Mr. Gigli," Dorothy Caruso said quietly.

"Me, I am jealous!" Caruso sang joyfully, looking anything but jealous. "You steal my role from me, yes?"

Gigli squinted at Caruso suspiciously. If the older tenor were indeed worried about being permanently replaced in *Mefistofele*, why was he acting so happy about it? Did he really mean he thought Gigli's performance so lackluster that he didn't have anything to worry about? Gigli managed to choke out a civil answer.

Caruso's mood changed abruptly; he became conspiratorial. "It fails tonight, does it not? The four ladies in the chorus, they are not hurt."

Gigli didn't understand. "What fails tonight?"

Caruso glanced quickly at his wife. "Whatever is causing so much trouble for the chorus." He'd promised Dorothy to stop talking about a curse. "The falling flat, it hits no one. No one is hurt tonight."

"The *performance* is hurt," Gigli said touchily. In his view the Metropolitan's chorus was unusually accident-prone, and that was the source of the mishaps that had been plaguing the opera house for the past few weeks. It didn't quite explain the woman with the knife in her chest, though. "We have to stop, while stage is cleared."

"Only *un momento*," Caruso said reassuringly. "When you sing again, everyone forgets the accident."

"That's true, Mr. Gigli," Dorothy added. "The performance resumed so quickly, no one had time to think about what had happened."

Gigli allowed himself to be persuaded. He relaxed a little and said, "Do you know the police question *me*? What do I know of the choristers' problems?"

"*Sì*, they question all of us," Caruso said. "They even talk to Doro because she is backstage some of the time." Dorothy nodded. "Right now, all they want to know about is the poor lady who is stabbed," Caruso went on. "That is no accident! But who hates her?"

"I do not even know her," Gigli said. "I do not know any of them, except as members of group of singers who are nothing but trouble! In no other house I sing in is chorus like this one tolerated—not for one minute!"

Caruso looked shocked. "It is not the lady's fault she is stabbed!"

"Of course not," Gigli said testily. "Her I do not blame. But the others—I think they invite trouble."

"You say they deserve what happens to them?"

Gigli threw up his hands. "I do not say this! I say they are troublemakers. Perhaps they make trouble for themselves?"

Dorothy saw the outrage building in her husband's face and started urging him toward the door. "We'll leave you to change now, Mr. Gigli. And we do thank you for such an exciting performance! Goodbye."

Gigli wondered at the odd look Caruso threw him as he allowed Dorothy to usher him out the door. *Cielo, it is strange evening all around,* Gigli thought. "Roberto! Assist me!" He quickly changed into street clothes, eager to get to a more friendly environment than what the opera house had provided that night. He left his valet to clean up behind him and hurried down the steps, almost bumping into a poorly dressed woman as he rushed out.

"Hey, there!" the doorkeeper called to her in a friendly way. "You're here mighty late, ain't ya?"

"Leave thing," Mrs. Bukaitis said. "Mistake."

"You forgot something? Well, better hurry up and get it, then. I'll be locking up in a few minutes."

The scrubwoman nodded and made her way to the substage area, which was not only deserted but dark. Mrs. Bukaitis pulled a flashlight out of her bag and aimed it upward. Following the night the trap door in the stage had given way, Edward Ziegler had issued the order that the pneumatic platform be kept in a raised position whenever it was not in use so that no one would fall again. The trap and the lift both had been needed in that evening's *Mefistofele,* but the stagehand in charge of working the lift had followed Ziegler's order and returned the platform to its up position as soon as the performance had ended. It was the underside of the platform that Mrs. Bukaitis was interested in.

She tucked the flashlight into an armpit and use both hands to work the lever, stopping the platform's descent at about six feet above floor level. She shone her light under the platform . . . yes, there it was. She stripped away the tape holding the rectangular box in place, and considered opening it right then.

No, better wait—wait and show it to Antanas. Antanas could tell her why the bomb had failed to go off.

"You must find new chorus master," Alessandro Quaglia told Gatti-Casazza in no uncertain terms. "Setti is not doing the job. He has no control over the chorus."

"Can anyone control the chorus?" Gatti murmured. "It is not simple matter of discipline, Maestro. They have reason for their anger."

"They need no reason! Their behavior is unprofessional and must not be tolerated. Do you see how they sabotage Gigli in *Mefistofele* last night?"

"I see. Do you see how falling flat almost kills four choristers?"

"Do you suggest one justifies the other?"

"No certamente." Gatti pulled at his beard. "I mean to say now is not good time for the, er, cracking down." Quaglia had come storming into the general manager's office, snow melting on his overcoat, demanding action, and Gatti was looking for a way to stop the conductor from pressuring him. "We must first end these 'accidents'," he said. "Then the chorus is more manageable."

Quaglia snorted. "They use the 'accidents' to demand more for themselves! Are they not asking for more money? Again?"

"My assistant handles all contract negotiations," Gatti said, ducking the question.

"How do you plan to stop so-called accidents? The police cannot stop them. How do *you* stop them?"

"Ah." Gatti sat up a little straighter. "The police cannot be everywhere during a performance—there are not enough of them. That is where I *can* do something. I employ firm of security protection agents to patrol the opera house before and during every performance . . . until the man behind these dreadful events is caught."

"Guards?" Quaglia thought a moment. "The man who is doing these things—he is very clever."

"But is he clever enough to stay hidden when *everyone* is looking for him? If nothing else, the presence of large numbers of guards discourages him, no? It goes on long enough. It must stop."

The conductor nodded slowly. "So we wait a little longer. Then, if it does not stop—then you replace Setti?"

Gatti told him he would think about it. Quaglia saw he was going to have to be satisfied with that and left. In the foyer, three scrubwomen were on their hands and knees; Quaglia wondered if one of them was the woman who'd discovered the hanging man in the chorus dressing room. He slipped into the back of the auditorium and sat down in the last row. The chorus master whom he'd wanted Gatti to replace had called an onstage rehearsal, ostensibly for the benefit of the new members of the chorus. But actually Setti was more worried about the regular choristers than the new ones, and he took every opportunity he could to rehearse them. Recalcitrant old singers and nervous new ones, both on the stage together. Quaglia wanted to hear what they sounded like.

What they sounded like right then was a gang of revolutionaries getting ready to storm the Bastille. They were shouting and waving their fists and clomping about the stage with unnecessarily heavy feet. Last night's falling scenery flat was the day's bone of contention, and the singers were making the most of it. Gatti's assistant was on stage with Setti, the two of them working at calming down the irate singers. But the choristers didn't want to calm down; they were feeding off one another's anger and excitement.

Finally Giulio Setti planted his feet, threw back his head, and roared: *"Sta'zitto!"* In the auditorium Quaglia flinched; so big a voice coming out of so small a man was a surprise.

The choristers were startled too, lapsing into a silence that could only too easily prove temporary. So Edward Ziegler stepped forward and began to speak rapidly. He told them Mr. Gatti had hired guards to protect them; the guards would be backstage, in the greenroom, in the chorus dressing room on the fourth floor. He explained that some guards would even dress in costume and accompany them on stage during performances. He promised them that this protection would continue until the person who had killed one of their number had been caught.

"So you see," Ziegler finished, "the management truly is concerned about ensuring your safety. We are doing everything we can conceive of to protect you. If you can think of anything else we could be doing, please tell us about it. We are open to suggestion."

There was a little *sub voce* muttering, but no one came forward with a specific suggestion; Ziegler had taken the wind out of their sails. One of the singers wanted to know how much the guards were being paid, but Ziegler pretended not to hear. "For the time being," he said, "just stay together, don't wander off alone. Try to keep a guard in sight at all times. Well, if that's all, I'll leave you to Mr. Setti now."

Ziegler hurried off into the wings but paused when he got there. He didn't want to run out on Setti if the chorus should still prove intractable. And besides, Gatti would be sure to ask him how the chorus sounded.

Setti said one word: *"Forza."* A few of the new choristers were carrying scores; they hurriedly located the choral music for *La Forza del Destino*. At Setti's indication, they began to sing.

Ziegler winced. Their attack was dreadful, everyone coming in at a different time. Setti let them continue awhile, until they were getting into the feel of the music, and then had them start over. The second time was a little better, but they still sounded more like a group of highly gifted amateurs singing together for the first time than the chorus of a professional opera company.

"Stop!" Setti cried. "You new people, you do not watch me! Put the scores aside. If you do not know the words, go *la-la-la*. But watch *me*."

This time, with every eye in the chorus on Setti's hands, the attack was crisp and sharp, the way it was supposed to be. Ziegler felt a tingle of excitement as the chorus began singing with enthusiasm; Setti was getting the ringing tones out of them that Verdi had intended when he wrote the music. They were beginning to sound like a real chorus when—for reasons known only to themselves—every tenor in the chorus started singing flat.

At the back of the auditorium, Alessandro Quaglia got up and left in disgust.

Ziegler stayed, waiting as Setti patiently rehearsed the tenors alone until he was satisfied they could stay on pitch. The reunited chorus tried again. This time they got all the way through one number without anything disgraceful happening; Ziegler released the breath he'd been holding. It would do. They weren't setting any new standards for choral singing, but it would do.

Setti called a break and hurried over to where Ziegler was standing. "Well? What do you think?"

"I think it's possible we may have a chorus again," the assistant manager said cautiously. "Not just yet, but there was a moment there—"

"Yes, yes!" Setti cried excitedly. "The singing, it is still in them! They *can* do it, if they will."

"If they will."

"And they will. I *make* them sing right. I must waste no time." The chorus master hurried back to his singers.

Ziegler nodded and left them to it, wondering if Setti could pull it off.

Rosa Ponselle had made her Metropolitan Opera début as Leonora in *La Forza del Destino*. She'd been taught the role one phrase at a time, slowly and painstakingly. When the night of her début arrived, it finally sank in on her that all those people backstage actually expected her to go out on that enormous stage alone and face that glittering Diamond Horseshoe of an audience all by herself. She was twenty-one years old and had never even seen a performance of *Forza*. She panicked.

But someone pushed her out on the stage, she sang, the audience loved her, and all was well. Now starting her third season at the Met, she'd learned more roles, sung more performances— and she still panicked. Part of the reason was that in *Forza* she was partnered with Enrico Caruso, whose pre-performance stage fright was legendary; Rosa couldn't help but pick up some anxiety from him. The rest of the reason was that she still thought of herself as an ex-vaudeville performer, one-half of a sister act, who was only slowly coming to feel that she really and truly belonged at the Metropolitan Opera.

Matters were not helped any by the fact that the backstage area was as crowded as Ebbets Field on the opening day of the World Series.

"Everywhere are police!" Caruso cried. "All the time, I am bumping into policeman!"

"Shut up, Rico!" Rosa screamed. "You're making things worse!"

"Do not tell your elders to shut up!" he screamed back. "You shut up!"

"In fede mia!" protested Pasquale Amato, that evening's singing villain. "Never do I hear so much noise backstage! Please—it is better without the screaming, yes?"

"It is better without the screaming *no!*" Caruso roared.

"Screaming is good for you," Rosa informed Amato in an uncharacteristically schoolteacherish manner. "It clears out the clogs in the respiratory system. Where's Setti?" She wandered away in search of the chorus master.

Amato looked at one of the guards. "Clogs?" The guard shrugged.

The new guards, mingling with those members of New York's finest assigned to the opera house, were there to reassure as well as protect; but so many uniforms backstage at once were having the contrary effect of making a lot of people nervous. The guards and the police were making *each other* nervous. The only ones not upset by the presence of so many strangers were the choristers. In fact, they wouldn't have minded if there'd been even more bodyguards in evidence. But police and private guards both had been busy; everything that could possibly pose a threat to the safety of the chorus was checked, double-checked, and triple-checked.

"Eh, Maestro," Gatti-Casazza said worriedly, "perhaps the choristers begin to feel more secure, do you think?"

"Does feeling secure make them sing better?" Quaglia said testily as a large policeman bumped into him. "I think not."

"Oh?" Gatti was surprised. "Ziegler tells me they sing well in rehearsal."

"Not when I hear them—ow! Watch where you step!"

"Sorry," a guard mumbled and elbowed his way through the crowd.

"Setti is optimistic," Gatti persisted.

"I hope he is right." Quaglia noticed Gatti's distraught air and relented a little. "I do not stay for entire rehearsal, you understand. Perhaps they improve after I leave."

"That must be—*per la vita mia!* What now?"

Rosa Ponselle had the chorus master backed up against a scenery flat and was laying down the law—at the top of her voice. "I'm telling you, Mr. Setti, if any one of those orangutans so much as crosses in front of me tonight, I'm going to kick him where it hurts the most!"

"Please, no—"

"Or if it's a woman, I'll tear her hair out—right there on the stage! I'm through with waiting until the act is over to complain! I'm going to start defending myself, right out where everyone can see! Do you hear?"

"Everybody hears," the chorus master sighed.

"Well, you make sure they all understand, now. I'm serious—I won't let myself be blocked off or pushed or stepped on or anything. I'm telling you, it's got to stop *tonight!*"

"Rosa!" Caruso sang out. "Do not bully Mr. Setti!"

"The chorus is his responsibility, isn't it? He's got to make them behave!"

Gatti insinuated himself into the one-sided argument and explained to the nervous young soprano that her declaration of independence could perhaps have been better timed. Eventually Rosa

let herself be persuaded that tonight was going to be different and
that she was worrying over nothing.

An older woman in peasant costume came up to them. "Mr.
Setti, we're going to be short one bass tonight. Spike is sick."

All talking stopped. Simultaneously Gatti and Quaglia and the
soloists figured out that 'Spike' was the name of an opera singer
and that he sang in the chorus and he was *sick.* . . .

"*Misericordia!*" Setti cried out. "Another one!"

"No, no, it's just something he ate," the chorus woman said
hastily. "He might feel well enough to sing later—he just can't
start."

"Where is he?" Gatti demanded.

"In the greenroom."

"Alone?"

"Of course not," the woman said indignantly. "A guard is with
him." She started to add something but found herself uncer-
emoniously pushed aside by a mob of people dashing to the greenroom to check on the state of health of a chorus singer named
Spike.

In the greenroom, a pale young man sat up on the settee where
he'd been lying and shakily lifted his fists to protect himself
against the horde bearing down on him. "What . . . what did I
do?"

"What is wrong with you?" Gatti demanded.

"How do you feel?" Amato asked.

"Lie down, lie down!" Setti urged.

"How long you feel this way?" Caruso wanted to know.

"Oh, is there anything I can do?" Rosa cried.

"Someone call a doctor!" Quaglia commanded the room at
large.

Spike's eyes grew larger as he understood that all these important people were worrying about his stomachache. "I don't need a
doctor. It's just indigestion."

"A doctor," Quaglia insisted. "We take no chances. Where is a
doctor?"

"One of my doctors, he is here!" Caruso cried. (Dorothy had insisted on it.) "I get him!" He hurried away.

Spike's mouth fell open at the sight of the most famous singer in the world running off to fetch *him* a doctor. "I took some Bromo-Seltzer."

Setti put his hand on the young man's forehead. "No fever. It could be indigestion."

"I know it's indigestion," Spike said. "In the dressing room, one of the men brought in a huge Italian sausage and I had some."

Amato's eyebrows shot up. "I eat sausage three, four times every week. It never makes me sick."

The young singer smiled ruefully. "Not all of us can eat garlic without paying a penalty. It always makes me queasy—I should have known better."

"Oh, you poor boy!" Rosa cooed. He was at least two years older than she. "Why not lie back down until the doctor gets here?" She sat beside him. "Here, let me help." With a minimum of maneuvering, Spike ended up with his head in her lap. "Isn't that better?" she asked.

"Oh, much better, yes."

"Where is that doctor?" Quaglia muttered.

Gatti pulled out his watch. "It is time. We must start the performance."

Quaglia shook his head. "I do not go into orchestra pit until I know this is not another attack on the chorus."

"I'm sorry, Maestro, but I must insist," Gatti said quietly. "You can do nothing here—"

Edward Ziegler came rushing in. "What is it? What is it?"

"A stomachache," Amato smiled, shaking his head. "From eating good Italian sausage."

"I heard one of the choristers had been—"

"No, no!" Gatti said. "Do not allow that rumor to spread! We do not know what is wrong yet—a doctor comes."

Ziegler walked over to where Spike was lying happily with his head in Rosa Ponselle's lap. "You don't look sick to me," he accused.

The smile on Spike's face was quickly replaced by a grimace of pain. He helped the effect by groaning a little. "A glass of orange juice might help." He pointed to a pitcher that stood on the small table next to the settee.

Rosa poured a glass. She put one hand under Spike's head to raise him up and held the glass to his lips. "How's that?"

He drank half the juice. "Better." She put the glass on the table. Spike laid his head back in her lap and grasped her hand. "How soft your hand is!"

"You must lie still," she whispered.

Ziegler looked at Gatti. "*This* is what everybody's so excited about?"

"Here is the doctor," Setti announced.

A thin man carrying a black bag followed Caruso into the green-room. It took him only a few pokes and prods to come up with a diagnosis. "Gas," he said bluntly and saw Rosa wince. "Excuse me, Miss Ponselle. I should have said a digestive problem."

Spike looked up soulfully at Rosa. "A *bad* digestive problem," he murmured. She made soothing noises and stroked his forehead.

"I have something here that'll have him up and around in no time," the doctor said. "Don't worry—it's nothing serious."

Only then did the others relax. Now it was official: No one was trying to poison the chorus. The men exchanged sheepish looks. "Look at us," Quaglia said sourly. "One chorister gets a tummy-ache and we all panic."

"I do not panic," Caruso sniffed. "I go get doctor."

"Now we start the performance," Gatti announced firmly and led the way out of the greenroom.

Rosa carefully lifted Spike's head off her lap. "Lie still, now. Take your time."

"Come back?" he asked hopefully.

She smiled and said maybe and followed the men to the stage. The curtain was going to be a little late tonight.

Gatti did a quick check; the soloists were in their places and

Quaglia was on his way to the orchestra pit. The general manager kept thinking of what the conductor had just said, about how quickly they'd all panicked once they thought another chorister might be in danger. Young Spike had been too interested in winning Rosa Ponselle's sympathy to be seriously ill; but was this to be the pattern from now on? Every time a chorus singer became indisposed, everything else would grind to a halt?

Gatti found himself a place in the wings where he could stand out of the way; general managers were fifth wheels during a performance. He mumbled a little prayer, hoping the audience had not had time to grow restless while waiting for the late curtain.

Out front, the talkative audience hadn't even noticed the opera was late in starting, and at least two of its members were grateful for the delay. Geraldine Farrar and Antonio Scotti had dawdled and were only just then arriving; they made their usual grand entrance into the artists' box—and found Emmy Destinn already sitting there.

"Emmy!" Gerry smiled bravely, not really welcoming the other soprano's company for the next few hours. "I thought you avoided Rosa's performances!"

"Not at all," Emmy answered sharply. "I just avoid Rosa."

"Now, Emmy," Scotti said reprovingly. "Rosa means well."

"She's a nosy little girl who's never been taught any manners." Emmy turned to Gerry. "And you—at a *Verdi* performance, Gerry?"

"I just don't sing Verdi—I do listen to him." Gerry had decided years ago that either Verdi's music wasn't right for her voice or her voice wasn't right for Verdi's music, a puzzle she didn't particularly care to resolve.

The truth was, they were all three there for the same reason. This was Caruso's first time back on the stage since the night he'd hemorrhaged. They were worried about him.

Quaglia had made his way to the podium and now faced the orchestra with both arms lifted in the air. Down came his arms and the orchestra sounded three powerful trumpet blasts, paused, and sounded three more. Then they were into the haunting, uneasy theme music associated with the opera's heroine.

Rosa Ponselle and Pasquale Amato opened the opera, and it wasn't until after Amato had exited that Caruso made his first entrance. He and Rosa immediately plunged into a long and dramatic duet, and the three singers in the artists' box held their breath.

They needn't have worried. The tenor's tone was pure and his control was perfect. He was holding back some, though—a cause for rejoicing because that meant he had decided to be sensible. But even holding back, Caruso still had more power than any other tenor in the opera company, including the sweet-voiced Gigli. It was going to be all right.

The full chorus didn't make its appearance until the second act, another cause for breath-holding. But whether it was because they were concerned about Caruso or because they just weren't in the mood for pestering Rosa, the choristers behaved themselves. They did nothing they weren't supposed to do. And they sang. They sang like the professionals they were, loving what they were doing and doing it well. A ripple of excitement began to run through the responsive audience.

"I am glad we do not miss this," Scotti whispered.

The excitement continued to build as the opera progressed; and upon the completion of her big final-act aria, *Pace, pace mio Dio!*, Rosa received a standing ovation. The two sopranos in the artists' box joined in with sincere enthusiasm; Scotti called out, *"Brava! Brava!"*

Whatever Emmy Destinn thought of Rosa Ponselle personally, the older soprano was still a musician before everything else; she responded wholeheartedly to the younger woman's performance. "How is it possible to have a voice like that?" she murmured.

"By special arrangement with God," Gerry answered wryly.

The opera came to an end, and the cast was called back for curtain call after curtain call. The audience finally began to leave, exhausted but happy. The three singers in the artists' box held court for a few minutes, but finally told their well-wishers that they were eager to get backstage. All the way down to the stage level they chattered happily, still keyed up by the performances they'd just heard.

So they were all three laughing and talking when they swept on to the stage behind the closed curtain . . . and found everyone there standing like statues. Singers, stagehands, guards—all frozen in place, identical expressions of shock on all their faces. The only sound was that of Rosa Ponselle crying, her face buried in Caruso's shoulder.

"Rosa!" Gerry gasped, hurrying over to her. "What is it? What's happened?"

"Spike's dead," Rosa sobbed. "Someone poisoned him after all."

☐ **5** ☐ "This," Captain Michael O'Halloran said to himself, "has gone far enough."

Even with the backstage area of the Metropolitan Opera swarming with hired guards as well as selected members of the New York police force, the madman on the loose had still managed to work his dirty deed. And if O'Halloran's best men couldn't put a stop to it, then O'Halloran himself was going to have to step in.

He'd resisted. When the stabbing of the chorus singer had been reported, it had been all O'Halloran could do to keep from grabbing his hat and dashing straight to the opera house. Even when the investigators he'd assigned to the case came back with word that the stabbing was only one of a series of suspicious-looking incidents, O'Halloran had confined himself to making suggestions and giving orders. He was a captain now; his role was to supervise investigations, not do the investigating himself.

O'Halloran had been involved in two earlier cases at the Metropolitan, back when he was still a lieutenant with the New York Detective Bureau. Both times, a Metropolitan singer had decided to play detective, imperiously meddling in the case without so much as a by-your-leave. First it had been Enrico Caruso, who'd stumbled and bumbled around and ended up accusing the wrong person. But much to everyone's surprise, his blundering had actually helped turn up the real killer in the end. The second time it was Geraldine Farrar who'd undertaken her own investigation; at the eleventh hour she'd stopped O'Halloran from arresting an innocent man.

He was simultaneously grateful to and exasperated with both singers. O'Halloran had no patience with amateurs who meddled in police business; but he had to admit that in those two cases the meddling had helped. He'd warned the investigators he'd assigned to this new case to be on the look-out for self-appointed detectives, but so far they'd reported no interference from anyone.

Because this time it's different, O'Halloran thought. Those other two times had dealt with a single incident each—violent death in both cases, horrible and unnerving, but at the same time manageable. Most people could cope with the idea of disaster striking and then moving on; you suffered your losses, picked up the pieces, and went on with your life. But the repeated, inexplicable *malevolence* of what was happening at the Met right now—that was something altogether different.

Captain O'Halloran shuffled through the various police reports on his desk, trying to get it clear in his mind the order in which the various incidents had taken place. Evidently the first of them had been the death of the woman chorister during a performance of *Samson and Delilah*. A stage urn had fallen on her head, killing her instantly. The episode had been labeled an accident at the time, understandably. Then one of the men in the chorus had hanged himself, or so it had appeared. Accident and suicide, no cause for suspicion yet.

But now O'Halloran's investigators were convinced that those first two deaths were homicides, and O'Halloran saw no reason to disagree with them. The next thing to happen had come during a performance of *I Pagliacci,* at a time when ex-detective Enrico Caruso was on the stage. A trap door in the stage floor had given way and two men had fallen thirty feet; one had died, the other had been seriously injured. Again, an accident—on the surface of things.

That, however, was the last such incident that could be dismissed as an accident without question. The stabbing of the chorus woman during a performance of *Carmen*—starring that other ex-detective, Geraldine Farrar—could only have been willful murder. O'Halloran mulled that over for a while. He accepted his detectives' theory that one person was behind all these frightening goings-on; to think otherwise would be to stretch coincidence beyond the breaking point. But between the *Pagliacci* staged 'accident' and the *Carmen* murder, the killer must have undergone a change of attitude. He was no longer satisfied with arranging murders that everyone was willing to accept as accidents. Now he wanted the world to know what he was doing; he wanted to be recognized. He wanted the chorus to understand he was out to get them.

O'Halloran frowned. That didn't jibe with the next incident, though—a flat had fallen to the stage during a performance of *Mefistofele,* barely missing four of the chorus women. A failure, from the killer's point of view, but one that again carried the appearance of an accident. Or perhaps that time it really was an accident? People in an opera house do not call the police every time a flat breaks loose from its moorings; and by the time O'Halloran's detectives had found out about it, it was too late to check the rope that had been used to raise and lower the flat. The rope had either been discarded or was being used elsewhere; one rope looks pretty much like any other. If it wasn't a true accident, then maybe the killer was having second thoughts about making his presence known. Or maybe he'd counted on someone's looking at the rope and seeing it had been cut.

The captain was inclined to think the latter was the true explanation. For when his latest attempt at murder had failed to be recognized as such, the killer had turned to the most obviously premeditated form of murder there was: poison. You can't say you administered a slow-acting poison in the heat of anger or in a fight. You can't say you thought it was sugar you were sprinkling on your victim's oatmeal, not if you expect to be believed. No, the use of poison was a calling card that no one could ignore or explain away. The sausage the victim had eaten part of and to which he'd attributed his indigestion had been taken to a police laboratory and analyzed; it contained nothing a good sausage should not contain. The poison had been added to a pitcher of orange juice the younger singer was drinking from in the greenroom.

O'Halloran's detectives had investigated the five victims' backgrounds and private lives but had found nothing useful. The man who'd been killed falling through the trap door had once been arrested for shoplifting when he was a boy; but other than that one misdemeanor, none of the victims had a criminal record. None of the five posed a threat to anyone else. There was no connection among them except the Metropolitan Opera; these five didn't even socialize together when they were away from the opera house. Singing in the chorus was the only thing they had in common.

O'Halloran was a man who took his work home with him, and his wife had grown so tired of hearing about the Metropolitan Opera that she'd urged him to take over the investigation himself. *It has to be stopped, doesn't it?* she'd asked reasonably. *So, stop it.* What she'd meant was *Stop talking about it and do something,* but O'Halloran had waited until the assigned detectives admitted they were stumped. Only then did the captain make up his mind to involve himself personally.

He'd start off by paying a visit to the opera house; then he'd decide whom to talk to. O'Halloran called for a police car, shrugged on his overcoat, and picked up his new gray Stetson. He'd reluctantly thought of saving the hat for special occasions, but his wife had convinced him that a Captain of Detectives needed to be well dressed all the time. That was one of the things he liked best about Bridget; she was always able to come up with sensible reasons for doing things he already wanted to do.

There was a spring in his step as he left the office. It was good to be working a case again, and he was determined not to let up until he'd learned why someone had set out to kill off the entire chorus of the Metropolitan Opera.

"I'm afraid," Geraldine Farrar told her friends. "For the first time in my life, I am truly afraid." Antonio Scotti wrapped a comforting arm about her shoulders. "Not even getting caught in Germany when the war broke out was as bad as this. This is the kind of fear that gets down inside your bones—does anyone understand what I'm talking about?"

"I understand," Emmy Destinn said quietly.

"Ah, Emmy." Pasquale Amato sat down beside her and patted her hand. "Do not think of the violent war years. Think of . . ."

"Think of now?" she asked wryly. "The non-violent postwar years?"

"*È vero,* it is not much better. A small war, inside our opera house."

"But how can you fight a war when you don't know who the enemy is?" Gerry cried. "This faceless killer moves among us like an invisible man and strikes whenever he pleases! I'm surprised the entire chorus hasn't resigned. I know I'd quit, if I were a chorister.''

"This morning, they say they quit—all of them," Gatti-Casazza muttered. The others gasped. "But Ziegler, he persuades them to stay," the general manager assured them hastily. "He promises each one a personal armed bodyguard. One guard assigned to one chorister, you see. These guards, they go with them everywhere—in the dressing room, on stage, everywhere.''

"*Cielo!*" Scotti exclaimed. "So many people!"

"It is necessary," Gatti said worriedly. "We must now find costumes for all the guards to wear. And the women choristers, they do not want men in their dressing room. So we must find women who know how to shoot the guns . . . and the expense! The budget, it is ruined. Ruined!"

They had gathered at the Carusos' Vanderbilt apartment in the morning after the latest chorus murder. Dorothy Caruso was trying to play hostess and listen at the same time, while her husband sat moodily in a corner, saying nothing. "Don't the police have any idea at all who is responsible?" Dorothy murmured.

Gatti shook his head. "They are as puzzled as we."

"We must do something," Emmy announced emphatically. "We cannot allow this to continue."

"What can *we* do?" Amato asked. "We—"

"I don't know—something," Emmy interrupted. "We can't just sit around watching this happen without trying to stop it."

"What can we do?" Scotti repeated, his face lighting up. "We can find the killer ourselves, that is what we can do!"

"Oh, Toto," Amato sighed.

"And why not?" Scotti went on enthusiastically. "We have experienced detective right here, do we not?" He gave Gerry a little hug.

"Oh, Toto," she sighed.

"*Two* detectives," muttered a tenor voice from the corner.

One and a half, Amato thought. "Toto, do you seriously ask

Gerry to go look for man who has already killed. . ."—he stopped
to count—". . .five people?"

"Ah." Scotti hadn't thought of it that way. "No, that is not
safe." He considered a moment, and then came up with a solution.
"I know! I investigate also! I stay with her every moment!"

"And do you carry loaded gun with you every moment?"
Amato asked with a touch of asperity. "Gerry, tell him you do not
look for this killer."

"Ah, Pasquale," she smiled, "don't you get tired of being the
sensible one all the time?"

"Yes," he admitted. "But someone must. *You* are not being
sensible now."

"I haven't said I'll do it."

"You do it," Scotti urged.

"She'll do it," Amato sighed.

"I'll do it if you'll help, Pasquale," Gerry said unexpectedly.
"With three of us sticking together, there can't be any real danger,
can there?"

"Me? You want me to be detective?"

"*Sì*, Pasquale!" Scotti beamed. "You make good detective!
Come now, say you help us investigate!"

"I have a better idea," Emmy Destinn said suddenly. "Why
don't we all investigate?" They all stared at her. "With seven
people out looking for an answer, one of us is bound to uncover
something, don't you think?" Dorothy Caruso suddenly remembered something she had to do in another part of the apartment and
fled. "Excuse me, I should have said *six* people," Emmy remarked dryly, not really surprised at Dorothy's flight. "Well, what
do you think?"

"I think it's a grand idea, Emmy!" Gerry said without hesitation. "Safety in numbers!"

She and the two baritones argued about it a little, and Amato
reluctantly found himself being persuaded to do the very thing he'd
been trying to talk the others out of doing. He turned to Gatti-

Casazza. "What do you think, Mr. Gatti? Do we help them investigate?"

Gatti shuddered. "I am terrified of this man, whoever he is. But Emmy is right—we cannot sit and watch and do nothing."

"Then you do it?" Scotti asked.

"Come vuole," Gatti acceded.

Scotti gave a cheer, the two women applauded his decision, and Amato nodded in resigned acceptance. None of them bothered to ask the sixth person in the room; they'd all assumed Caruso would be eager to jump in head first. So they were surprised when the tenor announced somberly, "An investigation is not necessary."

"Not necessary?" Gerry echoed. "Why ever not, Rico?"

"Because," he stood up to make his announcement, "I already know who is the killer."

There was a tense silence, which Emmy broke by saying loudly, "Well? Who?"

Caruso paused dramatically and then said, "It is Beniamino Gigli."

"Oh, for heaven's sake, Rico!" Gerry said in annoyance.

"Non è vero," Gatti objected.

"But it is true!" Caruso protested. "Gigli, he *hates* the chorus! So many years he works to get to the Metropolitan—and then when he does get here, the chorus, they make fool of him!"

"You could say the same of Rosa Ponselle," Emmy pointed out. "Except that part about working for years to get where she is."

"What about Giulio Setti?" Amato asked. "Tell us, Mr. Gatti—is he not in danger of losing his job because he no longer can control the chorus? Tell us true, please."

"I am forced to consider it," Gatti admitted unhappily. "But Setti is no killer—I know him for twenty years. Besides, my assistant has as much reason to hate the chorus as Setti."

"Edward Ziegler? Why?"

"His life is made miserable by the chorus. He must prepare their contracts, negotiate their demands, keep everybody happy . . ."

"He does all the dirty work, you mean," Gerry said. "Well, let's not forget Alessandro Quaglia, as long as we're naming names. He has no love for the chorus either."

"It is none of them!" Caruso cried. *"Per dio,* I tell you it is Gigli!"

"I hope you are wrong, Rico," Scotti said earnestly. "I and Gerry, we sing *Tosca* with Gigli after Christmas."

"Do you have any evidence, Rico?" Emmy asked. "No? I thought not. So you see, we do need to investigate . . . perhaps to prove you are right?"

Caruso thought about that. "True, it is best I have evidence when I turn Gigli in to police."

"Oh, definitely," Emmy said with a straight face.

"So, what do you say, Rico?" Gerry teased. "Do we have enough get-up-and-go left to do it one more time?"

He winked at her. "I think we manage. One last fling."

"Good, that's settled," Emmy said. "Well, Gerry, you are the expert. Where do we start?'

"When do we start?" Scotti asked eagerly. "Now?"

"Afraid not," Gerry answered him. "Quaglia has called a *Faust* rehearsal this afternoon—I'm going to be working."

"I accompany you," Scotti announced expansively. "I will be your bodyguard."

"And I will be yours," Amato grinned.

"We all go to the opera house," Caruso declared.

"That's where we'll start," Emmy nodded in satisfaction.

The small, damp fifth-floor room of the Elizabeth Street tenement building was the site of a great deal of frustration. An ad hoc committee of six was trying to figure out why Mrs. Bukaitis's bomb had failed to go off.

"I cannot find anything wrong with it," Antanas said. "The wires are all connected the way they are supposed to be."

"Perhaps the alarm clock does not work," a man with an ear missing suggested.

"It is a new clock," Mrs. Bukaitis said. "I paid one dollar for it." Someone murmured disapproval at the inflated price.

"Are you sure the clock was running?" the only other woman there asked. She was frail and had a bad cough; talking was an effort. "Maybe you forgot to wind it."

"I did not forget to wind it," Mrs. Bukaitis replied with a touch of irritation. "It was ticking when I left it."

"The dynamite," a gray-bearded man said. "It must be the dynamite."

Mrs. Bukaitis looked at Antanas, who shrugged. "It is the dynamite the city uses," he said. "I took it from a shed at a construction site."

"Unfortunately," the one-eared man sighed, "we have no way of testing it."

The last person in the room, who had remained silent until now, snorted in derision. "Amateurs! We are amateurs!" He was a dark, stocky man with a perpetual sneer on his face. "We cannot even build a bomb that works!"

"We are new at this, Lucien," the frail woman said. "It takes time to learn these things."

"And what if it had gone off?" Lucien plowed on, ignoring her. "What would it have accomplished? It would have blown a hole in the stage of an opera house." He gave his disgusted snort again. "An opera house!"

"Lucien," the gray-bearded man reprimanded mildly.

"Not just *an* opera house," Mrs. Bukaitis objected. "The *Metropolitan* Opera House—the favorite gathering place of the privileged classes of New York. It is these spoiled, self-indulgent Americans we must reach—"

Lucien swore. "We must make the Americans understand the war against oppression is not over just because they say it is over. And the way to do that is through a *military* strike. We should be planting bombs in the naval shipyard in Brooklyn, not in opera houses!"

The one-eared man disagreed. "If we want to attract the Americans' attention, we must hit them where they feel it most—in the purse. Wall Street, the new stock exchange they are building. That is where we should be placing our bombs, in Wall Street."

They all started talking at once and did not stop until Antanas roared for quiet. "We have been through all this before," he said. "We do not yet have access to the shipyard or to Wall Street, but Mrs. Bukaitis can come and go as she pleases in the opera house. It is a good place to test our bombs—which obviously need some testing." He looked at the glowering man. "And it is safer, Lucien. There are no armed guards in opera houses."

Mrs. Bukaitis pressed her lips together; she'd not told the others that the Metropolitan was now as tightly guarded as a military base. It was the first time in her life she'd had a chance to do something to help the cause on her own. In Vilnius, it had always been her late husband who made the decisions and took the risks. She was determined not to lose her first chance to prove herself; if Antanas knew about the guards at the opera house, he would order her to abandon her mission. She would bite off her tongue before she told him. "So what do we do now?" she asked.

"There is only one thing to do," Antanas said. "Start over. We must build a new bomb. And this time, we do it right."

Captain O'Halloran walked through the Broadway entrance of the Met and came to a quick stop. It had been five years since he'd last set foot in the Metropolitan Opera House, and the foyer was a lot smaller than he remembered. There was the box office off to the side, but there was no dramatic central staircase or other accoutrements of opulence. This part of the opera house looked more like the interior of a bank than anything else.

In the auditorium a rehearsal was in progress, but at the moment there was just a lot of talking going on. O'Halloran slipped into the last row and sat down, giving himself a few minutes to get reoriented. He suffered from mixed feelings; he was attracted to the opera house but leery of it at the same time. Twice in the past ten years he had stood on that immense stage and arrested a man; and both times he'd needed the assistance of eccentric, theatrical, self-aggrandizing opera singers to do the job. Sometimes O'Halloran thought all opera singers should be kept in cages. Other times he admitted he kind of liked them.

Some sort of argument was going on between the stage and the orchestra pit, but the captain couldn't make out what they were saying. He looked up at the sunburst chandelier suspended from the waffle-grid ceiling that had been painstakingly decorated with paintings and gold leaf. The fronts of the boxes on both sides of the auditorium were ornately carved, matching the six-story-high gold proscenium arch with the names of composers carved across the top. The stage, O'Halloran thought, must be close to a hundred feet wide. All in all, the opera house was a reflection of an earlier day, an age of prosperity and urbanity. A self-assured time, not at all like the present day with all its fears and uncertainties.

By the time O'Halloran's eyes had adjusted to the dim auditorium light, he could make out the figure of someone sitting about fifteen rows in front of him. A big man, filling the seat he was in and hunching over a little. Gatti-Casazza? O'Halloran didn't know the man on the podium in the orchestra pit, but the lady on the stage he was arguing with—the captain knew her. Oh yes, indeed he did know her.

"Quaglia, you are *insane!*" Geraldine Farrar screamed.

O'Halloran laughed to himself and stood up; some things never changed. He walked quietly down the aisle until he could see the face of the other man sitting in the auditorium—yes, it was Gatti-Casazza. He moved into the row behind the general manager and tapped him on the shoulder. "Hello, Mr. Gatti."

Gatti twisted in his seat and scowled, not recognizing him. "This is a closed rehearsal. You should not be here."

"Don't you remember me, Mr. Gatti? I'm Captain O'Halloran, of the New York Detective Bureau."

Gatti's face lit up as he remembered. "O'Halloran! *Certo, certo!*" He lifted a big paw to shake hands. "I am glad to see you, Captain. Are you come to find who is doing these terrible things to our chorus?"

"I've come to try. Anything happen today?"

"No, except the choristers no longer try to cooperate. Spike's death discourages them all. Maestro Quaglia, he takes them through the *Soldiers' Chorus* three times and they still do not sing it right."

O'Halloran filed the conductor's name away. "I'm going to nose around a little. I'd like you to come with me."

As the two men made their way backstage, the argument between soprano and conductor abruptly came to a halt. Quaglia gave the downbeat, the orchestra played, and Gerry began to sing.

But she sang only three notes before Quaglia made the cut-off sign. "It is still not right!" he protested. "If you just—"

"How can it ever be right when you keep interrupting?" she interrupted. "You had no reason to stop me then! Let's get on with it."

"No reason! You call three flatted notes in succession no reason?"

"I was not singing flat!" she screamed. "You think you have perfect pitch, Quaglia, but you don't!" She whirled to the other singers on the stage. "Did any of you hear me singing flat?" Nobody said a word. Gerry threw a look of triumph at the conductor.

Backstage, O'Halloran grinned and asked Gatti-Casazza, "Was she flat?"

"No," Gatti said worriedly. "Quaglia is mistaken. Everybody is in bad mood . . . argumentative."

O'Halloran looked at the various members of the chorus waiting backstage—so many of them! But he wanted to talk to as many as he could; a couple of them might know something they didn't realize was important. Then he saw that someone was already talking to a few of them. O'Halloran groaned. Surely Enrico Caruso wasn't playing detective *again*!

The tenor recognized him immediately. "Lieutenant O'Halloran! You are here! *Bene, bene!* Now we find the killer!" He grabbed O'Halloran's hand and pumped it up and down, grinning like a child who's just been given an unexpected treat.

"What do you mean, 'we', Mr. Caruso?" O'Halloran was pleased by the warm welcome but surprised by Caruso's appearance; the tenor did not look his usual robust self. "You haven't been doing my job for me again, have you? A little interrogating, maybe?''

"No, no!" Caruso grabbed his elbow and steered him away from the listening choristers. "I ask them not to make trouble for Gigli. They do it out of love for me, but they promise not to do it anymore, Lieutenant." He nodded complacently, as if he'd just made everything crystal-clear.

O'Halloran sighed. "It's Captain O'Halloran now. Who—"

"*Captain!* You are promoted! *Ne godo proprio!*" He pounded the policeman on the back. "*Captain* O'Halloran! *Magnifico!*"

O'Halloran endured Caruso's congratulatory thumping and asked, "Who is Gigli? You say the chorus was making trouble for him?"

"Beniamino Gigli, he is new tenor who tries to take my place," Caruso said in an offhand manner. "But the chorus, they do not want him to take my place. They know me long time, Captain. *Captain!* It sounds good, no?" He gave O'Halloran a whack on the shoulder and then got back to the subject. "The choristers play tricks—they upstage him, they drop props they are supposed to hand to him, they bump him when he has a high note. Not nice. They do same thing to Rosa Ponselle . . . they are jealous of Rosa, I think. But now they stop. I say, you must leave Rosa and Gigli alone. They promise."

O'Halloran had heard of Rosa Ponselle. He wondered if the opera world considered upstaging a heinous-enough offense to lead to murder. Dumb idea—even opera singers weren't that crazy. "Mr. Caruso, you aren't thinking of conducting an investigation yourself, are you? I hope we settled all that last time. You understand you're not to meddle in police affairs, don't you?"

The tenor drew himself up. "And why not? I am policeman too!"

O'Halloran stared at him. "What are you talking about?"

"Since last March I am policeman. Mayor Hylan says I am. For my silver jubilee!"

The captain remembered. The city of New York had honored Caruso on the anniversary of his twenty-five years in opera; as part of the ceremonies, the mayor had made the tenor an honorary member of New York's finest. As his first 'official' act, Caruso had gone to the opera house and arrested Gatti-Casazza. "Now, Mr. Caruso, I'm sure you understand what the word 'honorary' means. You can't—" He broke off when he saw a twinkle in the tenor's eye. "All right, all right, you've had your little joke. But I'm going to warn you anyway. I don't want you looking for whoever's been attacking the chorus singers. This man is dangerous— do you want to get yourself killed? Promise me you won't let me catch you playing detective."

With the request worded that way, Caruso was able to give his promise.

"And Miss Farrar too?"

"For Gerry, I promise nothing. I never know what she is going to do. You must ask her."

O'Halloran nodded and decided there was no time like the present—or as soon as she was off the stage, rather. He ambled back to where Gatti-Casazza was listening earnestly to something Emmy Destinn was saying. The captain just caught the end of it: "The ones I've talked to say anyone could have gone into the greenroom and added poison to the pitcher. The guards were guarding the people, not the room and its contents."

The police detective reintroduced himself; Emmy remembered him but not his name. "It's been a while, Captain O'Halloran," she said, putting old name and new rank together easily. "Are you in charge of the investigation?"

He said he was. "You've been talking to the chorus singers about the last murder?"

She frowned. "It is impossible not to talk about it."

"Yes, I'm sure. Let me ask your opinion of something. Do you think this new tenor—ah, Gigli, that's his name—do you think he's been sufficiently aggravated by the chorus to want to hit back?"

Both Emmy and Gatti-Casazza pooh-poohed the idea.

"Or Rosa Ponselle? What about her?"

"Of course not," Gatti huffed. "That is ridiculous suggestion."

O'Halloran noticed that Emmy had said nothing. "Is Miss Ponselle here today? No? Well, I'll talk to her some other time. Could you tell me—"

He was interrupted by a man Gatti introduced as his assistant. "Mr. Gatti, I think we're in for some trouble," Edward Ziegler said as soon as the amenities were over. "A spokesman for the chorus asked me to meet him here after rehearsal."

"They want something," Gatti said heavily.

"Probably more money," Ziegler nodded. "I had feared a mass resignation, but I thought we had that taken care of."

"They could still resign," Emmy said.

"They undoubtedly will, if this madman isn't found and stopped." He peered over his pince-nez at O'Halloran. "Any chance of that, Captain?"

"Of course there's a chance. We'll get him, Mr. Ziegler, don't you worry."

Ziegler said *hm,* excused himself, and hurried away. Gatti sighed and said, "Negotiating with the chorus—that is supposed to be only one of his duties. But now the chorus is taking up all his time."

A new uproar broke out on the stage. Geraldine Farrar came storming off with fire in her eye and headed for the stairs that led down to the auditorium. "I'll kill him!" she screamed. "God help me, I'll kill him!"

Running after her were Pasquale Amato and Antonio Scotti, both of them looking anxious. "Gerry, *carissima,*" Scotti cried, "he does not mean what he says! He has big mouth, that one, but he does not mean it!"

"Who does he think he is, talking to me that way? I'm going to take his head right off his shoulders, I swear!"

"Wait, Gerry, do nothing rash," Amato pleaded. "I remember you threaten to kill Toscanini on more than one occasion. Wait five minutes—take time to calm yourself."

"Toscanini always had a reason," Gerry snapped, "every time he yelled at me or interrupted me or got sarcastic. I may not have agreed with his reason, but he always did have one. That idiot out there on the podium—he stops me just to show he can. To prove his *authority*." She snorted. "That man is so insecure he's pathetic."

"So be kind, *gioia mia*," Scotti urged. "Leave his head upon his shoulders. He needs it."

She shot him a startled glance and laughed shortly. "He needs a new one."

Amato smiled; the crisis had passed. "Finish the rehearsal, Gerry, and I speak with Quaglia afterward."

"No, that is my job," Gatti-Casazza said, walking over to join them. "Quaglia exceeds his authority, but I talk to him. You sing, I talk."

"I'm not going to put up with this kind of harassment, Gatti."

"I understand. But do not walk out. I talk to him as soon as rehearsal finishes."

"If it happens again, I'm going to demand Quaglia's dismissal. I'm not joking."

Gatti blanched. "We do not talk of that now. Let me reason with him first."

The soprano reluctantly agreed, took a deep breath, charged back out on the stage, and yelled at Quaglia that she was ready.

Captain O'Halloran had watched the scene with interest, thinking he'd have to catch the outraged soprano the minute she left the stage. Angry people often gave things away that they otherwise kept well hidden. "Is she right?" he asked Emmy Destinn. "Was he just testing his authority?"

She gave him a sad little smile. "It is likely. Sometimes it seems to me that Quaglia is symptomatic of everything that is wrong in this house. I mean artistically. Quaglia's problem is that he succeeded Arturo Toscanini. Quaglia is a good, competent conductor—but Toscanini is a genius. So when Quaglia imitates Toscanini's behavior—the temper tantrums, the sarcasm—he simply calls attention to how far short of his predecessor he falls."

"And you say he's symptomatic of the Met? How?"

She made a vague gesture with her hands. "Take the chorus. It has degenerated from what it was before the war, but the choristers are acting as if they are stars. They demand more and more. And these attacks have certainly put them in the spotlight. They are receiving too much attention, both the good kind and the bad kind. But the malaise goes farther than that. Some of the principal singers—well, let us just say it's getting harder for them to give the great performances they used to give as a matter of routine. Unfortunately, this house is living on the memory of greatness.''

O'Halloran was shocked. He'd always had a mental picture of the Metropolitan Opera as something grand and solid and eternal, unchanged by the changing world around it. He didn't like Emmy's gloomy version of the way things were; he wanted her to be wrong.

Gatti-Casazza rejoined them, pulling nervously at his beard. *"Cielo m' aiuti!* Gerry wants me to dismiss Quaglia, Quaglia wants me to dismiss Setti, Setti wants to dismiss the entire chorus! *Sono perduto!''*

"Setti?" O'Halloran asked. "Who's he?"

"Our chorus master. He is with Metropolitan as long as I am. But he grows old . . . ,'' Gatti trailed off, shaking his head.

"Don't we all," O'Halloran murmured and turned to Emmy. "Miss Destinn, when I got here you'd just been talking to some of the chorus singers. I'd appreciate it if you didn't go around asking questions.''

Her eyes grew wide. "A series of murders has been committed—and you expect us not to talk about it?''

"I can't stop you from talking, I know that. But the less said the better—and I'll tell you why. Every time a story is repeated, it changes a little. Some detail is altered, or a new one is added, or something is left out. I've still got to talk to the chorus singers myself, so I'd like you not to encourage them to gossip.''

"Gossip! You call wondering how poison got into a pitcher of orange juice *gossip*?''

"Now, Miss Destinn, try to see my side of it—''

"Destinnova,'' she said haughtily. "Ema Destinnova.'' She turned on her heel and flounced away.

O'Halloran blinked. "What did she say?''

Gatti smiled. "Her new name. Emmy is very patriotic lady, Captain. When Czechoslovakia gains its independence, she changes her name to Ema Destinnova. We put the new name on the programs and sometimes the newspapers remember to use it— but to her friends she is still Emmy."

O'Halloran got the point; she didn't consider him a friend. "Well, whatever her name is, she just now told me something a bit disheartening." He repeated what Emmy had said about the Met's living on the memory of greatness. "Is it true? Have some of your people lost . . . er, well, you know what I mean."

Gatti tugged at his beard so hard O'Halloran was afraid he'd pull it out. "Emmy exaggerates," the general manager said reluctantly, "but there is some truth in what she says. Gerry sings beautifully today—she can still sing an exquisite Marguérite. But not at every performance, you understand? And Caruso's voice, it darkens more every year. Some say now he sounds more like baritone than tenor." Gatti bit his lip. "Baritone. Pasquale Amato at one time has the most beautiful baritone I hear in all my years in opera."

O'Halloran was surprised. "More beautiful than Scotti's?"

"Oh, yes. But the richness is gone from Amato's voice now. Scotti will last longer."

"So what Emmy Destinn said was true."

"*No completamente.* We are in period of transition, Captain. We have the great older singers reaching end of careers at same time we have new singers coming in to replace them. Ponselle, Gigli, next year Maria Jeritza." Gatti looked hopefully at O'Halloran, but the captain had never heard of her. "For me, it is time of both great excitement and great pain—eh, I do not make myself clear. Transitions are hard."

"You make yourself very clear," O'Halloran said. "I understand. Do you think—"

He was cut off by the sound of a woman's scream. "Gerry," Gatti muttered and shambled away, in no great hurry to find out what disaster had interrupted rehearsal this time. O'Halloran followed him to the side of the stage where Scotti and Amato stood watching.

Amato glanced at him, did a double take, and then said, "Lieutenant? Is that you? I do not recognize you without your derby hat! *Come sta?*"

O'Halloran took off the Stetson he was still wearing. "My wife bought me this one," he smiled, shaking hands. "And it's Captain now, Mr. Amato, not Lieutenant." Scotti didn't remember him and had to have his memory refreshed.

A war of words was being waged between center stage and the podium. "*Pazienza,* Gerry!" Scotti called softly.

"What is it this time?" Gatti asked mournfully.

"The same as before," Scotti said. "Interruptions, insults, sarcasm. Gerry tries to be nice to Quaglia, she truly does try." Amato nodded agreement. "But now," Scotti went on, "now I think she runs out of niceness."

"American singers!" Quaglia was screaming at the stage. "You are all lazy! You do not work!"

"Not work!" Gerry screamed back in outrage. "I've been working my . . . vocal cords off up here, and you call me lazy? Who do you think you are?"

"You do not try! You stand there and squawk like chicken and call it singing! Do you forget how to sing?"

A *deathly* silence fell.

Gerry walked slowly to the edge of the stage, placed her hands on her hips, and glared down at the man on the podium. "If you insult me one more time," she informed Quaglia evenly, "I'm going to come down there and ram that baton down your throat." She paused. "Imitating Toscanini's temper tantrums won't give you his talent, you know. So watch out . . . *Maestro.*" She pronounced the last word with just enough sarcasm to make it clear that Quaglia was in no way master there.

The conductor waited until she'd resumed her place upstage and then said to the violin section, in a voice just loud enough to be heard, "Eh, well—only a little longer. Next year Jeritza is here!"

"That does it!" Gerry shouted. "That really does it! Quaglia—I warned you!"

Quaglia stared at the baton she'd threatened to ram down his throat, tried to exchange looks with a few of the orchestra members (all of whom steadfastly refused to meet his eye)—and decided to run for his life. He sacrificed dignity to haste in his self-preserving flight up the auditorium aisle; the orchestra decided that meant rehearsal was over and started getting up to leave.

Backstage, Amato was laughing and holding out his arms to block the enraged soprano's rush toward the stairs. "You are too late, Gerry—he has made his escape!"

"The coward!" she fumed. "Wait until I get my hands on him!" Scotti and Gatti-Casazza were both making soothing sounds that were having little noticeable effect. "Gatti, that man must go!"

"We make no decisions now," he said firmly, "not in heat of anger."

"Who's angry?" she raged. "I have thought it over coolly and calmly and I have decided *Quaglia must go!*"

All the sound and fury gradually began to wane, but Captain O'Halloran hesitated. Talking to Geraldine Farrar while she was just everyday angry was one thing, but when she was coming off a monumental rage like this one . . . maybe it wasn't such a good idea. But he did need to ask her some questions. He went up behind her and cleared his throat, not even sure she would remember him.

The soprano turned and looked him straight in the eye. "O'Halloran!" she exclaimed. "It's about time you got here! Where have you been?"

The captain's mouth fell open. "Well, I—"

"Never mind that now. I have some questions I want to ask you—we *all* want to ask you. But not here . . . I've got to get out of this place before I lose my mind! We'll find some quiet place where we can talk—come along!"

O'Halloran smiled, and with a show of meekness fell in with

Scotti and Amato in following her off the stage. Gatti hesitated, wondering whether Edward Ziegler might not need his help in dealing with the chorus's latest demand. Then he decided his assistant could do the job perfectly well without any interference from him and hurried after the others.

As it turned out, Ziegler was just then wishing he had some help. The chorus and their various guards were crowded together on the Fortieth Street side of the stage, and their spokesman was presenting their new demand. He was a well-spoken American in his mid-thirties, chosen to speak because the chorus wanted no risk of misunderstanding.

"We want the Metropolitan to take out life insurance policies on each of us in the amount of fifty thousand dollars," the spokesman said. "And we want a double indemnity clause. That's essential."

"Insurance . . . on all of you?" Ziegler gasped, visions of a collapsing budget throbbing in his head. "Do you have any conception of what you're asking? Why, the cost of insuring all of you—"

"Cost!" the spokesman snarled. "We risk our lives every time we set foot in this place, and you talk to us of *cost*?" The other choristers muttered angry agreement.

Ziegler switched tactics. "I'm not at all certain we could find an insurer willing to underwrite such a policy. Frankly, you may be too big a risk. What with the police in on it now, outsiders are aware of what's going on here. I'm not sure we—"

"Well, then, you damn well better find an insurer, Mr. Ziegler," the man overrode his objection. "Because if you don't, this opera company isn't going to have a chorus." More mutters of agreement. "We'll wait twenty-four hours. If you don't have an insurer by this time tomorrow, we won't be coming back."

"Twenty-four hours!" Ziegler almost laughed at the absurdity of it. "That's impossible. No insurance decision is made that quickly—that's not a reasonable expectation."

"Reasonable!" someone snorted.

"It's not up to you to say what's reasonable! Not any more, it's not!" The spokesman was shouting now. "We've listened to your false assurances long enough!'' The mutter of agreement grew to a growl.

"*False* assurances?'' Ziegler echoed coldly. "We promised you individual bodyguards and we kept our word. You're being a bit cavalier in your accusations, aren't you?''

"Oh, now it's *our* fault, is it? Mr. Ziegler, you don't seem to hear what I'm telling you. You either get that insurance for us or the Met's going to have to shut down. Unless you want to try to put on operas without a chorus.'' Smirk.

"That might not be such a bad idea,'' Ziegler said, directing a frosty gaze at all of them. "You people have been nothing but trouble this entire season! A gang of second-rate musicians who aren't worth one-tenth of what you're paid—''

"Hey, wait a minute—''

"No, I will not *wait a minute*. You've done nothing but squabble among yourselves and demand this and demand that—and you don't even perform like professionals!''

"That's enough, Mr. Ziegler. Some of us have *died* here.''

"Yes, but only some of you. Unfortunately.''

There was a stunned silence. They were all shocked, even the guards. But none appeared more shocked than Ziegler himself. "My God, what have I said?'' he muttered. He looked at all the stunned faces staring at him and abandoned any hope of conducting a civilized negotiation that day. Without another word he turned and hurried away.

The choristers and their guards stood around looking at one another uncertainly for a while and then, because they didn't know what else to do, started drifting slowly out through the Fortieth Street exit. There were a few hushed comments exchanged, but no one really knew what to say.

When the last chorister had gone, Enrico Caruso stepped out from behind the teaser curtain where he had been hiding. "*Per dio*,'' he exclaimed softly. "It is not Gigli at all—it is Edward Ziegler!''

❑ 6 ❑

There was only one member of the Metropolitan Opera Company who spoke the Lithuanian language, and on Friday Antonio Scotti found him. He was an American-born chorus tenor named Tucciarone whose maternal grandparents had emigrated from a farm near the Lithuania-Poland border. When Scotti told him his services as a translator were needed, Tucciarone had hesitated. "It's been a long time, Mr. Scotti," he said. "I'm not sure how much I remember."

Scotti waved a hand airily. "Is like riding bicycle. You remember when you need to remember, yes? You come with me." He led the chorister into the Met's foyer. "She may know some English, I am not sure."

"She? Who is it?"

"Perhaps one of these ladies here." He pointed to the two women on their knees scrubbing away at the floor with stiff brushes.

"A scrubwoman?"

"As you say. Scusi, *signora,*" he said to one of the women. He told her he was looking for Mrs. Bukaitis.

Upstairs.

Ever since the notion first entered Scotti's head that he, too, could be a detective, he'd wondered why everyone had been so quick to dismiss as a possible suspect the very woman who'd reported finding the hanging man. He'd tried to convince Gerry that the woman might know more than she was saying, but the soprano hadn't been interested. He and Tucciarone found Mrs. Bukaitis sweeping out one of the rehearsal rooms.

The chorister spoke to her haltingly but evidently clearly enough to make himself understood. He introduced himself and Scotti, and told her the latter wanted to ask her a few questions.

"Ask her to tell us about finding the body in the chorus dressing room," Scotti said, giving Mrs. Bukaitis his most nonthreatening smile.

Her answer was rattled off so fast that Tucciarone had to ask her to slow down. She had opened the door and saw him hanging there, she said. There was no one else in the dressing room; none of the other choristers had arrived yet. She'd gone for Gatti-Casazza and led him back to the dressing room. No, she hadn't touched the man to see if he was still alive—she hadn't even gone into the dressing room. She'd opened the door, spotted the dead man, and gone for Gatti. That was all.

All the time she was talking Scotti studied her broad shoulders and her strong arms, thinking she would be quite capable of overcoming a healthy man in a struggle. "Now ask her what she is doing in chorus dressing room so close to performance time."

A strange look came over Tucciarone's face, but he repeated the question in Lithuanian and listened carefully to the answer. "She says she went back for a bucket she'd left there."

Scotti looked closely at the other man. "What is it? Something?"

"Mr. Scotti, I think she's lying. And I think I know why. We've had a problem with petty theft all year—small things taken out of the dressing room, sometimes cash. It's not a big problem, but every once in a while something just disappears. I think maybe she went to the dressing room to steal."

Scotti frowned. "Before the choristers arrive? Nothing is there to take!"

"Sometimes a few of us come in early and get dressed and go to the greenroom to wait—to avoid the crush in the dressing room. It gets awfully crowded in there with all of us trying to get ready at the same time. In between the time of the early arrivals and the time when the rest get there—that'd be a very good time to do a little pilfering."

Scotti noticed that while they were talking, Mrs. Bukaitis's eyes kept darting back and forth between them. They were alert and intelligent eyes, he thought, oddly out of place in one who held so menial a position. Mrs. Bukaitis almost looked as if she understood what they were saying. "Is something stolen from you?" he asked Tucciarone.

"I'm missing a pocket watch. It wasn't valuable, but it was mine and I hate being stolen from."

"Ask her if she takes it."

When the chorister asked her, a stream of loud, angry, unintelligible words erupted from the scrubwoman's mouth. Tucciarone looked at Scotti and shrugged helplessly; he couldn't keep up with her. But there was no doubt in either man's mind that the woman was telling them exactly what she thought of them, and none of it was flattering.

"Eh, thank her for her help," Scotti shouted to make himself heard. "I think we go now."

Tucciarone yelled something at the woman and the two men fled, pursued by the sound of Mrs. Bukaitis's voice giving vent to her outrage at their audacity in even suggesting that she might be a thief.

Beniamino Gigli played with the little dog in his lap the whole time Captain O'Halloran was interviewing him. They were in the tenor's hotel suite; Gigli on a sofa and the captain on a hard chair facing him. Gigli had said he was resting his voice and didn't want to talk, but O'Halloran had persuaded him to let him in.

Gigli had made no attempt to disguise his contempt for the Metropolitan Opera chorus. "Nowhere in Europe or South America do I suffer from such persecution by the *chorus!*" he declaimed. "Only in New York! Always there is soprano or another tenor who is jealous, one of the soloists, I mean. One expects that. But the *chorus? È imperdonabile!*"

"What's that?"

"I say their behavior is not to be forgiven! Gatti is too soft-hearted. Because someone is attacking them, he allows them to behave in ways he does not tolerate otherwise. Captain, you must find killer fast! We never have *normal* opera house until you do. Gatti is too lax." He bent over the dog in his lap and sang to it softly, seeking comfort from the small friendly body.

O'Halloran flipped through his notebook. "The way I understand it, it's Mr. Setti who's in charge of the chorus."

The tenor made a sound of annoyance. "That is another thing. Setti is too old for the job. But he is longtime friend of Gatti, so

Gatti keeps him on the payroll. He is soft-headed as well as soft-hearted, our general manager.''

O'Halloran was beginning to wonder if Gigli liked anybody at the Metropolitan. ''Were you in the opera house the night the woman was killed by an urn falling on her head? Between acts of *Samson and Delilah,* that was.''

''*Samson* is Caruso's opera. I stay home.''

''What about the night the man was found hanging in the chorus dressing room, ah, before a performance of *Mefistofele*? That was December sixth.''

''Of course I am there,'' Gigli said. ''*Mefistofele* is *my* opera.''

''Did you go to the chorus dressing room anytime that night?''

''I never go to chorus dressing room on *any* night. Why should I? I only hear about dead man, I do not see him.''

''Well, what about the night two of the choristers fell through the trap door? That was—''

Gigli cut him off with a slicing gesture that startled the dog. ''*Pagliacci.* Caruso.''

''You weren't there?''

''No!''

''*Carmen,* on the ninth? When the woman was stabbed?''

''No.''

''*La Forza del Destino,* when the man was poisoned?''

''No, no, no! I am there *one* night, when I sing! Questions, questions! Caruso, he just calls me on the telephone and asks me all these same questions! *Basta!*''

O'Halloran moaned. ''Caruso?''

''And he believes me when I say I am not there,'' Gigli said pointedly, ''and he promises not to bother me anymore. Ask the doorkeeper. He knows I am not there.''

''Now, Mr. Gigli, you must know how easy it is to slip around an opera house without being seen.''

The tenor dumped the lapdog on the sofa and stood up, stretching to make himself taller. ''I am a star, Captain O'Halloran. I am *always* seen.''

And that, O'Halloran understood, marked the end of the interview. It was just as well; there wasn't much else he could ask until he'd gotten one of his men to check on Gigli's story that he wasn't in the opera house on four of the five lethal occasions.

In the meantime, he might have another problem; it looked as if Enrico Caruso was ignoring his warning not to meddle. And from the grilling Geraldine Farrar had given him the day before, one might suspect that the lady too was thinking of putting on her detective hat again. In fact, all of them had been bursting with questions—Gatti-Casazza, Amato, and Scotti as well as Miss Farrar. O'Halloran couldn't really blame them; with five deaths taking place within a two-week period, they had the right to demand answers.

But O'Halloran had finally made them understand he wanted to ask *them* questions. There was a lot of hypothesizing and contradicting one another and outright guessing; but by the time they were finished, O'Halloran had a list of five names, people who had reason to hate the chorus. The two singers, Rosa Ponselle and Beniamino Gigli, whose performances were being sabotaged by the chorus. Edward Ziegler, whose thankless task it was to keep the chorus on stage and functioning without bankrupting the Met. Giulio Setti, whose loss of control over the chorus could well put an end to his career. And Alessandro Quaglia, whose long-standing dislike of all choruses had been aggravated by the undisciplined behavior of the present one.

Scotti had wanted to add a sixth name to the list of possibilities, that of the scrubwoman who'd discovered the body of the chorister who'd been hanged. Everyone had looked at him as if he were crazy.

Thinking back to the vitriolic rehearsal he'd witnessed yesterday, O'Halloran had asked Geraldine Farrar if she thought Quaglia was the killer—and was surprised when she said no.

"He's too . . . *small* to do something that big," she'd explained. "Look at him. He imitates Toscanini rather than develop a style of his own. He yells and screams just to prove he has the right to do so. He's even said he'd like to do operas with all the chorus parts cut out—because *this* chorus isn't up to scratch.

Those are the acts of a small man, but killing five people—well, that's an epic undertaking, isn't it? No, I just can't see Quaglia in the role of killer.''

O'Halloran had no way of knowing how accurate her analysis was, but it seemed to him that killing off chorus members was a poor way to make them perform better. Quaglia seemed to have the least to lose of the five—some damage to his reputation as a conductor so long as the chorus sang poorly, but that was all. Surely a conductor's livelihood didn't depend on how well the *chorus* performed, did it? Not to the extent that a chorus master's future did, certainly. O'Halloran decided to talk to Giulio Setti next.

Since the chorus wasn't rehearsing that day, Setti would not be at the opera house. O'Halloran thought he'd try his home on West Forty-second Street, across from Bryant Park. Setti lived in one of the few buildings in the neighborhood not yet converted to commercial use.

But when he got there, O'Halloran met Emmy Destinn coming down the front steps. "Well, this is a surprise, Miss . . . Destinnova," he remembered to say at the last minute.

"Is it? Why?" she said. "Setti is an old friend."

"And you just happened to go calling on an old friend at this particular moment? The way you just happened to be at the opera house yesterday?"

"Why shouldn't I be at the opera house?"

"Because you weren't singing in the opera they were rehearsing," O'Halloran explained patiently. "Why were you there?"

She turned a look on him that would have made a lesser man shrink. "Am I a suspect, Captain?"

"No, of course not."

"Then you have no right to question my movements." She sailed away.

O'Halloran decided to let it go for the moment. He climbed the steps and rang the doorbell; Setti himself answered the door. O'Halloran introduced himself and said he had a few questions to ask.

"I am not surprised," the chorus master sighed. "Come in, come in." He led the way into a fussily overdecorated room; the furniture was dark and heavy, Victorian, and polished to a sheen. The place dwarfed the man who lived there, but Setti seemed quite comfortable in his surroundings. He offered O'Halloran a seat and a cup of hot chocolate.

The captain accepted the former but declined the latter. "I suppose you know why I'm here, Mr. Setti. I need to ask you about these five deaths at the Metropolitan Opera. Let's start with the first one, during *Samson and Delilah*—"

Setti held up a hand. "Perhaps I save you some time, Captain. First, I am present at opera house all five times a chorister dies. Second, I see nothing unusual or suspicious during any of those five times. Third, no, I have no idea who is the killer. Are those the questions you wish to ask me?"

"On the button," O'Halloran grunted. "How'd you know?"

"I am asked them before," Setti said with a grimace. "First Pasquale Amato comes here, eh, forty-five minutes ago. He asks. Then Antonio Scotti calls on the telephone to ask. Then just before you arrive—"

"Emmy Destinn was here," O'Halloran nodded. "I ran into her as she was leaving. Same questions?"

"Same questions."

"Good Lord, are they *all* playing detective?" O'Halloran muttered to himself."

"*Scusi?*" But before O'Halloran could reply, Setti's telephone rang. The chorus master answered; and as he listened, a look of bewilderment came over his face. He covered the mouthpiece. "It is Gerry Farrar," he hissed. "Asking."

"Let me." O'Halloran took the phone and put on his 'official' voice. "Miss Farrar! I hope you aren't doing what I think you're doing. If you are, I want you to stop it right now."

"Who's that? Captain O'Halloran?"

"The same Captain O'Halloran who's investigating this case. There's no one named Farrar who's supposed to be investigating. *Is there.*" Not a question.

"Oh dear, that was subtle. I just wanted to ask Setti—"

"Don't. Don't ask him, don't *want* to ask him. Setti or anybody else. Do you understand me? You got lucky once, but this case is different. Keep out of it."

"Lucky! Well, I like that!" the soprano exclaimed indignantly. "I was a real help to you once—you can't pretend I wasn't!"

"No, I'm not denying that. But the situation is more dangerous this time, Miss Farrar. This man we're hunting doesn't seem to care whom he kills. You stick to singing and leave the detective work to me. Do you hear?"

"Captain O'Halloran," she said sweetly, "do you speak Italian?"

"Italian? No."

From the earpiece came a stream of angry words he couldn't understand, followed by the sound of a receiver being slammed down. O'Halloran smiled and hung up. "If she calls you back, tell her I ordered you not to talk to her," he told Setti, who responded with a look of relief.

The captain still wanted to go over the five killings one at a time, but the chorus master had nothing to add. He said he too had thought they were accidents at first, that the Metropolitan was having an unusually vicious run of bad luck. But when poor Teresa Leone was stabbed during a performance of *Carmen*—well, then there was no denying what was going on. He didn't know who was responsible, but . . .

"What is it, Mr. Setti? Anything you know might help."

"I do not *know* anything, Captain, but it seems to me the person doing these killings must surely be one of the choristers themselves."

"Why do you say that?"

"Eh, there is such discord in the chorus. Little factions, always quarreling. And one big schism—the Germans and the Austrians on one side, everybody else on the other. The chorus is still fighting the war, you see."

"Mr. Setti, I don't see how it could be one of the chorus— they're all watched too closely now. Maybe the first murders, but the chorus singers were under guard by the time someone slipped the poison into the orange juice pitcher.''

The chorus master shrugged. "The guards, can they watch all the time?"

O'Halloran snorted. "They'd better. Gatti-Casazza tells me each chorus member has a personal bodyguard now. That's going to be a hard defense to get past."

"Perhaps." Setti seemed unconvinced.

O'Halloran hesitated, and then took the plunge. "Mr. Setti—you're in danger of losing your job, aren't you? Because of the chorus?"

The older man's face grew red. "Quaglia!" he spat. "Quaglia, he tries to get Gatti to dismiss me! *Me!* I am with Gatti for twenty years, and this, this *newcomer* says I must go! *Follia!*"

"Then it's all Quaglia's doing?"

"*Così è!* Gatti, he never lets me go—never! But Quaglia, he hates choruses . . . and chorus masters! He wants to be rid of all of us." Setti realized what he had just said. "Do you think *he. . . ?*"

"I don't think anything yet." O'Halloran didn't tell the other man that Gatti-Casazza was indeed seriously considering letting him go; not for him to say. "Why does Quaglia hate choruses so much?"

"Eh, he always has trouble with choruses. The chorus at La Scala, one time they walk out on him! Right in middle of *Aïda*. Another time, the Covent Garden chorus petitions management—they ask for Quaglia's dismissal. They say he is too . . ." Setti had to grope for the word. "Dictatorial—they say he is too dictatorial."

"Did they get him fired?"

"No, but now he is not invited back so often as before. Same thing happens at La Scala."

"And now he sees it happening again here?"

By now Setti was beaming. "*Sì!* And so he kills them off, one at a time—"

"Wait a minute, wait a minute. How could he stab a woman

backstage during the performance of *Carmen* when he was out front conducting?''

"He stabs her before performance starts? She is found during first act.''

"That's right, she was.'' Obviously Quaglia's whereabouts were going to have to be checked into very carefully for all five deaths. And Setti's too, although it seemed to O'Halloran that the chorus master would be more likely to go after Quaglia than the trouble-making chorus. He tried to pin Setti down as to his exact movements during the five murder nights, but the older man said he was on the go constantly and couldn't remember where he was every minute.

Just as O'Halloran was about to leave, Setti let loose an unexpected cackle. "I just remember something, Captain. Do you know what Quaglia's first job in opera is? He is assistant chorus master!''

"Is that true? Where?''

"In Naples, a small house there. And Captain,'' Setti grinned, enjoying himself, "he is discharged! For incompetence!'' The chorus master went into a fit of cackling.

Well, you're certainly building a good case against your enemy, O'Halloran thought. "So you no longer think the killer is one of the chorus singers?''

"No, no—you convince me I am wrong.''

Hm. "So, Alessandro Quaglia was an assistant chorus master before he became a conductor. What did Edward Ziegler do before he became the assistant manager?''

"Ziegler?'' Setti was caught off-stride by the change of subject. "He is, ah, he is music critic for newspaper. Eh . . . the *Herald,* I think.''

"And you, Mr. Setti? What were you before you were a chorus master?''

A gnomish smile spread over the older man's face. "Captain O'Halloran, I am *born* chorus master.''

O'Halloran halfway believed him. He thanked Setti for his help and left, wondering whether the man really didn't know his position at the Met was in jeopardy or whether he was just putting a good face on it. Gatti-Casazza wouldn't think of firing him on Quaglia's say-so alone, O'Halloran felt sure; the chorus master had probably been slipping for some time. And Quaglia himself—the conductor's motive was looking a lot stronger than it had looked an hour earlier.

The sky was turning dark and the wind had picked up; the snow on the sidewalks was dirty and beginning to freeze. O'Halloran climbed into the police car. As he drove back to the station house, he remembered something Pasquale Amato had said yesterday. When Amato asked O'Halloran if he thought the killer was out to murder *all* the members of the chorus, O'Halloran had said he thought it was a distinct possibility.

Whereupon Amato shook his head sadly and said, "Captain, when the chorus is at full strength, it numbers one hundred forty singers. What kind of man sets out to murder one hundred and forty people? The killer, he is insane, you see. He must be insane, yes?"

He must be insane, yes. Such an undertaking was indeed insane. So insane, in fact, that O'Halloran now was beginning to doubt that killing off the entire chorus was the murderer's true goal. Hearing Amato put a number to it—one hundred forty people— well, that threw the whole enterprise into the realm of the absurd. But what, then? A slew of incidental murders to conceal the one significant one? Was that any saner?

Either way, Amato was right. They were looking for a madman.

Edward Ziegler sat at the desk in his office next door to Gatti-Casazza's, his head buried in his trembling hands. The cool, self-possessed assistant manager had lost control of himself—and in front of the chorus! How in the world could he ever negotiate with them now, when they'd heard him wish out loud that more of them were *dead*! Whatever had posessed him?

A throat-clearing sound made him look up. Enrico Caruso stood in front of his desk, having entered without knocking. The tenor looked ill at ease. "Mr. Caruso, I didn't hear you come in," Ziegler said, pulling himself back together.

"I must say something to you." He sat down without being invited. "I hear." He nodded soberly at Ziegler.

Ziegler waited but was rewarded only with more nodding. He asked, "What do you hear?"

"I hear what you say to the chorus yesterday. That not enough of them . . . die."

Ziegler took a deep breath and held it as he tried to decide how to handle this unexpected development. Appeal to his sympathy, that was it. "I need a vacation, Mr. Caruso. I've been carrying the burden of dealing with the chorus alone for too long—the stress is beginning to wear on me. I'm not thinking clearly. I would never have said such an unpardonable thing if it weren't for the killings that occupy my mind night and day—I wouldn't even have thought of it! In a moment of anger I blurted out my worst fear, and managed to turn it into a sort of curse."

"*Una maledizione,*" Caruso breathed.

"A slip of the tongue. Inexcusable, of course, but . . . these things do happen sometimes."

"You say you do not mean it?"

"Of course I didn't mean it!" Ziegler snapped. "Good God, even the chorus understands that!" He laughed bitterly. "Not that they'll let me forget it. Oh no—they'll *never* let me forget it!"

Jus then Gatti-Casazza walked in. "Ziegler, something we must—eh, Enrico, I do not know you are here."

Caruso nodded complacently. "*Sì,* I am here."

Gatti waited a moment but when Caruso didn't take the hint, he said, "I have urgent business to discuss with Ziegler. You come back another time, Enrico, yes? You talk to him later." Both he and his assistant stared at the tenor pointedly.

Caruso was not used to being made feel unwelcome and took his dismissal in poor grace. "I talk to *both* of you later," he said huffily as he left.

"*Cielo,* I think I am in for a scolding," Gatti smiled faintly.

"Do you see today's papers? No? An editorial in the *Times,* saying the Metropolitan should shut down as long as killer is, ah, 'on the loose'."

Ziegler shook his head decisively. "Impossible. If we cancel the rest of the season, we'll be so badly in arrears we'll never get out. We're already way over budget, what with hiring the bodyguards and all. And now the chorus is demanding that we take out life insurance policies on them for fifty thousand dollars each!"

To Ziegler's surprise, Gatti was not outraged by the demand. "*Sì,*" he mused, "is good idea. Insurance—it is the least we can do for them."

"If I can find a company willing to take the risk," Ziegler muttered. "Mr. Gatti, do you have any idea of how high these premiums are going to run? They'll bankrupt us! The only way I can see to pay for them is to extend the season a few weeks. Would the board of directors agree to that?"

"I think so. One or two members of the board, they too are saying we should cancel until killer is found. But the majority, they are firmly against cancelling. They say we must not give in to anarchic acts." Gatti pulled at his beard. "Anarchic. That is what they call these murders."

The telephone rang. Gatti's assistant picked up the receiver and said, "Edward Ziegler speaking . . . yes, what can I do for you?" He listened a moment and frowned. "Yes, I was there . . . in the greenroom." He listened again, and a look of astonishment appeared on his face. He glanced over at Gatti and made a vague gesture with the hand not holding the telephone. "As a matter of fact I do remember. It was Rosa Ponselle. May I ask why you—" He held the receiver away from his ear and looked at it accusingly. "She hung up." He did the same and remarked, "How extraordinary."

"What is it?" Gatti asked.

"That was Emmy Destinn. She was asking about the young man who was poisoned. She wanted to know if I remembered who it was who'd given him the orange juice to drink."

Good point, Gatti thought. He'd been there in the greenroom and Emmy had not, but she was the one who thought of it. Not that it made any difference—young Rosa couldn't possibly be the murderer.

"Mr. Gatti?" Ziegler said.

"Eh, she is worried and curious, as we all are. Now about extending the season—"

"Yes. Can I count on at least two weeks' additional box office receipts?"

Gatti nodded assent, already weary at the thought of the work involved in scheduling the extra performances. He was silent for a moment and then said, "Ziegler, this killer—do you think that is what he wants? To close the Metropolitan Opera?"

Ziegler's head jerked up. "Why, I don't know . . . that hadn't occurred to me. Why would anyone want to close us down?"

"I can think of no reason." Gatti stared at his assistant moodily. If the killer did want to close the Met, then Ziegler wasn't the killer because he wanted to stay open. But what if the killer's purpose was not to close the opera house, what if he wanted it to stay open so he could go on killing more choristers? Ziegler still wanted to stay open.

Gatti got up and walked heavily back to his own office. He didn't know the answer.

"I hate these tatty little places," Geraldine Farrar grumbled. "They don't even have champagne. And the people! Look at that man over there, at the corner table. I'm sure he's a gangster."

"He is proprietor," Antonio Scotti smiled. "Gangsters, they look more respectable, no?"

"I'm sure I wouldn't know. Toto, is this the best place you could find?"

Scotti had chosen the speakeasy for two reasons. First, it served real Canadian whiskey instead of the ersatz Scotch that was beginning to appear in bottles wearing counterfeit labels. Second, the band didn't start playing until midnight, which meant they could all talk without shouting. "*Sfortunatamente,* this *is* best place I find," Scotti said to Gerry. "It is not so bad, *cara mia.*"

"Stop complaining, Gerry," Emmy Destinn said. "You should see the one he took me to last Saturday. It makes this place look like the Ritz."

"Last Saturday I am in Brooklyn," Enrico Caruso mused. "It is not so good."

"'Not so good,'" Pasquale Amato sighed. "He hemorrhages on stage and calls it 'not so good'. *Cielo.*"

"He comes back too soon," Gatti-Casazza muttered into his beard.

"I am here, talk to *me*," Caruso demanded.

"You come back too soon," Gatti obliged.

"You do not say so when I sing *Forza*," the tenor snickered. Then he grew serious. "Why you interrupt me when I question Ziegler? How can I investigate when you tell me to come back later?"

"We keep crossing each other's paths," Amato complained.

A waiter appeared, looking as if their existence offended him. He slapped down their drinks, took their money, and left without a word.

"They do still have *un poco* to learn about charm, do they not?" Scotti smiled.

Gerry made a face. "I don't really like whiskey."

Gatti leaned across the table conspiratorily and whispered, "I am promised six cases of champagne before Christmas."

Five voices immediately demanded the name of his bootlegger.

By the time the waiter came back with their second round of drinks (for all but Gerry), they were ready to talk business. "This is only second day we investigate," Amato said, "and already we get in each other's way."

"Setti was annoyed when I talked to him," Emmy concurred. "He said he'd already answered the same questions twice by the time I got to him."

Amato nodded. "We duplicate each other's efforts."

"Too many cooks," Gerry agreed. "So what do we do?"

"We do not quit!" Caruso said indignantly.

"Of course we don't quit, Rico," Gerry said. "But we've got to get ourselves organized somehow. This way is no good."

"How?" Gatti asked. "We must all ask questions—we cannot take turns."

"I have a suggestion," Amato said. "Why not each of us concentrate on *one* person who has cause to hate the chorus? We each take one, er, suspect—and limit investigation to that one. What do you think?"

They all thought it over. Then Gerry said, "You know, Pasquale, that's not a bad idea at all. At least we'd stop bumping into one another."

"Yes," Gatti mused. "Is much more efficient that way. Not so much waste effort."

"I like, I like," Caruso beamed. "Emmy? Toto? You agree?" They did.

"Now we decide who investigates whom." Amato took out a notebook and a pen; writing it down would make it official. "*Con permesso,* I take Quaglia. I think the Maestro is more capable of killing than others." No one objected. "And Rico, you want Gigli." He started to write down the name.

"No, no—not Gigli," Caruso stopped him, to everyone's surprise. "Edward Ziegler."

"What is this?" Emmy asked. "I thought Gigli was your favorite suspect."

"I am wrong about Gigli," Caruso explained. "I make mistake. Edward Ziegler is the killer."

Gerry said, "I thought the purpose of the investigation was to find out who the killer is. You've already made up your mind! Again."

"*Non è vero,*" Gatti objected. "You are wrong this time also, Enrico."

"But I know something you do not know," Caruso told them, wide-eyed. He repeated the argument he'd overheard between Ziegler and the chorus as well as he could remember it, ending with the assistant manager's expression of regret that more of the choristers had not died.

The others were stunned momentarily, but then they were inclined to dismiss the statement as a lapse in taste as well as self-control. Scotti pointed out that everyone said things in the heat of anger that they immediately regretted. "You cannot accuse a man on so flimsy a basis," he added.

"*Flimsy!* He admits he wants them dead!"

"It is not evidence, Rico."

"Then I *find* evidence." He folded his arms across his chest and his face took on a stubborn set.

"Eh, well, then Rico investigates Edward Ziegler," Amato said, writing it down with a smile, "who is his new favorite suspect. That leaves Gigli uninvestigated." He looked around the table.

"I take him," Gatti offered. "I do not have favorite suspect."

"And I want Setti," Gerry said.

Gatti groaned. "Not Setti! Why do you suspect him?"

She lifted one shoulder. "He has the most to lose."

"Emmy?" Amato asked. "Who is your suspect?"

"Rosa Ponselle," she said without hesitation.

The others gaped at her. "Emmy!" Caruso cried. "You do not think young Rosa is *murderer*?"

"I think Rosa is a twenty-three-year-old woman who likes to play at being a little girl. That means she's capable of large-scale deceit."

Gerry smiled. "That also describes quite a few other people I know. All it means is that Rosa is postponing growing up as long as she can—a lot of girls do that, unfortunately. You don't really think Rosa's a killer, Emmy."

The other woman sighed. "Perhaps not. But she has as good a reason for hating the chorus as Gigli, and we're investigating him."

"This is true," Amato nodded. "It is not fair to investigate one but not the other. So—Emmy investigates Rosa." He wrote it down. "Eh, Toto, you are last one. Do we have any suspects left? Who is your choice?"

Scotti was silent a moment, and then he said, "While you talk this over, I am thinking. And I conclude this individual investigation is not smart thing to do."

"Oh, Toto!" Gerry exclaimed. "Why ever not?"

"Do you all forget why we decide in first place so many detectives are needed? So Gerry does not go looking for this dangerous man alone! No one of us must face a suspect alone—but that is what happens if we do it Pasquale's way, no?"

"*Cielo!* You are right!" Amato groaned. "I forget."

They all sat staring glumly at the table. They'd been so caught up in the planning that they'd overlooked the element of very real danger in their proposed undertaking. Every one of them was trying to think of a way to save the plan.

Suddenly Gerry sat up straight. "Why don't we work in pairs? That way when one of us needs to talk to a suspect, we just get our partner to come along! That would work!"

"*Sì, sì,*" Caruso said with a reawakening of enthusiasm. "That way we are all protected!"

"Not pairs," Amato said, "but teams! Teams of three—in case one person cannot go when needed, there is another to call. Eh, this is better. We work to eliminate suspects, yes? But if one suspect cannot be eliminated—"

"Then we contact the other team," Emmy finished for him. "If each team can narrow it down to one person—"

"Then the two teams get together and thrash it out," Gerry finished for *her.* "Oh, yes—that's the way to do it! What do you say, Toto? Will that satisfy you?"

He gazed at her dourly. "Will you really do it? Will you call me when you go see Setti?"

"Absolutely," she answered in a voice not to be questioned. "I have no desire to put myself in peril. I will call."

Scotti smiled and nodded. "Then I agree."

Subdued cheering greeted his announcement. Amato said,

"*Bene,* that is settled. Now all that is needed is for Toto to tell us whom he investigates."

Scotti cleared his throat. "Mrs. Bukaitis."

"The scrubwoman?" Emmy said in disbelief.

"You are not serious!" Gatti half-laughed.

"I am most serious," Scotti protested. "I talk to her. She is not just simple, ignorant woman who cleans the floors—there is more inside her head than that!"

"Toto, you waste your time," Amato smiled. "Why would a scrubwoman want to kill choristers?"

"Perhaps they catch her stealing," Scotti suggested. "Perhaps another reason."

"But—"

"No 'but'. I take Mrs. Bukaitis."

Gerry laughed. "Give up, Pasquale. Toto is going to investigate his scrublady whether the rest of us like it or not. Put her on the list."

Amato grumbled but added the scrubwoman's name, having to guess at the right way to spell 'Bukaitis'. "Now we divide into teams," he declared.

They argued about it a little but came to agreement fairly fast. The team of Farrar, Scotti, and Gatti-Casazza would investigate Giulio Setti, Mrs. Bukaitis, and Beniamino Gigli. The team of Destinn, Caruso, and Amato would investigate Rosa Ponselle, Edward Ziegler, and Alessandro Quaglia. They were all satisfied with their choices.

"Well, I feel as if we've accomplished something," Gerry said. "I think now I might manage another glass of Canadian—if anyone feels up to summoning that surly waiter."

"He does not know who we are," Caruso explained. "If he knows who we are, he does not treat us with disrespect." He waved an arm in the air until the waiter saw him. "So I tell him."

The waiter charged resentfully toward them and slammed an empty tin tray down on the table. He was gathering up their empty glasses when Caruso politely inquired as to his name. The waiter thought it over and decided it wouldn't hurt to tell. "Joseph," he admitted grudgingly.

"Joseph, I am most pleased to make your acquaintance," Caruso said in his best ingratiating manner. "Do you know that this lovely lady who sits to my left is the great Geraldine Farrar of the Metropolitan Opera?" He went around the table, introducing each in turn. "And I," he finished expansively, "I am Enrico Caruso! All of us, we are all with the Metropolitan Opera!"

Joseph picked up his laden tray and shouldered it. "I hate opera," he snarled, and charged away without taking their order.

❑ 7 ❑ The Belgravia had seen better days, Captain O'Halloran mused. The age-darkened stone of the apartment building looked dingy in the weak morning light, and the ornamental corner balconies all had the look of disuse to them. But the address was still a prestigious one, the corner of Fifth Avenue and Forty-ninth Street. Inside, the air of faded gentility was an even stronger reminder that the Belgravia had once been the ne plus ultra of luxurious apartment living. No po' folks allowed. O'Halloran took the elevator up to the eighth floor where Alessandro Quaglia lived. The conductor was expecting him.

Quaglia was dressed except for a brocade dressing gown that covered his boxer's physique. "Does this take long, Captain? I have much to do today."

O'Halloran murmured something noncommittal and took the chair Quaglia offered him. The first thing he wanted to find out was whether the conductor had been present in the opera house each time one of the choristers had died. He hadn't been there when the urn had fallen on the chorus soprano or when the tenor had been found hanging in the dressing room, Quaglia said; he did not conduct *Samson* or *Mefistofele*. But he'd been there the other three times.

"Do you ever attend an opera you're not conducting? Just to listen, I mean."

"No more. I go when I am younger and still learning, but not now."

"Why not?"

Quaglia's upper lip lifted. "I do not add to other conductors' prestige by sitting in their audience!"

"But singers go to hear *their* rivals."

"*Singers* are totally irrational breed of animal," Quaglia said in all seriousness. "You cannot ever, under any circumstances, expect rational behavior of singers."

O'Halloran thought of the conductor's battle with Geraldine Farrar and suppressed a smile. "If you hold such a low opinion of singers, why are you working in opera?"

Quaglia let out a sigh that seemed to come all the way up from his toes. "Because, Captain O'Halloran, the human voice is most beautiful musical instrument on face of the earth. The instruments we manufacture, they imitate it but they never reproduce it, not exactly. If you want to work with that exquisite sound the voice is capable of producing, eh, then you must work with singers. No matter how infuriating they are."

"Are you thinking of Miss Farrar?"

Quaglia started, and laughed. "Am I so obvious? Farrar is *senza dubbio* the best vocalist I ever work with. Her musicianship, it is near faultless. But the voice, *per sfortuna,* it deteriorates. She should not sing Marguérite . . . in *Faust*?" O'Halloran nodded. "The role is too high for her now," the conductor explained. "Yet once in a while—the last rehearsal, for instance—she finds the top notes to sing the role superbly."

"You told her she was flat."

"Did I? I do not remember. But my point is, you cannot tell her anything. She remembers the way she once sounds and does not admit the voice is different now. She is impossible woman."

O'Halloran tried a different tack. "Mr. Quaglia, did you ever work as an assistant chorus master?"

A look of distaste crossed the conductor's face. "Never! Assistant to chorus master—it is worst job in opera! Why do you ask?"

"I was told you started out as an assistant chorus master."

"Who tells you this?" he cried. "*Ella sbaglia!* I have nothing to do with rehearsing chorus!"

"What was your first job in opera?"

"Violinist, in orchestra. I am seventeen years old when I am hired," Quaglia added proudly.

"Where was this?"

"Naples. Il Teatro San Carlo."

O'Halloran asked the conductor to spell it for him and wrote it down. A wire to the Naples police politely asking for help ought to clear the contradiction up quickly enough. When Quaglia asked him again who had said he'd once been a chorus master, O'Halloran thought it better not to tell him.

The conductor leaned forward in his chair, his forearms resting on his thighs and his hands clasped between his knees. "Mr. Gatti? No, he has no reason to tell such a lie. It must be Giulio Setti—he once accuses me of encroaching on his territory." Quaglia snorted. "I would not have his job for ten times the money I am paid to conduct!"

O'Halloran asked him where he was when the first two murders took place. "The two times you say you weren't at the opera house."

Quaglia looked annoyed but answered. "When the hanged man is discovered, I am home. The first violinist calls me on the telephone and tells me. The other time—I do not remember."

The police captain made a note to check with the first violinist, thanked the conductor for his help, and left.

Antonio Scotti was in a part of the Metropolitan Opera House he hadn't even known was there. It was a small room in the substage area, the official resting place of mops, buckets, scrub brushes, five-gallon jars of ammonia, tin containers of brass polish and wax, bar after bar of lye soap. A clothesline holding drying rags was strung across one end of the room, and the sharp tang of some cleaning compound made the baritone's nose tingle. Crowded in among the cleaning supplies was a wooden bench, two discarded auditorium seats, and a low three-legged stool. In one corner stood an enamel coffeepot on an electric heater. The cleaning crew's greenroom.

"Another, ladies?" Scotti asked.

"Sure and that's a fine idea, Mr. Scotti," Mrs. Reilly said, holding out her coffee cup.

Scotti topped up her drink from the flask he'd had the foresight to bring with him; rye whiskey was not his favorite libation, but in these prohibitory days one took what one could find. He and the plump Mrs. Reilly shared the wooden bench. Mrs. Poplofsky, as long and lean as Mrs. Reilly was short and round, sat in one of the auditorium seats; and on the three-legged stool perched Just-Call-Me-Maude. Scotti filled their cups. The whiskey was tingling pleasantly in his veins, and the three scrubwomen were looking a little more content with their lot in life.

"Perhaps she does not talk much because of difficulties with the language," he said, continuing a line of conversation he'd initiated.

"Nooo, that's not it," said Mrs. Reilly. "She's just not what you'd call a friendly soul, doncha know."

"Mebbe she can't talk English," Mrs. Poplofsky said in a tone of secrets-sharing, "but that don't mean she can't understand it." She closed one eye conspiratorially.

Scotti raised an eyebrow. "You mean when you speak English to her—"

"I mean she understands what it suits her to understand," Mrs. Poplofsky nodded. "Oh, she's a deep one, she is!"

Mrs. Reilly laughed. "Deep! That one? Sure and you're mistaken, Mrs. Poplofsky. She's by way of bein' standoffish, that's what she is!"

Scotti looked at Just-Call-Me-Maude. "What do you think?"

She giggled and said she didn't know.

Mrs. Poplofsky took out a box of cigarettes, offered one to Scotti (who declined), and toed a scrub bucket into position to use as an ashtray. "She's up to something, mark my words."

Scotti took a swallow from the flask cap he was using as a glass and thought to himself that Just-Call-Me-Maude had a rather sweet face—or was that the whiskey's opinion? "Mrs. Bukaitis is up to something? What?"

"Can't rightly say what it is," Mrs. Poplofsky replied, "but she's alla time going places she has no business going."

Scotti suppressed a desire to cough; Mrs. Poplofsky had taken only two puffs of her cigarette but already all the breathable air in the basement room was filled with smoke. Nobody else seemed to mind, but then they were all getting a bit glassy-eyed. "Where does Mrs. Bukaitis go that she should not go?"

"Well, once I caught her trying the door of Miss Farrar's dressing room, and everybody knows that *nobody* cleans that room except Miss Farrar's own maid. And another time she was nosing around that platform thing they got out there—you know, the platform that goes up through the trap door in the stage?''

Scotti sat up straight. "Is this before or after the chorister falls to his death?''

Mrs. Poplofsky thought back. "After.''

"Oh.'' Scotti sank back, deflated.

"Poor man,'' Mrs. Reilly said sincerely. "Tumblin' down like that, not knowin' what's happenin' to him. Dreadful, just dreadful.''

Mrs. Poplofsky crossed one long leg over the other. "Funny thing 'bout that time. She had a box she kept trying to hide from me.''

"Her cigar box?'' Mrs. Reilly asked.

"Naw, bigger'n that.'' She blew out a cloud of smoke.

Just-Call-Me-Maude hiccupped.

"Mrs. Bukaitis keeps her personal things in a cigar box,'' Mrs. Reilly explained to Scotti.

Scotti nodded as if that were something he'd been wondering about. He rubbed an itching nose; the combination of cigarette smoke and cleaning compound was making it hard for him to breathe and he was growing woozy. A little whiskey should clear his head—but the flask cap was empty.

"You too, huh?'' Mrs. Poplofsky said pointedly.

Scotti poured her some rye. "Maude?''

"Yespleaseandthankyou.'' She held out her cup. But when Scotti turned to Mrs. Reilly, only a drop was left in the flask.

"Awr, now ain't that a cryin' shame,'' she said mournfully.

"Do not distress yourself, dear Mrs. Reilly,'' Scotti said happily as he reached into a pocket and pulled out a second flask. "*Per servirla!* We still manage to ward off the cold!''

"Glory be!'' cried Mrs. Reilly. "Now there's a sight for sore eyes!''

Just-Call-Me-Maude laughed and spanked one thigh with her free hand.

"I like a man who thinks ahead," Mrs. Poplofsky said, closing one eye meaningfully and holding out her cup still again.

When they had further fortified themselves against the winter, Scotti said, "The box she tries to hide from you, Mrs. Poplofsky—what kind of box is it?"

"I dunno, just a box. About so big." She demonstrated with her hands, trailing cigarette ash.

"Her lunch?"

"Nooo, couldn't be," Mrs. Reilly said. "She brings her lunch wrapped in paper."

"Mrs. Poplofsky, you are sure this is *after* trap door breaks open?"

She guffawed. "I was sure until you found that other flask." She stretched a long arm down to stub out her cigarette in the bucket at her feet. "Now you got me addled."

Just-Call-Me-Maude fell off her stool.

"Aow, there she goes," Mrs. Reilly sighed. "Come on, lass, up with ye." She hoisted the other woman back up on her stool and explained to Scotti, "She's not used to spirits so early in the day."

He wondered why her face was growing blurry and turned back to Mrs. Poplofsky. "*Per favore,* try to remember," he entreated her. "Is important."

She scrunched her face up in the effort of concentration. "You know, Mr. Scotti, now that I think on it, I ain't all that sure it was after. It mighta been before."

"*Che fortuna!*" the baritone cried, exuberantly flinging out an arm and knocking over a row of mops that had been standing in their buckets next to him. "Oh—*scusi, scusi!*"

"Ah, don't you be worryin' yerself about them mops, darlin'," Mrs. Reilly laughed. "You can't hurt 'em."

Scotti fought down an urge to rest his head on Mrs. Reilly's motherly bosom. "Do you see what she does with the box?" he asked Mrs. Poplofsky.

He was answered by a snore. Mrs. Poplofsky's head had sunk forward on her chest.

"Ah, poor dear," Mrs. Reilly crooned. "She works hard, she needs her rest."

Just-Call-Me-Maude was weaving unsteadily on her stool, humming a little tune to herself and smiling at no one in particular. It was beginning to seem to Scotti that he'd spent half his life in this close little room among the mops and the brooms and the lye soap. He fumbled his watch out of his vest pocket, but the Roman numerals on the face were a blur. He held the watch out to Mrs. Reilly. "Tell me the time?"

She squinted at the watch. "It's gone a quarter past the hour of eleven."

Scotti moaned. He was supposed to meet Gerry fifteen minutes ago; she was going to be furious! "I must go." He got shakily to his feet—and stared helplessly at the barrier of spilled mops that separated him from the door.

"Never you mind," said Mrs. Reilly, disposing of the mop obstacle with a few well-placed kicks of her surprisingly small feet. "Allus wanted to do that," she muttered. "Now you lean on me, dear. You're not lookin' any too steady."

Scotti placed one hand on her plump shoulder and let her lead him to the door. "I think you take me all the way out, yes?"

"Be careful!" Just-Call-Me-Maude squeaked unexpectedly.

"Of what?" he asked, but Mrs. Reilly was already leading him away.

She took him to the Seventh Avenue scenery doors, which were standing open to accommodate the shifting of stage flats out into the street. A light snow was falling, ignored by the stagehands maneuvering the scenery through the gaping double doors. "Now, Mr. Scotti, what you're needin' is a brisk walk in the fresh air," Mrs. Reilly told him. "Invigoratin', it is. You take deep breaths, hear, and you'll be feelin' right as rain in no time."

"Thank you, Mrs. Reilly, I follow your advice."

"And be sure you come back to see us again," she laughed. "You're allus welcome!" She waddled away toward her basement kingdom, still laughing.

Scotti stepped out onto Seventh Avenue, where the stage scen-

ery was stacked on the sidewalk exposed to the elements, waiting
for the trucks that would haul it away to a warehouse; the Metropolitan Opera House had no room to store its own scenery. Scotti
followed Mrs. Reilly's instructions and took a deep breath of the
December air—which cut through his lungs like a knife. This was
supposed to make him feel better?

Walk it off. He strode purposefully toward the corner and looked
up at the street sign: Thirty-ninth Street. Gerry lived on West Seventy-fourth; he was heading in the wrong direction.

She was going to be furious. Thirty-nine from seventy-four was
what? He puzzled over it a minute and then decided that anything
that hard to subtract was bound to be too far to walk. He hailed a
taxicab.

In Gerry's apartment building, the elevator motor said, *She's
going to be furious. She's going to be furious* all the way up. Down
the hallway, there's the door. After two or three attempts, Scotti
located the doorbell and pushed it. She's going to be furious.

And then she was in the doorway, blocking his entrance. "Do
you have any idea," she asked icily, "what time it is?"

"You are furious," he said sadly.

"You were supposed to be here at eleven o'clock! I've been
waiting for you the better part of an hour!"

"I am inves, I am inveshigay, I am asking questions."

Gerry peered at him closely. "Toto, are you tipsy? What have
you been doing?"

He pulled himself up to his full height. "I," he announced with
dignity, "am this morning *carousing*. With other women. With
three other women. Are you not jealous?"

The corner of her mouth twitched. "What other women?"

He ticked them off gloved fingers. "Mrs. Reilly. Mrs.
Poplofsky. And Just-Call-Me-Maude. Three of them."

Gerry blinked and said, "I think I'll wait to ask for an explanation of that one. Right now, you'd better get some coffee in you.
Come on in."

Two cups of coffee later, Scotti was able to tell her of his morning's visit with selected members of the Met's cleaning crew. To

his surprise. Gerry seized on Mrs. Bukaitis's trying to get into her dressing room as the most important matter he'd uncovered. "Maybe I should add another lock," she said.

Scotti said it wouldn't hurt. "I think she steals. But, *cara mia,* the important thing is that she does something around the stage platform. The platform that is right under the trap door!"

"Honestly, Toto, you can't think that's evidence of anything?" Gerry objected. "A scrubwoman standing in one place instead of another place? Your Mrs. Popplesofty didn't actually see her doing anything, did she?"

"Poplofsky. She saw her trying to hide a box."

"A box. Oh, that sounds ominous, that does. Toto, I'm glad you had a nice gossip with the girls, but don't make too much of it."

He was hurt. "At least I try."

She gave him a quick kiss by way of apology. "And you'll go on trying. And so will I, if we can ever get started. We'd better hurry—it's after noon, and Setti may already have left. Come on, let's go."

They took Gerry's limousine to Setti's house on Forty-second Street and got there just as the man himself was coming out the door. They offered him a ride; Setti, who usually walked the short distance to the opera house, squinted up at the snow and accepted. When they were all tucked in comfortably under the lap rug, the chorus master asked why they wanted to see him. "More questions, I suppose. Why does everyone think I see something nobody else sees?"

"Oh, we're all being asked questions," Gerry said with a show of casualness. "But there's something you're in a position to know that nobody else is. It's about Teresa Leone. Didn't you miss her before the performance started?"

He shrugged. "I count heads, I end with right number."

"Un momento," Scotti interrupted. "Teresa Leone—which one is she?"

"The mezzo-soprano who is stabbed," Setti said. "Right before *Carmen."*

Gerry asked, "When did you take your head count?"

"Eh, twenty minutes before curtain, perhaps fifteen."

"Mm, that doesn't leave much time. I suppose the killer just waited for any chorister who strayed away from the others. What do you do after you make your count, Mr. Setti?"

"Usually I listen to complaints. I do not stab the singers."

"Of course not—I didn't mean to imply you did." *Not yet, anyway.* "But do you move around a lot? Do you remember actually seeing Teresa during that fifteen- or twenty-minute period?"

"I move around, yes." Setti wrinkled his forehead. "I think I see her, right before curtain."

"But didn't one of the other choristers say she'd gone looking for Teresa a *half hour* before the curtain . . . and couldn't find her?" Not true; Gerry had made that up just to see what Setti would say.

"Eh, then perhaps I am mistaken," was what he said. "Or she is. I do not remember—no one knows these details are important until later." At that moment the chauffeur pulled up to the Broadway entrance of the Metropolitan. "Now I must bid you adieu, Miss Farrar," Setti said. "I have busy day awaiting me and I can answer no more of your questions." He nodded to Scotti, climbed out of the limousine, and went into the opera house.

"And so, *carissima*?" Scotti asked. "What do you learn?"

"I learned I need to know a lot more about interrogating people," she said frankly. "Maybe he's only pretending he ended up with the right number when he counted. Who's to check up on him? Maybe she was already dead by then."

"He could make mistake when he counts," Scotti suggested.

"Yes, that too, I suppose," Gerry sighed. "Well, that was a waste of time. When I retire from the opera," she said dryly, "I don't think I'll be opening a detective agency."

"Of course not," Scotti teased. "Who would consult eighty-five-year-old detective?"

Gerry laughed. "You may still be singing in your eighties, but I won't. I always said I'd retire at forty."

"You always *say* it, yes."

"And I mean it, Toto. I'll be forty in, let's see, fourteen months. Only fourteen more months! Oh dear."

"You do not retire," he said firmly. "Not for many, many years. No. You do not."

"One more season, that's all. One more, and then it will be time to stop."

"No! You do not talk this way! Gerry, you must not say you go! How can I sing when you are not here? Do not even *think* of leaving! *Ne la prego!*"

She saw she was distressing him and let the subject drop.

Gatti-Casazza hated what he was doing.

Across the table from him, a stick-thin young man was shoveling in food as if he hadn't eaten for a week. *Doesn't Gigli feed him?* Gatti wondered. The young man's name was Roberto; when Gatti had invited him to share a noonday meal, he'd told his guest to choose any restaurant he liked. Roberto had chosen the one in the world's largest hotel, the Pennsylvania, at the corner of Seventh Avenue and West Thirty-second Street. Neither man had been in the capacious new hotel before, and both were impressed by so much open floor space in one of the highest-priced areas of real estate in the world.

Roberto was Beniamino Gigli's valet, and Gatti had set for himself the unpleasant task of prying information out of him. Roberto had hinted that he could use fifty dollars for a new winter coat, and Gatti had agreed to the amount. He, Giulio Gatti-Casazza, general manager of the Metropolitan Opera Company, was going to bribe the valet of one of his star singers to give away secrets about his employer! *Vergognoso!* Shameful, shameful. Even worse, the fifty dollars would have to come out of his own pocket.

The way Roberto was eating, the meal could well cost another fifty. Gatti decided the valet was just a pig. A skinny pig. "How do you enjoy your meal?" he asked.

"Needs wine," Roberto answered around a mouthful of lobster.

"*Sì*, a good meal, it is not complete without wine. I wonder why the Americans do not understand that."

Roberto belched delicately and patted his mouth with a napkin. It wasn't until dessert that Gatti could force himself to start the questioning. According to the valet, his employer went almost nowhere without Roberto in attendance. Gatti took that with a grain of salt but started asking anyway as to the tenor's whereabouts on the nights the murders took place. Gigli was in the opera house on the *Mefistofele* night, when the chorister had been hanged with his own suspenders. Of the other times, Roberto said Gigli was home every time except once, when he went out to play cards.

Gatti wasn't sure whether to believe him or not. He did not think Roberto was lying to protect Gigli, but he could be lying to protect himself; if he admitted he didn't know anything, he might not get his fifty dollars. Gatti seized on the one specific thing the valet had said. "How do you know he is out playing cards?"

"Because he takes me with him!"

"No, no—I mean how are you so sure of which night this is?"

"Eh, that is easy. The card-playing, it goes on until four o'clock in the morning! And I, I must be up at six to take the dog out to do his business! It does not matter if I get no sleep—every day I must go out with the dog and come back with the newspapers. And the day after the card-playing, I am so sleepy I can barely make out what the headlines say. But when I can, I see that a man falls through the stage at Metropolitan Opera and dies!"

"Pagliacci," Gatti murmured.

"Sì, during *Pagliacci.* I rush home and wake Mr. Gigli—I remember he is very angry. Then I show him newspaper . . . and he turns white like ghost! I remember he says, *'Misericordia!* In the opera house, they are dying—and I worry because Scotti takes my money!'"

"Scotti?" Gatti asked, startled. "Antonio Scotti?"

"Sì, Mr. Antonio Scotti. He is big winner in the card-playing."

Gatti let the smile he was feeling spread slowly over his face. Now if Toto could just remember which night it was he cleaned out Beniamino Gigli . . .

The waiter arrived with the check—not quite fifty dollars. Roberto cleared his throat. "I tell you what you want to know?"

"Yes, Roberto, I think perhaps you do."

Roberto cleared his throat again.

Gatti nodded and took out his wallet. Slowly, because it hurt, he counted out five ten-dollar bills. "There you are, Roberto. Fifty dollars, as we agree."

"And another fifty not to tell Mr. Gigli." The valet smiled at him innocently. "Do you want Mr. Gigli to know you ask questions about him behind his back?"

Gatti ground his teeth and opened his wallet again.

Mrs. Bukaitis emerged on to the south side of Delancey Street and paused to get her bearings. She didn't like Delancey; too many people, too much traffic, too much noise. The street had been widened on the south side when it was made the approach to the Williamsburg Bridge; now anyone crossing the street had to watch out for a continual string of streetcars as well as the automobiles that showed so little respect for those on foot. The newer buildings on the south side sported dentists' signs in almost every other doorway; all the remaining doors opened into offices of one sort or another as well. Nobody lived there.

But it was the older, north side of the street that was Mrs. Bukaitis's destination. Uptown, the policemen who'd directed traffic had long since been replaced by electric traffic lights, but Delancey Street had neither. Mrs. Bukaitis chose her moment and darted through a gap in the traffic. She sheltered briefly in the second of the two streetcar stations that trisected the street; she stood shivering and staring out at the bridge to Brooklyn that she'd never crossed. The bridge's pedestrian walkway was empty; the wind blowing off the East River was cruel in December.

Pulling her coat collar close, Mrs. Bukaitis crossed the remaining lane of traffic and stepped to the safety of the sidewalk in front of Wildman's Men's Shop. The north side of Delancey was all old tenement buildings, with stores on the ground floor and barely livable rooms above. Mrs. Bukaitis headed west until she came to a dingy café and went in. If the place had a name, nobody knew it. The grease on the windows reflected a yellow tint over the cheerless brown interior; a Christmas wreath had been nailed to one wall in a halfhearted attempt to add a little color to the place.

Mrs. Bukaitis looked around quickly; Antanas was not there yet. Opening the big black bag she'd brought with her, Mrs. Bukaitis pulled out the pocket watch she'd 'found' in the chorus dressing room at the Metropolitan. It was still early; Antanas would be there before long.

The café's cook-owner always kept a large kettle of soup simmering on the stove. Into the kettle went any leftover bits of vegetable or grain or fat or fish or fowl that came to hand; the regular customers called it surprise soup. Mrs. Bukaitis asked for a bowl.

The wind outside made the window glass rattle in its frame. Mrs. Bukaitis sat at a battered table where she could keep an eye on the door and warmed her hands over the steaming soup bowl. There were perhaps half a dozen other customers in the small café, all of them talking and eating at the same time. Mrs. Bukaitis ate her soup in silence. She'd just finished when Antanas came in. He was carrying the box under one arm.

He slid into the chair opposite her and kept the box on his lap. In a low voice he told her, "He says this one is all right. He says the only reason it might not go off is if the dynamite's no good."

"Isn't there any way to tell?" she asked.

"Not without testing other sticks from the same batch. I don't want to do that—it might give us away. We'll let *this* one be the test. If it doesn't go off this time, I'll have to get some different dynamite."

Mrs. Bukaitis nodded. "I'll set it on Monday."

"Why not today?"

"Because on Monday Geraldine Farrar is singing. Every seat in the house will be taken."

"Where are you going to put it?"

"The same place as last time. Even the rich Americans will find it hard to ignore a gaping hole in the stage floor."

Antanas ran his tongue over his lips. "You mustn't let yourself get caught, you know."

"I'm not afraid."

"That's not the point. There aren't enough of us yet that we can afford to lose even one member of the cell."

"I'll be careful."

At that moment a uniformed policeman came into the café. He stood just inside the door, hands on hips, exuding authority. All conversation ceased. Mrs. Bukaitis felt something pressing against her legs and realized Antanas was trying to pass her the box under the table. She took it and slipped it into her large black bag.

The policeman was looking for someone. He walked among the tables, inspecting each face carefully. Then he walked over to the cook-owner and asked him something; the man shook his head. The policeman gave them all the once-over again and finally departed, leaving the café door standing open. Everyone in the place let out a big breath. The café's owner closed the door and returned to his soup kettle.

"At least you won't be bothered by police at the opera house," Antanas muttered.

Mrs. Bukaitis said nothing.

"Mr. Setti's called a rehearsal in five minutes, Captain. I should be—"

"That's all right," O'Halloran assured her. "I've already spoken to Mr. Setti and he knows I'll be talking to several of you. You are. . . ?"

"Contralto."

"No, I mean your name?"

"Oh. Irene Matera."

"Have a seat, Miss Matera. Here on the bench." They were in one of the Met's smaller rehearsal rooms—a piano, a piano bench, and six uncomfortable-looking straight chairs lined up along one wall. No window. It was Sunday, but not a day of rest. O'Halloran leaned against the piano and tried to assess the fortyish woman sitting on the piano bench. He'd sought her out because she was American of Italian extraction; the Italian-born choristers pretended not to understand what he was saying, and the Germans barely condescended to speak to him at all.

A few minutes of questions and answers convinced him Irene Matera was going to be no help in establishing the presence or absence of anyone; she stated flatly that everyone was there every time there was an attack on the chorus. *Everybody* was a suspect, as far as Irene Matera was concerned.

Toss out a few names. "What about Mr. Setti? Surely you'd notice if he, uh, disappeared for a while during a performance?"

"Oh, Setti's all over the place. Nobody can keep track of him."

"What about Mr. Quaglia?"

She made a *humph* sound. "What about him?"

"Does he come backstage before a performance?"

"Before, during, and after. Just try to keep him away."

"*During* a performance?"

"During the intermissions, I mean. He likes to pester the soloists with last-minute instructions. It makes him feel as if he's in charge."

"And he isn't?"

She shrugged but didn't answer.

"What about Beniamino Gigli?"

"We promised Mr. Caruso we wouldn't bother him anymore," she said defensively.

"That's not what I mean. Was he backstage during any of the performances he wasn't in?"

"Probably. There are always a lot of people around who shouldn't be there."

"Do you positively remember seeing him on one of the nights he wasn't singing?" O'Halloran insisted. The contralto reluctantly admitted she didn't. "How about Rosa Ponselle?"

A change came over Irene Matera. From a normal, pleasant-looking woman she metamorphosed into something suggesting an avenging fury. "Rosa Ponselle," she said acidly, "is a bitch. She wouldn't be singing here at all if she weren't sleeping with Caruso."

O'Halloran was taken aback, but he managed to say mildly, "I understood Rosa Ponselle was a genuine singer, a good one."

"She is a good singer," the woman admitted, "but so am I.

And *I'm* still in the chorus. I've been studying opera since I was thirteen years old—but Caruso brings in his vaudeville tootsie and overnight she's made a star! Now I ask you, Captain, is that fair?''

The naked envy emanating from the woman made O'Halloran take a step back. ''And so you've been sabotaging her performances?''

''We've stopped. We promised.''

''I don't understand. You obviously resent Caruso for what you see as a wrong done to yourself, but you also undermine Gigli . . . out of loyalty to Caruso?''

''That was the men,'' she said sullenly. ''Their god Caruso can do no wrong.''

Ah, now it made sense. The male choristers resented Gigli and the women resented Rosa Ponselle—and they probably helped each other in badgering the two stars. It had become a vicious game, in which the prize lay in seeing how much they could get away with. Not the most wholesome of atmospheres. ''And I suppose you suspect one or both of them of killing choristers to get even,'' O'Halloran said dryly.

Irene Matera unexpectedly laughed. ''Not Ponselle. She doesn't have the nerve. Do you know she hides from us? She's hiding right now, in the star dressing room.''

''Now?''

The woman nodded. ''She won't wait offstage during rehearsal. She hides in the dressing room until it's her turn, and then somebody has to go up and get her.'' The chorus woman laughed again. ''She's afraid of us.''

And isn't that something to be proud of, O'Halloran thought sourly, already on Rosa Ponselle's side even though he'd never met the young lady. He abruptly told Irene Matera she could go, without adding his usual thanks-for-your-help.

Because years had passed since he'd last prowled the offstage areas of the Metropolitan Opera House, it took O'Halloran a while to find his way to the women's dressing rooms on the Fortieth Street side of the house. Placards in four languages lined the corridor walls: *Visitors are requested to delay until after final act, dogs are not permitted backstage.* He knocked on the star dressing room door.

"Who is it?" a young voice asked suspiciously.

O'Halloran identified himself and was told to come in. He opened the door to see a pretty young brunette curled up in a padded wicker armchair, an open book lying on her lap. The captain shivered; the room was cold. "Don't you have any heat in this room?"

"I turned it off. I sing better in low temperatures."

O'Halloran started to ask why but then decided he didn't really want to know. Instead he asked if she could account for her whereabouts on the five murder nights.

She gasped. "Am *I* a suspect?"

"Everybody's a suspect, and nobody is. Help me cross your name off the list."

Rosa told him she'd been in the opera house during the *Carmen* and *Forza* murders, but as well as she could remember she'd been at home the other three times.

"Anyone with you?"

"I live with my sister. She's better at remembering dates than I am."

O'Halloran nodded and asked, "You were singing in both *Carmen* and *Forza*?"

"Just *Forza*. *Carmen* is Gerry Farrar's opera. I came to watch and listen."

"Any particular reason?"

She grinned impishly. "I intend to sing *Carmen* someday. If Gerry ever lets me."

O'Halloran grinned back. "Don't hold your breath." He let the grin fade. "Now I have to bring up an unpleasant subject. The way the chorus has been treating you—"

"Oh, those wretched people!" she exclaimed. "Look, Captain. . . ?"

"O'Halloran."

"Captain O'Halloran, I'm sorry as I can be about what's been happening to them. Nobody should have to live in fear of their lives like that, and when you catch the guy who's doing it I hope you boil him in oil. But that doesn't alter the fact that the choristers just aren't very nice people. They want me out of here, and they've been doing everything they can think of to make me look bad!''

"I understood they'd promised Caruso to stop bothering you."

"Well, yes, the last time I sang they didn't make any trouble. But I don't trust them!''

Recalling Irene Matera's bellicose jealousy, O'Halloran thought she was wise not to. "One of them told me you're having an affair with Caruso."

Rosa threw her book at his head.

He ducked just in time. "Hey!"

"I am so sick of that story! Sick, sick, *sick* of it!" she screamed. "That's just one of the ways the chorus tries to make me look bad—spreading rumors that I slept my way into the Met! Well, I didn't! There's not a word of truth to it!" She was out of her chair, pacing angrily.

O'Halloran picked up the book. *This Side of Paradise.* "You mean Caruso just heard you singing in a vaudeville house and—"

"No, it wasn't like that. I don't even know if he's ever *been* in a vaudeville house! I was taking a voice lesson and someone who works for Caruso was there and heard me and he told Caruso and Caruso came to hear me at my next voice lesson and he told Mr. Gatti and Mr. Gatti called me in for an audition and *that's* how I got into the Met!" She stopped for breath. "Caruso was just being kind and helpful. There's nothing illicit between us—he treats me like a daughter or a niece. And now we're both being smeared by this ugly rumor . . . just because he was kind!"

O'Halloran put the book on the dressing table. "Well, the rumors will stop eventually."

Rosa had calmed down a little. "Caruso isn't even remotely interested in me *that* way—thank goodness!" She paused, thinking. "No, Geraldine Farrar is more Caruso's idea of what a woman should be." Her face took on a wry look. "Indescribably beautiful, the epitome of high fashion—everybody's dream girl!"

The captain smiled at her. "Jealous?"

"Of course I am!" she admitted cheerfully. "We all are. Except Emmy Destinn. Emmy lives in her own world. She doesn't have much to do with the rest of us."

O'Halloran remembered the lady in question coming out of Setti's house just as he himself arrived there. "You might be surprised. I know she's been asking questions about these murders— she probably calls it 'investigating'."

"Emmy? I know Gerry once did something like that—"

"Her too. And Caruso. They fancy themselves detectives, you see. You wouldn't be doing any of that, would you?"

"Any of what? Investigating, you mean?" Rosa looked astounded at the suggestion.

"That's what I mean. Are you?"

"Are you crazy? Why would I pretend to be a detective? I wouldn't *dream* of going around asking questions and sticking my neck out! Not on your life!"

"Bless you, my child," O'Halloran sighed, and left.

□ **8** □   *"Idiota!"* Antonio Scotti grabbed his hair with both hands. "Why do I not think of it? I forget, I forget!"

"Then it is true?" Gatti-Casazza asked.

"Sì, sì—he is here all night!"

The Geraldine Farrar team of detectives was meeting in Scotti's apartment in the Knickerbocker Hotel to compare notes. "Are you sure of the date, Toto?" Gerry asked. "That's important."

"It is night trap door falls open in *Pagliacci,"* Scotti said. "I remember thinking when I hear, this terrible thing happens while I am busy relieving Gigli of his last singing fee. It is same night."

"And he is here playing cards all the time?" Gatti persisted. "He does not go out for a while?"

"Only to visit the amenities. He comes right back, to this very room."

"Eh, then," Gatti smiled, pleased with his work. "Now we remove one name from list of suspects, no?"

"Gigli is not good card player," Scotti offered by way of general information.

Gerry made an apologetic sound. "That was smart detective work, Gatti—but I'm afraid we can't take Gigli's name off the suspects list just yet."

"Perchè non? He is here playing cards all night with Scotti! Other men are here too, they are also witnesses. How can he wreak havoc at the opera house and be here playing cards at same time? No, Gerry—Gigli has good alibi."

"But he didn't have to be at the opera house *that night.* He could have sabotaged the trap door earlier. Whoever the killer is, he didn't have to wait for the actual performance."

"È vero," Scotti nodded. "She is right, Gatti."

Gerry said, "Here's something to consider. What was the last opera performed before *Pagliacci?"*

"Mefistofele," Gatti answered. Gigli's opera. "But that does not mean he is guilty!"

"No, of course it doesn't. But it does mean he had a good

opportunity to fix the trap door so it would give way the next time a lot of weight was put on it.''

"You mean he can fix it right after *Mefistofele* performance ends.''

"Or the next day," Gerry said. "He'd have had plenty of time.''

Gatti slumped in his chair. "I do not think Gigli is guilty.''

"Neither do I," Gerry admitted promptly. "But if we're looking for evidence to eliminate suspects, we just don't have any for Gigli yet.''

The general manager groaned. "*Cielo!* And I think I do such good detective work!''

"But you do!" Scotti said, trying to cheer him up. "That was smart, going to Gigli's valet.''

"But not very nice," Gatti said despondently. "And it is for nothing!''

"Well, murder isn't very nice either," Gerry said. "Don't worry, Gatti—you're going about your investigation the right way.''

But it wasn't his proficiency as a detective that was bothering Gatti. It was the loss of the hundred dollars he'd paid the valet Roberto that he was mourning. He'd had no idea detective work could be so expensive.

Emmy Destinn resisted the temptation to finger the Flemish lace, remembering how Caruso had squawked the last time she'd touched it. "What is it you want me to see, Rico? Something new?''

"See? I do not ask you to come because I want you to see.''

Enrico Caruso had his own art gallery. A quarter of a century of accumulating antiques and *objets d'art* had resulted in a collection that took up too much room to live with comfortably. So the antique watches, velvets, brocades, bronzes, enamels, candlesticks, paintings, and the like had to be given their own resting place, a rented gallery on Fiftieth Street near Fifth Avenue.

Emmy turned away from the lace. "If you don't have something for me to look at, why did you want me to come here?"

"I ask Edward Ziegler to meet me here, and we agree not to face suspects alone, no? So I call a teammate. You are my protection!"

"But why here? Why not just talk to him in his office?"

"Too many interruptions," Caruso growled. "I try in office, but always are interruptions. Here is better."

Caruso fidgeted while Emmy amused herself looking at his collection as they waited. After a while she too began to fidget. "When is he coming?" she asked.

"He is supposed to be here now," Caruso worried.

"Well, I can't wait all day. He's not going to tell you anything anyway. What do you expect him to say? 'Yes, you are right, I did it'?"

"You do not know, he might."

"Oh, don't be absurd, Rico! Don't you have a plan? What are you going to ask him?"

"I think we just talk, and maybe he gives something away."

Emmy was astounded. "That is your plan? Wait for him to give himself away? Oh, Rico, that is plain silly! *You* are silly. Shame on you, wasting my time like this."

He looked pained. "Emmy, you do not even try to be agreeable any more!"

"I do not *feel* agreeable!" she snapped.

"I already know that!" he snapped back. "Everybody at the Metropolitan Opera knows that! Ever since you come back from Prague, you are *grouch*."

Sputtering, Emmy grabbed up the Flanders lace and wrapped it around her shoulders.

"Emmy, take care!" Caruso cried. "The lace, it is fragile! I tell you before! Now put it back!"

"Lace is meant to be worn," she snarled, "not spread out on a table and stared at!" But she put it back.

Fortunately that was the moment Edward Ziegler opened the door to the gallery and let himself in. "Sorry I'm late, Mr. Caruso—I was meeting with the new insurance underwriters and couldn't get away." He spotted Emmy. "Oh, Miss Destinn. I didn't know you'd be here."

"She knows all," Caruso nodded, trying to look Solomon-like.

"All?" Ziegler peered at them over his pince-nez. "Are you referring to that unfortunate slip of the tongue when I was negotiating with the choristers? You aren't going around telling everyone about that, are you?"

"The choristers, they talk, yes? So what does it matter if I—"

"Yes, yes, I suppose you're right," Ziegler said irritably. "What is it you wanted to see me about?"

Caruso looked surprised. "*That* is what we talk about. You and the chorus."

"What about them?"

"You do not like the choristers, no?"

"I'm not too fond of the ones we have at the moment, you might say."

"Might I also say you go so far as to hate them?"

A look of comprehension crept over Ziegler's face. "I? You think . . . *I* am the one killing the choristers?" He worked his mouth wordlessly a moment. Then: "How dare you accuse me? How *dare* you?"

Caruso was uncomfortable; he wasn't very good at confronting people. "Mr. Ziegler, can you tell us someone you are with at time of murders? Some person who can give you alibi?"

"Why should I? You're not the police!"

"No," the tenor sighed. "I am Caruso and you are Ziegler and we must work together in the opera house. *Mi dica, di grazia*— one name? One murder?"

Ziegler was still angry but he made the effort to think back. "Well, during *Forza* . . . when the chorister was poisoned—"

"No, not that one," Caruso interrupted. "The poison, it can be put in pitcher any time, yes? Perhaps *Carmen*?"

"This is preposterous! How do you expect me to remember that far back?"

"Not so far. Please try. The time right before the curtain."

Ziegler scowled, trying to remember. Suddenly his face lit up. "Quaglia! I was talking to Maestro Quaglia—I'm sure of it! Yes, that was the night two of the orchestra members called in ill and Quaglia was complaining that our orchestral pool was inadequate, that it should be maintained at the same level as our pool of contract singers. We talked right up to curtain time, I'm sure of it!"

"*Bene!*" Caruso cried. "You see, you do remember! Now, *Pagliacci*—"

But the Met's assistant manager had had enough. "Mr. Caruso, I don't know what you think you're doing, but I'm not going on with this. I don't have to account for myself to you."

Caruso put on his best menacing leer. "Do you prefer to account to Captain O'Halloran of the police?"

"Yes, as a matter of fact, I think I would prefer that."

Caruso hadn't expected that. "Eh, um, so you, uh." Ziegler crossed to the door and opened it.

"Mr. Ziegler, one word before you go," Emmy said, speaking for the first time. "Right before *Pagliacci*, you came to my dressing room and you spoke German to me. Why did you do that?"

He looked puzzled. "Why did I come to your dressing room?"

Emmy let her exasperation show. "You know perfectly well what I mean. Why did you speak German to me? You've known for two years that I do not permit that language to be spoken to me."

Ziegler showed a little exasperation himself. "How can I possibly remember a thing like that? I'd probably been talking to some of the German choristers and just forgot to switch when I spoke to you. That happens sometimes, when you speak four languages."

"I speak five," Emmy said, "and it's never happened to me."

"Which simply proves what a truly superior person you are," he said, bowing sardonically. He left without another word.

Caruso walked over to the door and looked out through the barred window, watching Ziegler as long as he was in sight. "Emmy," he asked, "who is it that investigates Maestro Quaglia?"

"Pasquale."

He nodded. "I think I must ask Pasquale to check on this *Carmen* alibi Ziegler gives us."

"Yes," she murmured after a moment, "that is exactly what you must do."

The Met's doorkeeper scratched the bridge of his nose. "That's a tall order, Mr. Amato. A couple hundred people come troopin' in here ever' night."

"I know I ask a lot," Pasquale Amato replied, "but please, try to remember."

"Why do you wanta know when the Maestro was here anyway?"

"It is these killings," the baritone said, looking for the best way to shade the truth. "If one person is backstage all five times a chorister dies, then perhaps that person sees someone else who is here all five times—you see? So I ask myself, who can be here all five times? And I answer myself, perhaps Maestro Quaglia? Perhaps he sees someone who does not belong here?"

"Why doncha just ask him?"

"I think I check with you first." Amato was on shaky ground there, so he hurried on: "*Di grazia,* do you remember? Is he here?"

The doorkeeper scratched his nose again. "He don't come for the Germans. He's never here when we're doin' one of the Germans."

"But no chorister dies during a German opera. What about the Italian or French operas he does not conduct?"

"Yeah, ever' once in a while he drops in. Never stays long."

"Was he here during *Samson and Delilah? Mefistofele?*"

But the doorkeeper couldn't remember, and Amato had to settle for a maybe. Quaglia wasn't at the opera house; Monday's opera was *Zazà,* which he did not conduct. It was just as well, as Amato wasn't ready to confront him yet. The conductor could have been backstage during the crucial times—*but wait!* Amato suddenly thought. What were the 'crucial' times? Three of the killings could have been rigged hours ahead of time—the falling urn, the broken trap door, the poisoned juice pitcher. Amato shook his head; trying to pin down times wasn't the answer. He'd have to find some other line to follow.

"Mr. Amato!" a voice called. "I do not think you rehearse today."

Amato turned to see the chorus master approaching. "No, Mr. Setti, I come to see you," he improvised, steering the older man out of earshot of the doorkeeper. "It is about Maestro Quaglia that I wish to speak. I know he has trouble with choruses in past—"

"*È vero!*" Setti smirked. "Quaglia knows nothing of choral singing. He does not know how to tell the chorus what he wants— I think because he does not know what he wants himself. So he blames choristers for his own imprecision."

"Eh, he has no trouble telling soloists what he wants," Amato remarked dryly. "When does it start, this hating of choristers?"

"At La Scala," Setti guessed, "or perhaps Covent Garden. You know chorus petitions against him there?"

"*Sì*, I—"

"Do you know why? Because he tries to strangle a chorus tenor! He loses control of himself completely . . . and they fight!" Setti looked out of the corner of his eye to see how Amato was taking that.

Amato was taking it with a great deal of astonishment—because he knew Setti had just told him one enormous lie. The Covent Garden chorus had protested in a dispute over what they claimed was Quaglia's lack of consistency. The chorus would have perhaps one full rehearsal with the soloists and orchestra before a performance; Quaglia would conduct their music one way at the rehearsal and another during the performance. There had been no fight, no attempt at strangling. Amato knew, because he'd been singing at Covent Garden at the time it all happened.

Openly pleased with the effect his bit of 'news' had created, Setti pushed it a little farther. "A man of uncontrolled violent impulses, our Maestro. I do not wish to make accusations, but . . ." He held his hands out, palms up, leaving it to Amato to finish the sentence any way he wished.

Amato at last found his voice. "No, no, you are right—we must take care not to start accusing one another."

The chorus master scowled; that wasn't the response he'd been angling for. "But it does not hurt to be careful, eh? Do not allow yourself to be alone with him, Mr. Amato."

Amato glanced at a stagehand sweeping the floor and then looked back to the doorkeeper. Right then he was more worried about being alone with Setti than with Quaglia. He mumbled something and found an excuse to get away; the chorus master was suddenly making him nervous.

Very nervous.

Emmy Destinn was in something of a bind. First of all, she'd taken on the task of investigating a murder suspect that no one seriously believed could be guilty, including the investigator. Emmy wasn't overly fond of Rosa Ponselle, but the only thing she had by way of evidence against her was that Rosa had poured out the poisoned orange juice for the unfortunate chorister who picked the wrong time to get thirsty. Calling that little bit of nothing 'evidence' was stretching it a bit. Anyone could have picked up that pitcher of juice and poured a glass; it was mere chance that it happened to be Rosa.

Second, there was the problem of *how* to investigate. There was no point in talking to the choristers; every one of them would swear to having seen Rosa Ponselle lurking backstage when she had no business being there, a knife in one hand and a vial of poison in the other. Rosa lived with her sister, but there was no point in talking to her either; she would swear on a stack of Bibles that Rosa had been home every night, knitting shawls and singing hymns.

But the main obstacle was one that Emmy reluctantly acknowledged as virtually insurmountable: it was just too improbable to think that the younger woman would jeopardize her future simply to get even with a bunch of ill-mannered hecklers. Rosa Ponselle didn't have the world at her feet yet, but it was only a matter of time. She was on the right track, she had Gatti-Casazza guiding every step of her career, she was fresh and young and still had it all ahead of her. Emmy tried to remember what *that* felt like.

Rosa and her sister lived in an apartment building on Ninety-seventh Street near Riverside Drive. Perhaps the doorman?

Emmy took a taxicab farther uptown than she'd ever been before. When she arrived at her destination, she was annoyed to learn that the apartment building had no doorman. But there was a doorbell labelled BUILDING SUPERVISOR. She pushed it.

The man who answered the door was in his late forties. Thin lips, tight jaw, suspicious eyes—constipated-looking. "No vacancies," he told Emmy, "and we don't keep no waiting list."

Emmy sized him up quickly and reached into her purse for a twenty-dollar bill. "I will pay you one dollar a minute for your time," she announced.

The man's eyes narrowed at the sight of the twenty, and he motioned Emmy inside. The first thing she saw in the tiny foyer was a bicycle propped up by the side of the staircase. The building supervisor was struggling to get the door to click as he pulled it to. "Fool latch is broken again," he muttered. "I'm gonna have to fix that before they all start yelling." He glanced at Emmy. "Twenty minutes?"

"At the most." She pointed to the bicycle. "Is that. . . ?"

"Belongs to one of the tenants. A singer, she says." He led Emmy down to a large basement room that seemed to be a combination living room–bedroom–kitchen–workshop–office. The man let her find her own seat and then said, "First of all, I gotta know who I'm talking to."

"Ema Destinnova," she said, and waited.

No flicker of recognition. "What can I do for you, Mrs.?"

"Tell me your name?"

"Bridges." Nothing else.

"Mr. Bridges, can you hear when people come in and go out of this building?"

He pointed to the ceiling. "Steps run up right over there."

"Can you tell from the sound who's climbing them? Or coming down?"

Mr. Bridges allowed the ghost of a smile to appear. "You're kinda new at this, ain't you, Mrs.? Who you wanta know about?"

"Rosa Ponselle," Emmy sighed.

"*Her* I can always tell," he snorted. "She never walks. She runs up the stairs, she runs down the stairs. Never walks."

"That sounds like Rosa," Emmy muttered.

"You know her, huh?"

"We work at the same place." Emmy tried asking whether Rosa had gone out or not on certain dates, but the man just laughed and said he didn't keep records of the tenants' comings and goings. Emmy had expected no less. "Has she ever said anything to you about, well, about some people who were bothering her?"

He started to shake his head but then stopped. "Wait a minute—once she was madder'n a hornet about something. She wasn't talking to me, she was talking to her sister—I was in the kitchen fixing a leaky faucet. She kept saying *they* did this and *they* did that, and the sister seemed to know what she was talking about. Is that what you mean?"

"It may be. Can you remember anything specific she said?"

He thought back. "Well, she said somebody jarred her elbow when she was about to pick something up. And she complained about some guy who planted himself right in front of her and wouldn't move. Buncha things . . . oh yeah, I remember she told her sister she thought somebody was putting them up to it or egging them on or something."

"Somebody? Did she say who?"

"Yeah, but I don't remember the name."

"Quaglia? Setti? Ziegler?"

"What was the second one?"

"Setti? Giulio Setti?"

Mr. Bridges scrunched up his face. "Could be. I know it wasn't Ziegler, and I don't think it was the other one."

"Alessandro Quaglia."

"Nope. It was Setti. I'm pretty sure."

Emmy spent a dollar's worth of time thinking about that. Rosa was impetuous and could just be hitting out at any available target. Or she could actually know of something that had convinced her Setti was behind all the badgering. Emmy wondered if Rosa would tell her if she just asked her straight out. Or . . . "Mr. Bridges, did Rosa say why she suspected Setti of being behind it?"

"Naw, not really. She just said something about him building sympathy."

"Building sympathy for himself?" Using the chorus's all-round bad behavior to excuse his doing a less-than-perfect job with them? It was possible. "Did Rosa mention what she planned to do about it?"

"I don't remember nothing more, Mrs."

Meaning her time was up. "Well, thank you, Mr. Bridges, you've been an enormous help. Now I wonder if I might use your telephone before I leave?"

He shook his head. "Didn't get none put in."

Emmy forced herself to smile and said goodbye. Out on the street, she paused a moment. She'd chosen a time to snoop around Rosa's apartment building when she knew the younger woman would be at the opera house. She'd wanted to call to make sure Rosa hadn't left yet; Emmy thought a good heart-to-heart was next on the agenda. Well, if she missed her at the opera house she'd just have to try another time.

The bad weather had eased up a bit. The snow had stopped and the wind had died, for which Emmy rendered silent thanks; she was almost as uncomfortable in the New York winters as the Italian singers were. She walked to Riverside Drive and started the business of hailing a taxicab. When after nearly ten minutes of continuous arm-waving and no cab had stopped, Emmy no longer had to worry about getting cold; she was warmer than she liked inside her fur-lined coat.

She should have brought the limousine. If she couldn't get a taxicab to stop for her, what was she to do? It was too far to walk to the opera house—nearly sixty blocks. She hated the subway; she was convinced it wasn't safe. There were streetcars, but the only one Emmy knew about ran down Third Avenue—a *long* trudge across town. She couldn't go back to the apartment building and use the phone to call a teammate to come get her, because Mr. Bridges 'didn't get none put in.' So how was she to get back downtown?

The answer came immediately. Rosa's bicycle.

It had been nearly thirty years since Emmy Destinn had been on a bicycle, and she hadn't particularly enjoyed it even then. But if she must, she must. She made her way back to the apartment house and tried the door instead of ringing for Mr. Bridges. The faulty latch gave way, and thirty seconds later Emmy was walking Rosa's bicycle east on Ninety-seventh Street.

She wasn't even going to try Riverside Drive; too much traffic. She waited until she got to Broadway to try riding the flimsy-looking machine. The first few attempts consisted mostly of pushing along on one foot and then overbalancing the other way and pushing along on the other foot. But at last she got both feet on the pedals at the same time and went wobbling down Broadway—on the sidewalk. She prayed fervently that no one she knew would see her.

Emmy had forgotten how uncomfortable bicycle seats could be. But thank God hemlines were shorter now; she would never have been able to manage in the voluminous skirts she wore before the war. Emmy's legs tired quickly, but much of Broadway was a gentle downhill slope in the direction she was going and she could coast now and then. Almost-frozen slush lined both sides of the sidewalk, so she had to concentrate on steering right down the middle. Whenever a pedestrian yelled at her to get off the sidewalk, she'd just pedal faster—in case a policeman was in the vicinity.

Once she'd settled into a sort of rhythm, she started thinking about Giulio Setti. Emmy had known Setti almost as long as she'd known Gatti and Caruso and the others. She couldn't say she knew him well, but still he would not have been her nominee for the role of killer. Not that she thought him incapable of killing; the war had taught her that anyone was capable of anything. But Setti's normal way of dealing with conflict was to negotiate, to compromise, to work things out. That, however, was back when choruses behaved themselves and worked hard at their art. Now Setti could do nothing but watch helplessly as his whole life was being changed, his future jeopardized by conditions he couldn't seem to control. Maybe something had just snapped.

Emmy pedaled past the Colonial Club and Christ Church. Past hotels and apartment buildings—the Ansonia, the St. Andrew, the Sherman Square, the Doulton. At the intersection of Broadway and Amsterdam, a boy threw a snowball at her. Emmy snickered at him when he missed.

Even if Rosa Ponselle did have proof that Setti was encouraging the chorus to behave badly, it didn't automatically follow that the chorus master was also the killer. But such uncharacteristic behavior must mean *something* . . . if Rosa did indeed know what she was talking about. Funny thing, Emmy thought, Rosa seemed to have changed from being a suspect to being a source of information. Well, if her 'information' turned out to be useless, she could go right back to being a suspect again.

Crossing Columbus Circle, Emmy ran out of luck—she took a spill; the front wheel of the bicycle hit a patch of ice and down she went. The only thing injured was her dignity, but she did have the wind knocked out of her. A passing automobile stopped and the driver got out; two men left the sidewalk and hurried out into the street where she sat. Any other time Emmy would have welcomed such solicitousness, but now she just wanted everyone to pretend they hadn't seen her. Two of the men got her back to her feet and the third picked up the bicycle. Embarrassed, Emmy muttered her thanks and pedaled away as fast as she could.

By the time she reached Fiftieth Street, every muscle in Emmy's ample body was screaming for mercy. Her buttocks were cramped, her back ached, the calves of her legs felt as if they had hot needles stuck into them. All she needed to make her misery complete was for it to start snowing. Hastily she glanced at the sky, as if afraid her errant thought had been overheard. But the weather ignored its cue, and the snow held back.

Doggedly she pedaled on, hoping she wasn't too late to catch

Rosa. Ten more short blocks and at last she was at the Fortieth Street entrance of the Metropolitan Opera House. She struggled through the door, and the machine that had seemed so flimsy when she started out now weighed a ton as she dragged it up the few steps to the stage level. Breathing heavily, Emmy swore a sacred oath never, ever to get on a bicycle again, not even to escape earthquake, tidal wave, or the coming of Armageddon.

"That's *my* bicycle!" a young voice shrieked. "What are you doing with my bicycle?"

Emmy groaned. "How can you tell? They all look alike."

"That's my bicycle," Rose insisted. "And you stole it!"

"Rosa, I am on the verge of dying from pain and exhaustion. If you—"

"You *stole* my *bicycle*!"

"I did nothing of the sort!" Emmy snapped, impatient with the girl's nonsense. "It's right here, isn't it? I just borrowed it because I didn't have any other transportation. I didn't hurt it."

Rosa placed her hands on her hips and squinted one eye. "I left it at home. What were you doing at my apartment building?"

A small crowd of interested observers was beginning to gather. Emmy sighed. "Could we go upstairs and talk?"

"We can talk right here and we can talk about why you stole my bicycle. Mr. Bridges didn't let you take it, did he?"

Emmy was tempted, but she resisted, "No, Mr. Bridges doesn't know anything about it. He wasn't even in the foyer when I—"

"*Aha!*" Rosa pounced. "So you know who Mr. Bridges is! What were you doing snooping around my home? Explain yourself!"

At that point Emmy simply gave up. She was in no condition to lock horns with this belligerent young woman; her epic two-wheeled voyage down Broadway had been for nothing. She'd just call Gerry Farrar and let her question Rosa, let *her* find out if the young singer knew something important about Giulio Setti. Setti was her suspect, after all. Let Gerry do it.

She turned her back on Rosa and walked out.

*   *   *

Enrico Caruso peered through a side window of the back seat of his limousine, watching a crowd of pedestrians who all seemed to be carrying packages. Christmas was only a week away, but Dorothy was doing most of his shopping for him this year. Caruso pressed a hand against his side; the pain had come back.

The limousine turned into Christopher Street, and Caruso shifted his attention from the people to the buildings. He was not good at remembering addresses, but he was sure he'd recognize the building when he saw it. He was looking for the home of an old friend, a bass-baritone who'd been singing at the Metropolitan since before Caruso had first come to New York. Tommaso had been then and still was now singing in the chorus. He was the only chorister Caruso had ever met who sincerely had no desire to advance to solo parts.

Tommaso liked singing in the chorus. He had neither a solo voice nor ambition; he was comfortable being part of a crowd. A Neapolitan by birth, Tommaso had made a point of welcoming the new tenor from Naples when Caruso had come to the Metropolitan back in 1903. He'd helped the newcomer learn his way around, invited him home to dinner with his family, and helped him find a tailor. Within a month Caruso was feeling completely at home in New York, but he never forgot the kindness the chorister had extended to a stranger.

"Here!" Caruso commanded. "Stop here!"

The chauffeur pulled over to an empty place by the curb and waited, engine idling. Caruso opened the back door for a better view of the brick building. Star-shaped tie-rods about halfway up the side. A third-story window with one corner rounded instead of angled. Yes, it was Tommaso's place. "You wait," Caruso instructed the chauffeur.

Unfortunately, the chorister lived on the third floor, so Caruso was panting by the time he rapped on the door with his gold-headed cane. Tommaso answered the door with a napkin tucked into his shirt collar. "Rico! You come at good time! We eat, yes?"

Caruso went through the motions of declining but did allow himself to be persuaded to accept a small plate of spaghetti. Tommaso's wife's idea of 'small' was the same as Caruso's, and the tenor ended up consuming a full pound of the pasta. Tommaso's two boys weren't at all shy with their famous visitor, and Caruso enjoyed the company even more than his little snack. His side had stopped hurting; he'd have to tell his doctor of his discovery that spaghetti flavored with góod fellowship could cure pain.

When they'd all finished eating, Tommaso led his unexpected guest into the front parlor where they could talk without fear of interruption. "Eh, my old friend, I know you come to wish us happy Christmas," Tommaso said, "but I think there is something else too, yes?"

"You are right, Tommaso," Caruso said, sinking into a large armchair. "I wish to ask you about Mr. Ziegler. I hear what he says to you, to the chorus." He explained about being behind one of the stage curtains when the assistant manager had blurted out the wish that more of the choristers were dead.

Tommaso shook his head sadly. "That is ugly moment, that. I always think he hates us. Now I know he does."

"Then you think he means what he says?"

"'Means'?" The chorister thought a moment. "I think he wishes us all dead, at one time or another. I also think he is sincerely horrified when five of us do die. He worries about what the public thinks, you see. It does not look good, somebody killing choristers."

"Then you do not think he is killer himself?"

"Mr. Ziegler? Eh, no. Why would he kill choristers?"

Caruso shrugged. "You make much trouble for him."

Tommaso laughed. "It is his job, handling trouble. And he does get the life insurance for us that we demand. No, Mr. Ziegler understands what singing in the chorus is like. He knows why we do what we do."

"He understands . . . what you mean, he understands?"

"Because he knows from experience! Do you forget he is once chorister himself?"

Caruso's mouth dropped open. "I never know this! He sings in Metropolitan chorus?"

"No, no, not the Metropolitan. The old Manhattan Opera—you remember? Mr. Ziegler, he is young man then."

"How do you know this, Tommaso?"

"Two of our chorus, they sing at the Manhattan at same time. They say he has good voice for opera, good quality—but the voice is not flexible. They say he is not good *singer*." Tommaso paused. "I think they make fun of him. He is there only one year."

"He quits after one year?"

"I am not sure, I think he is let go. Then he becomes music critic for newspaper! And he looks down his nose at chorus."

Caruso closed his eyes and thought about that for so long that his host suspected he'd fallen asleep. But then he sat up and said, "Tommaso, consider. He is failure as chorister. He takes job with newspaper where he can criticize choruses to his heart's content. He becomes Mr. Gatti's assistant and finds most of his time is spent trying to solve problems the chorus creates. He does not see things from your side anymore, not for long time. Perhaps this year the chorus . . . pushes him over edge. He goes a little crazy, he starts hitting back. Is possible, no?"

Tommaso frowned. "But he is same now as always. He is not crazy man."

"Ah, but he can lose control of himself! You see it once yourself."

The other man rubbed both eyes as if they hurt. "I do not know, Rico, I do not think so. He is too reserved, too frosty—"

"Cold-blooded?"

Tommaso smiled. "I do not mean that. I just cannot imagine Mr. Ziegler risking his own position for any reason. No, if anyone goes a little crazy and starts hitting back, as you say, I think it is Mr. Gigli. He has temperament for killing, that one."

"So does Gerry Farrar, but you do not suspect her, do you?" Caruso was a little put out; he wanted his old friend to agree with him. "You do not still cause trouble for Gigli and young Rosa?"

Tommaso was innocence personified. "Me, I do not cause trouble for either of them, not ever! It is the others who play the mean little tricks." He stopped to remember a few and couldn't help smiling. "But I never take part, I do not cause trouble, not for Mr. Gigli and not for your protégée."

Caruso hesitated, but then said, "Do you hear rumor, Tommaso? About Rosa and me?"

His friend made an angry sound. "I hear, and I say it is crazy! I know Ponselle does not get roles *that* way! She sings because of Mr. Gatti's promise, no other reason!"

"Promise?"

"You remember, during war he promises subscribers that Metropolitan Opera will be at least half American. So he hires Rosa Ponselle to help keep that promise."

Caruso sighed. "I think he hires her because of her singing. But it is nasty rumor, about Rosa and me . . . and not true! She is a *child*. I fear Doro will hear."

"Do not worry, Rico. The rumor, already it begins to die. Your Doro will hear nothing."

Reassured, Caruso thanked the other man and got up to leave. "You think about what I say. About Mr. Ziegler?"

"I think about it, *sì.*"

"The killings, perhaps they stop? There is no attack since *Forza.* This is good news, no?"

"It is the guards who prevent more killings. So many guards— they are everywhere!" Tommaso chewed his lower lip. "But when there are no more guards, when Mr. Gatti tells them all to go home—what happens then?"

Caruso didn't have the answer to that.

□ **9** □ Ruggiero Leoncavallo's four-act opera *Zazà* was first performed in 1900 at the Teatro Lirico in Milan, where it flopped. Three years later the San Francisco Opera tried it, and it flopped again. In 1909 a new production was bravely mounted at the Coronet Theatre in London. *Big* flop.

Then in 1919 Gatti-Casazza revived the opera as a starring vehicle for Geraldine Farrar—and suddenly *Zazà* was a razzle-dazzle, everybody-talking-about-it, *roaring* success. The first and only time.

The reason wasn't hard to understand; *Zazà* was, quite simply, the most risqué production the Metropolitan Opera had ever mounted. *Scandalous!* the horrified first-night audience cried and rushed out to buy tickets to see it again. *Shocking!* the newspapers bellowed and reviewed the opera over and over. *Almost as good as a girlie show* was the word on the street, sending non-music-lovers by the score to the yellow brick opera house at Thirty-ninth and Broadway. *Zazà,* to Gatti-Casazza's delight, became the hottest ticket in town.

When Gatti first considered reviving the opera, he knew something spectacular would have to be done with the production. They couldn't count on the music alone to do the job; it just wasn't good enough. It was sometimes hard to believe that *Zazà* had been written by the same man who gave the world the dramatic and exciting *I Pagliacci*. The ultra-lyrical third act, in fact, sounded more like Massenet than Leoncavallo; that distinctive Leoncavallo 'voice' was missing in *Zazà*. The opera needed help.

Gatti's solution had been to ask famed theatrical producer and director David Belasco to stage the opera. Belasco had directed for the Met before, to everyone's mutual satisfaction. He was always welcome in the opera house, in spite of the fact that for years he'd been trying to lure Geraldine Farrar away from opera to the Broadway stage. When Belasco heard the *Zazà* music, he understood the problem immediately. He decided to direct the opera as if it were a stage play, a play in which all the dialogue just happened to be sung instead of spoken. He set out to make what was going on in the plot so visually enticing that the audience wouldn't listen to the music too closely.

So he started off by suggesting that in one scene the star pick up an atomizer bottle, lift her skirts, and perfume her panties. The entire opera company gasped and waited for their volatile soprano to take David Belasco's head off.

It didn't happen. She thought about his suggestion, smiled . . . and did it.

Then she went him one better. In the seduction scene in the first act, she dropped her blouse for a moment. Geraldine Farrar, the first singer at the Metropolitan Opera to go topless. The day following the première, one of the critics wrote: "Geraldine Farrar has two excellent reasons for appearing in the role and last night she displayed both of them."

That had been the year before, and *Zazà* was still going strong. Gerry was well aware that if the opera had been staged before the war, she'd never have been able to get away with it. But times were changing—skirts grew shorter and shorter, people were restless, novelty was not only welcome but actively sought after. The timing was perfect.

Early Monday evening Geraldine Farrar arrived at the Metropolitan on the arm of Antonio Scotti and trailed by her maid. They lingered outside the door a few moments to chat with the crowd of gerryflappers that had already gathered. After the performance the crowd would be so thick and so noisy and so excited that a line of policemen grasping hands would be needed to hold them back; it had been that way since the first performance of *Zazà* last season. Gerry loved it.

Backstage, the usual mob of chorus singers, personal guards, and police took up every square inch of floor space. Gatti-Casazza was trying to talk to five people at once and didn't see them come in. Upstairs, they were surprised to find Emmy Destinn waiting impatiently outside Gerry's dressing room. She was not dressed for the opera.

"Emmy!" Scotti exclaimed. "Is something wrong?"

"Gerry, I've been trying to get you on the phone for hours," Emmy said accusingly.

"I wasn't taking any calls today," Gerry answered as she unlocked the door and went inside. "I don't like distractions on the day of a performance." *You should know that,* her tone implied.

The others followed her in, and the maid started laying out Gerry's make-up and first-act costume. Scotti moved a chair three inches and offered it to Emmy, then took his usual seat beside Gerry's dressing table. The small dressing room was crowded with four people in it.

"Is Rosa Ponselle coming tonight?" Emmy demanded peremptorily.

"Rosa? Not that I know of," Gerry said. "Why?"

"She thinks Setti is behind the way the chorus has been treating her." She immediately had everyone's full attention, including the maid's.

"Why does she think that?"

"That's what I couldn't find out." Emmy went on to explain her talk with Rosa's apartment-building supervisor and why she hadn't been able to ask Rosa about it herself.

Scotti was delighted. "You *steal* her bicycle?"

"I borrowed it," Emmy snapped. "Stop that inane grinning, Toto—it's not funny." The maid giggled but broke off when Emmy shot her a dark look. "Gerry, since Setti is your suspect, I'm telling you about it. Do what you like—I wash my hands of it."

Scotti couldn't resist asking, "Does Rosa call the police?" Emmy didn't deign to answer.

Gerry was thinking. "You know, Emmy, she could just be looking for someone to blame."

"There is one way to find out. Ask her."

"I'll do that. In the meantime," Gerry glanced at Emmy's street clothes, "since you're obviously not going to be out front tonight, how about keeping an eye on Setti during the performance? Try to hear what he tells the choristers."

"He's not my suspect," Emmy said, annoyed that Gerry wasn't sticking to the plan. "I just came here to tell you—"

"Yes, I understand, and I appreciate your taking the trouble and thank you. But as long as you're here. . . ?"

"Why can't Toto watch him? He's on your team."

Gerry went behind an Oriental screen to undress. "Toto," she said dryly, "has his own job cut out for him. Toto is going to protect us all from scrubladies."

"I check with Mr. Ziegler," Scotti explained, unperturbed by the sarcasm, "and he tells me the cleaning crew finishes before six o'clock. So if Mrs. Bukaitis is even in the building, that means something is awry."

"Awry, huh." Emmy sighed. "Gerry, we are on different teams. But very well, I will help this one time. Hereafter, we stay with our plan."

"*Ella ha troppa bontà,*" Scotti murmured, and kissed her hand.

From behind the screen, Gerry said, "Hadn't you two better start your, er, patrols?"

"*Sì, carissima.* Come, Emmy—to work!" The two of them left and descended to the stage level.

At the bottom of the stairs they ran into Gatti-Casazza. He smiled at Emmy and said, "I know why you are here tonight! You look for another bicycle, yes?"

She sagged. "Rosa complained to you?"

"Rosa says nothing. But it is all everyone else talks about! The lady who steals bicycles!"

"*I didn't steal it!*" Emmy roared. "Oh, what's the use?"

"No use," Scotti teased. "You are branded for life."

"How is Gerry tonight?" Gatti asked. "She is nervous? Worried?"

"She is very calm," Scotti assured him. "Nothing happens since *Forza,* no? The guards, they do good job."

"I hope they do good job," Gatti frowned. "I also hope we do not grow complacent." On that doubtful note he left them.

"He is worried," Emmy remarked.

"It is his job to worry," Scotti soothed. "Look—there is Mr. Setti. Now I must go search for my scrublady."

They parted. Emmy followed Setti as he darted hither and yon backstage, listening to him listening to complaints from the choristers. Scotti busied himself asking the stagehands and the guards if they'd seen any scrubladies backstage.

"What do you want with a scrublady, Mr. Scotti?" a voice behind him asked. "Did you spill something?"

Scotti turned. "Captain O'Halloran! I do not see you there." He lowered his voice. "I do not look for just any scrublady. I look for Mrs. Bukaitis."

O'Halloran knew the name. "The woman who found the chorister hanging in the dressing room?"

"She is the one. I think she hides truth about herself!"

O'Halloran pulled a long face. "You too?"

"Che cosa dite?"

"You're playing detective too? Miss Farrar and Mr. Caruso and Miss Destinn and now you?"

"Sì, sì," Scotti smiled broadly. "Pasquale and Gatti too!"

"Pasquale Amato? I thought he had better sense. And Mr. Gatti?" O'Halloran tried to imagine the slow-footed general manager in hot pursuit of clues and couldn't do it. "What do I have to say to get through to you people? *Keep your nose out of it!* Don't meddle in police matters. Do you understand?"

"No, Captain, I do not understand. Surely you welcome help?"

"I have all the help I need, thank you. *Professional* help. Mr. Scotti, you're not a detective. You've had no training. All you'll do is muddy the waters and make things more difficult for *me*. Now do you understand?"

Scotti thought about it a moment and then said, *"Sì,* now I understand."

"Good." O'Halloran clapped the baritone on the shoulder and continued on his rounds.

"I must avoid muddy water," Scotti said to himself and resumed his search for Mrs. Bukaitis.

O'Halloran was checking the deployment of his men. A man

was stationed in the fourth-floor chorus dressing room, with two other men in the halls within calling distance. Two were in the greenroom. The others all patrolled constantly, checking the props room, the wings, the substage area, the catwalks above the stage, the wardrobe room upstairs, even the unused rehearsal rooms. Policemen in white tie and tails mingled with the audience. With the personal guards Gatti-Casazza had hired for the chorus singers, the killer would have a hard time getting to anyone now. *Maybe we've got him stopped,* O'Halloran thought.

The opera started.

Five or ten minutes into the first act O'Halloran moved to a place in the wings where he could see the stage. He watched Geraldine Farrar move with grace and authority through a role that had defeated all the sopranos who'd previously attempted it. O'Halloran didn't know anything about opera, but even he could see the lady on stage was in her element.

"Where does that dog come from?" Gatti's outraged voice boomed from behind him.

A shaggy yellow dog had trotted out on to the stage, tail wagging happily, obviously fascinated by this strange new playground he'd found. He sniffed at the furniture, almost tripped one of the singers, and jumped up on a chair where he could see better. Gerry made the mistake of trying to incorporate the dog into the action and patted him on the head—whereupon the dog started following her around the stage wherever she went. When Gerry sang a series of high notes, her new friend decided to make it a duet and howled along happily. The audience tittered.

But then the dog caught sight of the conductor's baton. He raced down to the edge of the stage and wagged his tail furiously. Back and forth his head went, then up and down, matching the movements of the baton. He dashed away four or five steps, then came back, then dashed away again. When the conductor failed to throw the shiny white stick for him to fetch, the dog barked at him.

Gerry had had enough. She grabbed the dog by the scruff of the neck and started dragging him toward the wings. He was puzzled and resisted, but she didn't loosen her grip. At the side of the stage she thrust the dog straight at O'Halloran and hissed, "*Arrest* this animal!"

The audience good-naturedly applauded her action. A stagehand took charge of the dog, and O'Halloran watched as the performance quickly settled into its proper groove once again. There was a lot of coming and going, and then Gerry was on stage alone with the tenor. Someone jostled O'Halloran; he drew his eyes away from the soprano long enough to see he was surrounded by male choristers and their guards, all eagerly watching the stage.

Out on the stage, Gerry Farrar was as aware of her offstage audience as of the one out front. *Zazà* was the kind of opera she loved—a seldom-performed piece in which the soprano appeared in almost every scene, virtually carrying the opera alone. *Zazà* told the story of a café singer who abandoned her career for her lover, only to learn he was already married to someone else. It was an *acting* opera, a display-case opera; and speaking of displays . . . it was time for the seduction scene. She performed her mini-strip-tease and got her usual audible response from the audience. Quickly covered again, she eased downstage right to the acoustically preferred spot on the stage and caught a glimpse of Captain O'Halloran's startled face staring out at her from the wings.

The first act was drawing to a close when Gerry became aware of a loud muttering from backstage, and even one or two voices raised in what sounded like anger. A quick glance to the wings on both sides of the stage told her she'd lost one of her audiences. *What* was going on? She was growing angry—until she remembered the last time this had happened. *Carmen.* When the chorus woman had been found with a knife in her chest.

God, not again! she prayed. Out of necessity she forced all thought of what might be happening backstage out of her mind and concentrated solely on her singing. The curtain finally closed and Gerry ran off the stage, almost knocking down the tenor she'd sung the scene with. Stagehands, singers, and guards stood with their backs to the stage, staring at something she couldn't see. "Let me through!" she cried. The crowd parted just enough to make a path for her. She wriggled her way to the front.

And saw an unfamiliar woman—Mrs. Bukaitis?—being held by both arms, on one side by Antonio Scotti and on the other by a uniformed policeman. "Toto?"

He shot her a look of triumph. "I catch her, Gerry! I catch her myself!"

"You . . . caught her? Doing what?"

"Fastening *that* to platform under stage!"

That, Gerry now saw, was a box Captain O'Halloran was holding. He removed the lid and showed her the homemade bomb inside. He said, "She was trying to blow up the stage, Miss Farrar."

While I was on it. Suddenly her knees gave way and the whole backstage area began to revolve around her. Then hands were gripping her and she felt a chair being pushed against the back of her legs. "Gerry—sit!" Gatti-Casazza's voice commanded out of nowhere. She sat.

Then Emmy Destinn was there, forcing her head down between her knees. The floor stopped heaving, and the near-faint passed. Gerry was immediately on her feet again. Emmy murmured, "So Toto was right."

O'Halloran handed the bomb to one of the police officers, who gingerly carried it out of the opera house—to everyone's audible relief. The captain said, "Come along now, Mrs. Bukaitis. You've got a lot of questions to answer at the station."

Gatti-Casazza held up a hand to stop him; he had a question he wanted an answer to right then. "Why?" he asked Mrs. Bukaitis. "Why you do this terrible thing?" Then he gave an exasperated shrug and said to O'Halloran, "I forget—she speaks no English."

"Of course I speak English," Mrs. Bukaitis said scornfully. "You assume I am ignorant because I scrub floors! It was easy to fool *you.*"

"I know it!" Scotti cried. "I say she understands—I am right!"

Gatti persisted. "But why? Why do you want to kill?"

Mrs. Bukaitis cursed in her own language. "My countrymen are being killed every day and you do nothing about it!"

O'Halloran asked, "So how is killing innocent people going to stop that?"

"It is to make you pay attention! You squander money on luxuries like opera while men and women in my country are being enslaved! Free Vilnius!"

O'Halloran scowled. "Who's Vilnius?"

"It is a place, you fool, not a person! The capital city of Lithuania. Poland enslaves Vilnius, and the rich and powerful United States does nothing! You turn your backs! You do not deserve your safety and comfort!"

"An anarchist," Scotti breathed.

O'Halloran was shaking his head in disbelief. "So you think the best way to get the United States to help you is to blow up the stage of its leading opera house? Did I get that right?"

"To make you listen!" Mrs. Bukaitis screamed. "To prove we are serious!"

"I *know* it is anarchist!" Scotti exulted. "All the time I say it is anarchist! Gerry, do I not say it is anarchist?"

"Yes, Toto, that's what you said," Gerry agreed. She muttered to Emmy, "He's going to be impossible to live with."

"Anarchist—that is your word," Mrs. Bukaitis objected. "I am a patriot."

"A pretty bloodthirsty one," O'Halloran said dryly. "There was enough dynamite in that box to blow the roof off this place."

Scotti was thinking. "*Un momento* . . . I think this is not first time she tries. Perhaps first time the bomb, it does not go off? Therefore more dynamite this time?"

O'Halloran swallowed a laugh. "That's not the way it works, Mr. Scotti, but what makes you think this is the second time?"

"Mrs. Poplofsky," he said promptly.

"Who?"

"Poplofsky," Gatti-Casazza repeated slowly, as if the name should be familiar.

"You should know her, Mr. Gatti," Scotti said, "she works for you." He turned to O'Halloran. "Mrs. Poplofsky is scrublady here in opera house. One time she sees Mrs. Bukaitis trying to do something with mysterious box—by the platform under stage! That is first bomb, yes?" Mrs. Bukaitis muttered under her breath.

O'Halloran took out his notebook and asked Scotti to spell Mrs. Poplofsky's name. Scotti made a stab at it. O'Halloran said, "She works here, you say? Where can I find her?"

Scotti said, "Underneath stage is a room filled with brooms and soap and mops. There is place to sit down and drink coffee. Mrs. Poplofsky goes there about ten-thirty in mornings." Everyone gazed at him in admiration for possessing this esoteric bit of knowledge.

Gerry walked over to the scrubwoman and looked her over from head to toe. "You almost killed me. I've never met anyone before who wanted to kill me."

Mrs. Bukaitis sneered. "You, somebody else—what difference does it make?"

"*What difference does it make?*" Gerry screamed. "Did you hear what she said—*what difference does it make?*"

Emmy spoke up. "Is that why you murdered the choristers? Because it doesn't matter to you who dies?"

"What do I know of your precious choristers?" Mrs. Bukaitis jeered. "They are nothing to me."

"I do not understand," Gatti said. "Do you say you do not murder the choristers?"

Mrs. Bukaitis spat in the direction of the general manager's shoes. "You Americans!" she snarled. "You understand nothing!"

"I am Italian," Gatti protested faintly.

"And I am Czechoslovakian," Emmy said proudly.

"Well, *I'm* American," Gerry growled. "Do you want to try spitting at me?"

Mrs. Bukaitis considered it, saw the expression on the soprano's face, and decided discretion was the better part of survival.

"All right, folks, I think that's enough," Captain O'Halloran said. He motioned with his head and Scotti reluctantly gave up his hold on Mrs. Bukaitis's arm. A uniformed officer stepped up to take his place, and the two policemen marched the would-be bomber off between them. "I'll let you know when the hearing's set," O'Halloran said to Scotti. "You'll be needed to testify."

"I testify with pleasure," Scotti announced. "I and Mrs. Poplofsky."

When O'Halloran left, everyone started talking at once. There were a few hysterical laughs and some outright cheering. Only Gatti seemed to remember that they were supposed to be performing an opera; he did his version of hurrying around, getting things going again.

"Emmy," Gerry said, low, "do you think she did it? Do you think she murdered the five choristers?"

Emmy hesitated, and then muttered. "No."

Gerry shook her head. "Neither do I."

Scotti came swooping down on them. "Eh, what you say now? Gerry, you laugh at me, *carissima*," he reproved. "You think I am foolish to investigate scrublady, no? But now—you think I am foolish now?"

She looked at him with an expression he'd never seen before. "You saved my life, Toto," she said simply.

They wrapped their arms about each other and stood there shuddering for a moment or two, at last letting it sink in what a truly close call they all had had.

Rosa Ponselle decided it was time she and the Metropolitan's chorus master had it out.

On Tuesday, the day after *Zazà,* the chorus was just finishing a rehearsal in the roof theatre. Rosa waited outside, bravely facing the stream of choristers as they left. Setti was always the last to leave; she went inside and closed the door behind her. "Mr. Setti, we have to talk."

He smiled pleasantly. "But of course, Miss Ponselle. I fear I have only uncomfortable chairs to offer here—"

"I'll stand. Mr. Setti, why are you doing it? What did I ever do to you?"

He blinked. "I do not understand."

"Oh, you understand, all right. They aren't bothering me right now, I admit—but how long is that going to last? When will they start again?"

"They . . . you speak of the choristers?"

"Of course I speak of the choristers! Who else? What I want to know is why you put them up to it. Why did you?"

"Put them . . ." Setti's face fell as he at last understood what she was saying. "You accuse me? You say *I* cause them to . . . you are wrong! You cannot be more wrong! I try to get them to *stop.*"

"Oh, don't do that! Don't tell *lies.* I heard you, Mr. Setti!"

He looked so honestly puzzled that Rosa felt a twinge of uncertainty. "You hear me . . . say something?" Setti asked. "What do you hear?"

"Right before *Forza,* I heard you telling some of the choristers to box me in, not to let me move around so much. You actually told them to stand on my feet to keep me from moving if they had to! Now don't lie about it, Mr. Setti—I heard you!"

The chorus master looked as if he didn't know whether to laugh or cry. "But it is not *you* I am talking about, Miss Ponselle! Yes, I say these things—out of desperation, I might add. But not about you!"

"Oh, sure!"

"Consider. Do you hear me say your name? Think back."

Rosa was uneasy. "Well, I don't actually remember hearing my name. But you had to be talking about me. Who else could it be?"

"I speak of Irene Matera. She is contralto—you know her?"

Rosa didn't know many of the choristers by name, but she did know Irene Matera. "Oh, that one." *That one* had been making trouble for Rosa since the first time she set foot on the Metropolitan stage.

"Eh, she crosses in front of you," Setti said. "Almost every performance, she finds way to cross while you are singing. I tell her not to do this, but she ignores me. So before *Forza,* I find four choristers I can trust and instruct them to stop her from crossing. Do you remember *Forza?* Does anyone cross in front of you?"

Rosa was dismayed. "No. That was the first time this season someone did *not* cross in front of me. Oh my."

"If you are not certain, I give you names of choristers I instruct to—"

"Not necessary, Mr. Setti, I remember perfectly well. How could I forget? That was the night Spike died." She was silent a moment and then said, "Oh, Mr. Setti, I owe you a whopping big apology. I heard something and I jumped to conclusions and I got it all wrong." She rolled her eyes upward. "Lord, this is embarrassing! Can you ever forgive me?"

He smiled. "But of course! Do not feel bad."

"Well, I do. I suspected you of doing something to hurt me and all the time you were just trying to help me. Dumb, *dumb*. I am so sorry."

"Do not concern yourself, dear Miss Ponselle. It is what happens here that makes our judgment faulty. Singers are killed and we get nervous and suspicious of one another."

"I s'pose. It was still dumb."

"Then I too am 'dumb'. I tell you something," he added confidentially. "Before that Lithuanian bombing woman is caught, I suspect one member of the company of being killer!"

"Really? Who?"

"Maestro Quaglia," he admitted. "Please—*mi faccia questo piacere,* do not tell him I say so."

"Wouldn't dream of it. What made you suspect him?"

The chorus master shrugged. "He is sour man—sour inside, you understand? From disappointment, failed expectations. No matter how hard he tries, he cannot be Toscanini!"

Rosa laughed. "Oh, how I wish I'd been here in those days— before the war, I mean! Toscanini's been gone . . . what, five years? And you're all still talking about him!"

"Maestro Toscanini, he is very special man."

"He must be. Is it true he and Gerry Farrar had an affair that lasted seven years?"

Setti was shocked. "Miss Ponselle, we do not speak of such things!"

"I know," she complained, "and I surely wish someone would! All the rest of you know all these juicy things about each other and

I don't know a *thing*. Not for sure. I think it must have happened—Gerry and Toscanini, I mean.''

"Miss Ponselle," the chorus master said sternly, "do you forget so quickly how unkind gossip can be? I refer to rumor that says *you* have affair with married man."

With Caruso. "Oh dear, I thought that nasty bit of business was over and done with! I'm not having an affair with *anyone*." She bit her lip. "I did it again, didn't I? Jumped to conclusions."

"It is hard not to hear gossip in the opera house," Setti conceded, "but you do not have to repeat it!"

Yes, Daddy. "Don't worry, I won't. Not anymore. And I won't go around accusing people of things, either. Mr. Setti, you don't hate me, do you?"

"Of course not," he smiled. "How can anyone hate you?"

"Well, thanks for being so nice about it."

Rosa left the roof theater feeling a lot better than when she'd gone in; it was best to get these things out in the open. She was on the bicycle recently recovered from that bicycle thief Emmy Destinn and well on her way home before she realized he hadn't really answered her question about Gerry and Toscanini.

Enrico Caruso gave a dinner party on Wednesday, two nights after Mrs. Bukaitis had been arrested. He invited only the two teams of self-appointed detectives, since the dinner party was to honor Antonio Scotti's emergence as *investigatore supremo*. Dorothy Caruso had grown accustomed to entertaining on short notice; she'd long since memorized the telephone numbers of the necessary caterers and florists. Gatti-Casazza supplied the champagne—his bootlegger had come through.

Emmy Destinn and Geraldine Farrar refrained from voicing their reservations about the 'solution' to the crimes that had been plaguing the Metropolitan; they didn't want to throw a damper on Scotti's big evening. He *had* caught a potential bomber and he deserved to be honored for that. But Mrs. Bukaitis's potential as a destroyer of opera houses would not have been realized on Monday after all, as it turned out; the dynamite she'd used in her bomb had been defective.

"Not a very good bomber, eh?" Pasquale Amato grinned over the oysters Rockefeller. "Captain O'Halloran, he says the dynamite is stolen from place where they build new bridge. The man in charge—the foreman, he says box of dynamite is set aside so they can send it back to manufacturer. That is why it is so easy to steal."

"How big a box was it?" Dorothy asked. "It's hard to think of one woman stealing a whole box of dynamite by herself."

"Captain O'Halloran thinks she has help. Several times she says 'we' plan to blow up stage for the attention."

"I don't understand why she waited until the place was swarming with people to set her bomb," Emmy remarked. "Why didn't she just take care of it earlier in the day?"

"Because of Mrs. Poplofsky!" Scotti cried gleefully. "After we talk, Mrs. Poplofsky too becomes suspicious of Mrs. Bukaitis. She watches her like hawk—Mrs. Bukaitis *cannot* fix bomb earlier in the day!"

Gerry raised an eyebrow. "Lucky for us the detective business is so contagious."

Gatti-Casazza watched glumly as his champagne disappeared more rapidly than he had dreamed possible. "Does she admit to killing the five choristers?"

"That is strange thing," Amato said. "At first she says no, but then she stops answering all questions and talks only of how the Poles must be driven out of Vilnius. Now when the police ask her do you kill this chorister or do you kill that chorister, she just says what do you think, or do you not know, or I tell you when Vilnius is free."

"How odd," Gerry said. "It sounds as if she wants to be blamed."

"It makes her more important, you see."

"But . . . *murder*! Surely she wouldn't risk a death sentence—"

"Ah, but she is already convinced she is going to stand before a wall while firing squad shoots at her! She refuses to believe this country has one penalty for murder and another for attempted murder. It is explained to her many times, but she does not believe.''

Emmy asked, "How do you know all this, Pasquale?''

"I and Toto, we go to police station and ask!''

Scotti laughed. "The captain, he is not overjoyed to see us, but he answers our questions. He feels obligated to me, you see, and this captain, he does not like to feel obligated. He feels same toward Gerry and Rico. Three times singers solve crimes for him— this cannot be good for the captain's self-esteem.''

"I think you are wrong, Toto,'' Caruso said. "Captain O'Halloran, he is good man. He does not resent us when we truly help.''

Everyone laughed out loud at that. Scotti said, "Mrs. Bukaitis makes mistake—she grows impatient. Killing choristers one at a time, it is too slow. So she thinks with one big bomb—*boom!* Many at once! Bomb is great time-saver!''

"Do not joke,'' Caruso said sharply. "Do not ever joke about bombs!''

Startled, Scotti looked at his friend . . . and understood. "You are right, Rico. I forget. I do not joke about bombs again. Forgive me.'' Just the past summer Caruso had been singing in Cuba when someone threw a bomb at the stage; bombs were not to be treated lightly.

"Well, backstage is going to seem positively deserted now,'' Gerry said lightly, deliberately turning the subject. "With all those policemen and private guards gone. Not that I'll miss them.''

"The police are gone,'' Gatti said. "Not the guards.''

"You haven't discharged the guards?''

"Not yet.''

Emmy asked, "Why not? Do you think there is still danger?''

Gatti hedged. "I think they stay a little while longer.''

The two sopranos exchanged a look. Gerry said, "Gatti, you've never in your life spent a penny you didn't have to and those guards are costing you a fortune. You must have some reason for keeping them on.''

The general manager made a noise of exasperation. "I have no
. . . *reason*. I just think it better that they stay a little longer."

Gatti's tacit admission that he wasn't satisfied that the real killer
was in jail cast a slight pall over the dinner party. Good hostess
Dorothy immediately called for dessert and tried to start a conversation about the Chicago Opera, now back in business after the
war. No one was interested.

"I think tonight we meet to disband our investigating teams and
to celebrate Toto's victory," Amato remarked, "but now I am not
so sure. Mr. Gatti, do you say we should continue looking?"

Gatti thought about that. "I do not think it hurts to investigate a
little more."

"Bravo!" Gerry cried. "I wasn't going to say anything, but I
feel the same way. I'm convinced the attempted bombing and the
murders are two separate things. Emmy?"

Emmy nodded. "Sorry, Toto. I agree with them."

Scotti looked as if he'd just been told he'd never sing again.
"But Mr. Gatti—you do not worry sufficiently to make your presence known at the opera house tonight, no? You are here instead,
are you not?"

"Ziegler is there. He takes my place."

"Ziegler!" Caruso exclaimed. "He is my suspect."

"What is the opera tonight, Mr. Gatti?" Dorothy asked
brightly, still hoping to get away from this morbid subject.

"*Lucia*," Gatti answered shortly.

"Gigli," Caruso muttered. Edgardo in *Lucia di Lammermoor*
was another of the roles he was sharing with the new tenor.

They finished their dessert in silence and left the dining room.
No one wanted to go home with the question of further investigations left unresolved, but no one seemed to know how to approach
the subject. Gerry joined Emmy at the window and for a few moments the two sopranos looked quietly out at the night lights of
New York's skyline. Gerry said, "Gatti was a surprise, wasn't he?
If we could just come up with some specific reason for going on
with the investigation! We need something solid to convince the
others."

"I know," Emmy said. "I've been racking my brain trying to think of something. But the truth is, I am like Gatti—I do not have a *reason*. A conviction, yes. But not a reason."

Just then Dorothy Caruso came up to them, looking ill at ease. "I must ask your help," she said. "This is supposed to be a party, but everyone is standing around like mourners at a funeral. I am going to suggest we play a parlor game. If you two agree to play, then the men will play."

Gerry took her hands. "Dorothy, I know this must be dreadful for you—and I'm truly sorry you got caught up in it. But we can't just drop the subject. What if the killer is still loose?"

Dorothy shook her head. "I don't want to think about that."

"I know you don't, but *we* must think about it, you see," Gerry said gently. "Every time I've gone into the opera house these past few weeks, I've had to wonder if anyone was going to die that night. We can't just pretend nothing has happened."

"I wish you would."

"We're going to have to talk about it, decide what we're going to do. Would you rather we went somewhere else to talk?"

"You don't have to listen," Emmy said tactlessly.

Dorothy blushed but held her ground. "Yes, I do have to listen. Stay here. If it concerns Rico, it concerns me."

Emmy relented. "Of course it does." She managed a half-smile.

Off to the side, Caruso was also smiling as he stood watching these three fine women all under his roof at the same time. Across the room Gatti-Casazza watched Caruso watching the women. Caruso had proposed marriage to all three women, and he'd kept proposing until one of them said yes. Gatti cleared his throat. "We must talk," he said.

"Yes," Amato agreed, "we must."

No one said a word.

The atmosphere was beginning to grow tense when a maid appeared and said Mr. Gatti was wanted on the telephone. Gatti excused himself and followed her out.

The maid's appearance had broken the tension. "I tell you what

I think," Amato said. "I think we are presumptuous to go on investigating after police make arrest. It is like saying we know better than police."

"The police can be wrong," Gerry murmured. "Pasquale, the five murders were all individual acts—personal and up close and full of risk. But bombing, that's killing from a safe distance. They're just too different to be done by the same person."

"Pah! Who is to say how a killer thinks?"

"Someone had better say," Emmy declared dryly. "Gerry has a point—more than one person is involved. Mrs. Bukaitis is responsible only for the bombing part."

"*Only* the bombing?" Scotti exclaimed indignantly.

"You know what I mean. There's somebody else who hasn't been caught."

"Captain O'Halloran, he is satisfied," Caruso said. "Is he not?"

"Quite satisfied," Amato said. "He even thanks Toto."

Gatti-Casazza came back into the room, his step even slower than usual. One look at his face and everyone knew something was terribly wrong. Gatti had to swallow twice before he could speak. "That was Ziegler. It is not over. It is still happening."

A dead silence crept over the room. "Tell us," Gerry whispered.

"Someone fires a gun backstage tonight. Twice. Two times he shoots at chorus baritone."

Scotti swallowed. "Is he. . . ?"

Gatti's expression lightened. "No! He is not even hurt! Ziegler says the man with gun must fire from great distance—because of the guards, you understand? He misses first time, fires again, misses second time, everyone starts shouting, he runs away!"

"*Per dio*," Caruso breathed heavily, "you do right when you keep the guards!"

"Did anyone see him?" Amato asked, appalled.

Gatti shook his head. "Ziegler says it happens too fast. He says killer is obviously man not used to handling guns."

"It is not over," Amato said dully. Dorothy began to cry.

"Do not cry, Doro," Caruso said, on the verge of tears himself.

"One good thing," Gatti said, getting over his initial shock. "We eliminate Beniamino Gigli from list of suspects. He is on stage singing at time shots are fired!"

"Good, good!" Gerry cried. "That's a start!"

Scotti still couldn't believe it. "Mrs. Bukaitis is not murderer?"

"No, Toto," Gatti said. "She is bad woman, but she is not murderer."

"Then my investigating—it is for nothing!"

"That's not true, Toto," Gerry said firmly. "You stopped a bomber before she could build a working bomb. *You saved a lot of lives.* No one else in this room has done that." Scotti straightened his shoulders.

"Gatti!" Emmy cried, having just thought of something. "When did this shooting take place?"

"Eh, ten, fifteen minutes ago, Ziegler says."

"Call Rosa Ponselle. Get her on the telephone—be sure you talk to her and not to her sister. If Rosa is at home right now, we can eliminate another suspect!"

"Oh, Emmy," Caruso said, wide-eyed. "You are smart lady!"

Dorothy found Rosa's number for Gatti, and everyone pushed after him into the hallway where the telephone was. They all held their breath while the connection was being made. "Rosa?" Gatti said in a voice higher than usual. "Is it you?" He nodded to the others; there was no mistaking Rosa Ponselle's voice. "I have bad news." He explained to her what had just happened as the others drifted back into the sitting room.

"Well, Gerry, you wanted something solid to convince the others," Emmy said. "Now you've got it." Gerry thought that was a tasteless remark and said so; Emmy shrugged and turned away.

"Let's see where we stand," Gerry said. "Rosa Ponselle was at home at the time of the shooting. Beniamino Gigli was on stage."

"And Mrs. Bukaitis is locked up in the jailhouse," Scotti said gloomily.

"So we've just eliminated half our suspects," Gerry went on. "Well, I can tell you right now who our team's candidate is—

Giulio Setti. He's the only one left. I presume he was at the opera house tonight?" This last was directed toward Gatti, who was just then coming back into the room.

"Of course," Gatti said. "He is always there."

"Our team has two suspects left," Amato said, "Ziegler and Quaglia."

"Ziegler is there," Caruso was quick to point out.

"Who conducts tonight?" Amato asked.

"Bodanzky," Gatti said. "But Quaglia is there also!"

"*Cielo!*" Amato exclaimed. "Quaglia never goes to listen to other conductors work! Why is he there?"

"Because Ziegler asks him to come. Bodanzky, he is ill. An hour before curtain, he tells Ziegler he cannot conduct tonight. So Ziegler calls Quaglia. Then Bodanzky says he is feeling better, he thinks he can conduct after all. Ziegler asks Quaglia to stay, in case Bodanzky cannot finish the performance."

"So he wouldn't have been there at all if Bodanzky hadn't gotten sick," Gerry said. "But he *was* there, so we can't eliminate him. All our remaining suspects were there—Quaglia and Ziegler and Setti."

Amato nodded. "One of those three."

One of those three.

□ **10** □ Captain Michael O'Halloran cursed himself for a fool. He'd let himself be distracted from the pursuit of a killer by the ravings of a political fanatic. He'd been too quick to accept Mrs. Bukaitis as the perpetrator of the Metropolitan chorus killings, too quick to pull the police out of the opera house. Thank God Gatti-Casazza had kept the guards he'd hired; the general manager had shown a better feeling for security than he had.

It was the omnipresent guards who had forced the killer to fire his gun from a distance—not a great distance, but enough to make him miss. He could have moved in close and got his man, but not without getting caught. Perhaps he could have gotten the guard as well; but the chorus singers stayed together in small groups pretty much all the time now. No single chorister-guard pair was going to wander off alone and become an easy target. The killer might have gotten one or two in close, but he couldn't have gotten six or eight.

O'Halloran was puzzled by the variety of methods the murderer used. First an urn bashing a woman's head in. Then a hanging. Then a death resulting from a fall. Then a stabbing. Then a falling piece of scenery, which missed. Then a poisoning, which didn't. And now a shooting, which also missed. It was as if once the killer had crossed over the boundary and committed that first murder, he'd found a pleasurable excitement in what he'd done. So he'd made his vendetta into a game, varying his approach each time for the sheer morbid enjoyment of it.

The captain leaned back and put his feet up on his desk. Whoever this man was, he was sicker than most O'Halloran had come up against. Sicker and slicker and still anonymous. And he was a member of the Metropolitan Opera Company; outsiders had not been permitted backstage since the night Teresa Leone was stabbed. The killer could be a singer, a conductor, a stagehand, an orchestra musician, a member of management. Nor had O'Halloran totally ruled out the possibility that this killer of choristers might be a chorister himself, unlikely as that seemed.

But there were some with more reason to hate choristers than others. O'Halloran had received answers to the wires he'd sent to the Naples and London police. Giulio Setti had lied when he said Alessandro Quaglia's first job in opera had been assistant chorus master. Quaglia had told the truth when he said he'd started out as a violinist in the orchestra. But he had lied about something else; he'd not begun his career at the prestigious San Carlo Opera as he claimed but at a slightly lesser house, an old theatre called Il Fondo. Of the two lies, O'Halloran thought Quaglia's the more understandable; everyone puffed up his credentials on occasion.

So it looked as if Setti were deliberately pointing the finger of suspicion at Quaglia. The chorus master might be trying to blacken the conductor's name as a way of protecting his own position at the Met, since it was Quaglia who'd been most vocal in demanding the other man's dismissal. Or was Setti honestly convinced that Quaglia was guilty? Quaglia had told O'Halloran that he'd been at home at the time the one chorister was hanged and in fact had learned of it only when the first violinist telephoned and told him. O'Halloran checked with the violinist, who verified Quaglia's story . . . to a point. The violinist had not called until around eleven o'clock, hours after the chorister had died. So, no alibi for Quaglia.

The answer O'Halloran had gotten from the London police was especially illuminating; Quaglia had had so much trouble with the chorus at Covent Garden that his invitations to return had become fewer and fewer and might have ceased altogether. Quaglia's signing a contract with the Metropolitan had made an open break unnecessary; Covent Garden didn't wish to alienate a conductor they found serviceable and reliable although 'uninspired'.

Uninspired. From what O'Halloran understood of opera folks, that was one of the most insulting things you could say about a musician. But Covent Garden had reason not to be too fond of Maestro Quaglia. According to the police report London had sent, Quaglia had once tried to strangle a member of the chorus. Covent Garden had tried to smooth things over, saying that the two men had gotten into an altercation and had both gone for the other's throat. No one was hurt, and no charges had been filed; the whole affair had been pretty well hushed up. But the report made it clear that the police considered Quaglia to be the instigator of the fight.

What if Quaglia didn't know he was a second-rate conductor? What if he just saw that he wasn't receiving the respect accorded Toscanini and the other great conductors, nor was his work on the podium recognized as being the superior kind of music-making he obviously thought it was? A true second-rater would then look about for someone or something else to blame. In this case, the chorus would make a perfect scapegoat. Before Covent Garden there'd been trouble at La Scala, and now there was more trouble at the Metropolitan. Perhaps there were even incidents with other choruses at other opera houses that O'Halloran didn't know about. But Quaglia could reason that the recognition he felt due him had been denied by three major opera companies, and all because he'd been undermined by the destructive behavior of the choruses. Quaglia's resentment could have been building for years until he reached a day when something just broke, when he had to take action to right what he saw as a dreadful wrong.

Self-preservation was a strong motive.

Unfortunately, Giulio Setti had the same motive. His case was much more direct: he'd lost control of the chorus and was in danger of losing his job. At his age he couldn't hope to go on to another major opera company; for Setti it was a matter of hanging on in New York or retiring. And in spite of everything that had been happening, it was obvious the man loved his work. The chorus master could have set out to kill off the worst trouble-makers in the chorus as a means of sustaining a way of life he loved. The only problem with that theory was that Teresa Leone, the chorister who'd been stabbed, hadn't been a troublemaker.

The difficulty was that O'Halloran couldn't quite see how Setti could have managed the killings physically. He'd long since passed his prime, and he was not a big man. Two of the killings required a certain amount of strength. Well, perhaps only one; he could have taken Teresa Leone by surprise—the body showed no sign of a struggle. But how in the world could Setti have managed to hang a healthy, good-sized man less than half his age?

Quaglia, on the other hand, was built like an ox. He could have managed it.

There was one other man who might feel threatened by the chorus, although the nature of that threat wasn't quite clear to O'Halloran. Edward Ziegler's job put him in constant contact with the chorus. He negotiated their contracts, he listened to their complaints. It fell to him to find a proper response whenever the choristers threatened to strike—which had already happened a couple of times this season. Considering all the trouble the chorus had been causing lately, O'Halloran could see how Ziegler might grow to hate the choristers.

But why kill them? Ziegler's job was not threatened, as Setti's was. Ziegler was not denied his proper prestige and recognition, as Quaglia thought *he* was. What was to be gained? Nothing, speaking from a rational point of view. But that's where it got tricky; the killer, of course, was anything but rational. Clever. Sneaky. Crafty. But not rational.

If there was any one person at the Met who epitomized rationality and civilized self-control, O'Halloran thought, it would have to be Edward Ziegler. An elegant, reserved, high-class man—a bit frosty, perhaps a little more proper than he really needed to be. Conventional wisdom had it that it was exactly that type of person who blew up the worst if he ever lost control; the resulting behavior was all the more shocking because of its contrast to what one expected of such a person. Like Quaglia, Ziegler appeared to have enough physical strength to overpower another man and hang him.

O'Halloran tried to visualize Ziegler losing control of himself and couldn't do it. Could a man like that kill out of mere hatred? Not that hatred was ever really *mere*. O'Halloran wondered if there was something missing, perhaps something in Ziegler's background he didn't know about. The trouble was, the man seemed so damned sane!

They all did; they all three appeared to be sane, law-abiding, and respectable. True, Quaglia was given to indulging in temperamental outbursts—like the screaming match with Geraldine Farrar.

But that sort of exhibition wasn't all that unusual in an opera house; it wouldn't be wise to attach too much importance to it. Nevertheless Quaglia had already demonstrated a potential for violence at Covent Garden. On the whole, of the three with the most obvious motives, O'Halloran thought Alessandro Quaglia the most likely suspect.

But 'likely' didn't win court convictions; what he needed was some one piece of hard evidence. And he didn't have the foggiest notion of where to get it. After mulling it over for a while, Captain O'Halloran decided to fall back on an investigatory technique he'd used during his lowly detective days. It didn't win him any friends, but it sometimes got results.

He would go to Quaglia, to Setti, and to Ziegler and tell each one individually that he was the prime suspect in the case. Then he would sit back and watch. He'd watch their reactions, what they did next, what they failed to do. He would invite each man to make a mistake.

And then he'd wait to see who accepted the invitation.

Geraldine Farrar sat listlessly turning the pages of the *Times*. She'd cut her practice session short that morning; all her top notes were missing. There was no point in trying to force a sound that just wasn't there.

She read the political news first. Only last month Gerry had participated in the nation's electoral process, the first time in her life she had been permitted to do so. There was fighting in Ireland. Twenty thousand aliens a week were landing on American shores. The mayor of New York was asking for 769 more patrolmen.

Then Gerry saw something that made her heart skip a beat. It was a photograph of the man with whom she'd had the first serious romance of her life, when they were both nineteen—the former German Crown Prince, Frederick Wilhelm, who was now living in exile on the Dutch island of Wieringen. The photograph showed him in a blacksmith shop, learning how to make a horseshoe. *Oh God, Willi!*

She turned the page so violently she tore it. After a moment she forced herself to pay attention to the clothing advertisements. Skirts were still getting shorter, making no concession to winter winds. Gerry marveled at and rejoiced in the change in women's clothing styles; for *centuries* women had worn skirts that went all the way down to the floor, skirts that were graceful to look at but which successfully impeded women's movement. Then almost overnight skirts were revealing an ankle, then a calf, and now the more daring styles were actually showing a knee! A revolution as well as a revelation.

Tomorrow was Christmas Eve, and the paper featured page after page of gift suggestions. Gerry's shopping was done, and even then the maids were busily wrapping her presents in bright-colored paper. She'd decided on the fur coat for Scotti. Idly she wondered what his gift to her would be. Last year he'd given her emeralds.

Merry Christmas. A killer is loose.

Once the thought had intruded, she made no attempt to drive it away. Her investigating had produced nothing conclusive about 'her' suspect; she could prove Giulio Setti neither guilty nor innocent. Since Mrs. Bukaitis and Beniamino Gigli were now both off the suspects list, Scotti and Gatti-Casazza were helping her by questioning the choristers.

She herself had concentrated on talking to the stagehands, for two reasons. First, she didn't quite trust anything the choristers might have to say; and second, she'd always had good rapport with the Metropolitan's backstage crew. But the stagehands hadn't been able to tell her anything she didn't already know, and none of them could truthfully remember where Setti had been every moment he was in the opera house. And so far the choristers hadn't been any help to Scotti and Gatti. *Scotti and Gatti,* sounded like a vaudeville team.

Oddly, the attempted shooting during *Lucia* had had one beneficial effect. The chorus baritone who'd been shot at told everyone who would listen how his guard had pushed him into a corner at the sound of the first shot and then proceeded to shield his body with his own. This impressed the rest of the choristers, who seemed to realize for the first time that the Met's management truly was trying to protect them. Also, and perhaps more important, the intended victim was a *German* singer, the first ever to be attacked. That convinced the Italian contingent—that is to say, the majority of the choristers—that they were not being singled out for persecution. As a result, the chorus was now more cooperative and better behaved than it had been all year.

But that was the only good thing to come out of so much trouble. Gerry had followed up the lead Emmy Destinn had given her, but it led to nothing. Rosa Ponselle told Gerry that she'd been mistaken about Giulio Setti, that the chorus master had in no way been responsible for the chorus's badgering of her. Since Rosa seemed embarrassed when she made this admission, Gerry was inclined to take her word for it.

All of which left her exactly nowhere. How do you look at three sane-appearing men and decide which one has gone quietly but murderously crazy? Setti still seemed to her the most fragile of the three, the one most likely to break under pressure. And the pressure on Setti was great, had been great since the end of last season. The other two had no such direct threat hanging over their heads; their futures were safe. Gerry found it difficult to think of either of them as a killer; it was too improbable. Quaglia might be a possibility, but Ziegler she dismissed altogether. There was no way that starchy, overly formal man was going to get his hands dirty committing a *murder*. Unthinkable.

But one thing she knew for certain: Setti dreaded nothing so much as a forced retirement. *Me too,* she thought wryly. But there was a difference between them. Setti would hang on as long as he could; Gerry, on the other hand, was repelled at the thought of experiencing what Setti was going through now—the mutterings that it was time to quit, the looks of disappointment, the hints that it might be wise to start thinking of other things. For Gerry, the dread was of unsold seats in the opera house, of desertions from her army of gerryflappers, of the lessening of the demands made on her time and talent. No, that was not for her. She'd come in at the top, and she'd go out at the top.

And it was time; the signs were already beginning to appear.

Gatti had told her that next year she'd have to share to role of Tosca—long an exclusive Geraldine Farrar property—with that Jeritza woman from Vienna. That was the first step in the dethroning process; lord knew she'd seen it happen often enough to other singers.

She still had one more season in her. And she'd make it one to remember! She'd make every single performance stand as a reminder of the glory days that were slipping away from them all. The world had changed so much—there was no center now, no focus. And there seemed to be so many more people now than there were before. Where did they all come from? Where were they going? And what would they do when they got there? The world had changed, and it was going to change even more. The handwriting was on the wall: adapt or die.

One more season—and then what? What kind of life was there for her when she no longer had an opera stage to perform upon? She'd been a star too long to content herself with sitting in a rocking chair and twiddling her thumbs. She liked being a star. She didn't want to give up being a star. Did she have to stop being a star altogether just because her voice was going?

For the past decade David Belasco had been importuning her to star in one of his plays.

"Bella!" she called to the maid. "Get my blue coat and have Albert bring the limousine around front. I'm going out."

On the way to Belasco's theatre it occurred to Gerry that this might not be the best of times to descend upon the producer. David Belasco was having problems of his own; the high priest of the American theatre was under attack by a raucous gang of postwar theatre people for what they called the 'ornate hokum' he produced. Belasco had given over forty years of his life to staging plays better than anyone else in the country, and now the theatre he loved so deeply was turning against him. It angered Gerry and scared her at the same time. It could happen to anyone in the public eye.

The Belasco Theatre on West Forty-fourth Street was the same beehive of activity it had always been. A harried-looking young man told her 'the Governor' was upstairs in his private rooms. Gerry took the stairs to the top floor, where an equally harried-looking middle-aged man ushered her in to The Presence.

And there he sat, enthroned behind the desk mounted on a Ming dais, waiting to receive the reverence due him. "Gerry—what a pleasant surprise!" He rose to greet her. "Here, let me take your coat. Please sit down, my dear, and tell me why I am blessed by a visit from the world's leading soprano—who could be the world's leading actress if she would only place herself in my hands."

She smiled. "Thank you, David. Is now a good time to talk?"

"Anytime you wish to talk, dear lady, is a good time." As courtly as ever. "Allow me to wind up this call and then my time is yours." Only then did she realize he'd been talking on the telephone.

Gerry welcomed a few moments' grace to reorient herself while Belasco talked about a casting problem with whoever was on the other end of the line. It had been six or seven months since she'd last seen her old friend, and she was surprised at how much stouter he'd grown in that time. The hair was all white now, but he still wore a black suit and the reversed collar that gave him the air of priestly authority he so carefully cultivated. The air was heavy with the scent of burning joss sticks and the lighting was dim; the effect was one of a temple where one came to worship. Some things never changed.

"What about the Cornell girl?" Belasco was saying. "She's contracted for one more play."

Gerry looked around. David Belasco's private rooms were legendary, with their labyrinths of shelves and glass cases and alcoves stuffed with art treasures and stage props, everything from suits of armor to antique velours to trinkets worn by the Borgias. But the total effect wasn't quite as colorful as Gerry remembered it, somehow. Many of Belasco's treasures had the slightly coated look things get when they're left in the same place too long. From where she sat, Gerry could see dust on the tops of two of the display cases.

"He may be well-known in England," Belasco said, "but no

one's heard of him here. Explain to him what life in New York can
be like without money. A long-term contract will protect him from
that.''

The beginning of a headache was making itself felt. Gerry
hoped the producer wouldn't expect *her* to sign up for life.

Belasco hung up the phone and made a sound of mild annoyance. ''Sometimes I think I'll never understand this new generation of actors. Here's a man fresh from the London stage, and he
wants to act for the Theatre Guild for a pittance when he can earn
ten times the salary elsewhere! And why? Because the Guild calls
itself an 'art' theatre company! What am *I*—a vegetable dealer?''

''Young people don't always know what they want,'' Gerry
murmured.

''He's not that young—he's thirty. Have you seen the kinds of
plays the Guild has been putting on? They take themselves so seriously—all this heavy soul-searching, this exploration of an 'inner
life', whatever that is! They have no sense of what theatre is
about. People want to be entertained when they come to a play-
house. They want spectacle, melodrama, farce! They don't want to
be—what is the term?—*psychoanalyzed*.''

''That's certainly been true for as long as I can remember,''
Gerry sighed, ''but these are new times, David. Maybe audiences
want something different now.''

''Oh, we all have to keep up with the times,'' he said airily,
''but the basic appeal of the theatre never changes. It must supply
something that is missing in our dreary everyday lives. All this
dark pessimism the new playwrights keep giving us . . . I must say
I find it unwholesome.''

''Have you thought about producing any of the new playwrights? Perhaps you could provide whatever's missing.''

''Impossible, Gerry. I must have something to work with! Have
you heard of a fellow called O'Neill? Well, he is being praised as
the new 'voice' of American theatre. But, my dear, *the man can't
write!* Such wooden dialogue I have never before encountered in
all my years in the theatre! And such gloomy subject matter! No,
the fad for that kind of play is just that—a fad. Mr. O'Neill won't

be around long. You must understand that all this new drama is merely temporary . . . it will pass, it will pass. And when it does, then the theatre can go back to being what it has always been.''

Gerry's headache blossomed. ''What are you planning now?''

''I'm thinking of a French play that should adapt well to the American stage, a contemporary piece called *Tiger Cats*. Two marvelous acting roles—and no preaching! There's no place in the theatre for a pulpit, something the Theatre Guild would do well to remember.'' He blinked at her. ''But my dear, you must forgive me! Here I am rambling on about these upstarts in the theatre when you have a far more serious problem in the opera house. Do the police have any idea of who's responsible for the killings?''

''I don't think so. But there are enough policemen and guards backstage that we're probably as safe as it's possible to be—with a madman in the house. The guards were able to prevent a murder, you know—the last time he tried.''

''So I've been given to understand. And the attacks have all been confined to members of the chorus?''

She nodded. ''Someone has a terrific grudge against choruses. He's mad, of course.''

Belasco leaned back in his chair and steepled his fingers. ''I seem to remember a certain soprano who took it on herself to uncover a killer not too many years ago. And succeeded! Are you by any chance planning a repeat performance, Gerry?''

She smiled wearily. ''I've tried, but it's not the same this time. This time it's ugly and vicious—and sometimes I'm afraid. I *hate* being made to feel afraid!'' She was silent a moment and then muttered, ''Damn him to hell and back!''

He laughed. ''That sounds more like the old Gerry.''

''The problem is,'' she went on, ''I'm pretty sure I know who the killer is. But I have no evidence! And I can't think of any way to find some.''

Belasco sat up straight. ''My dear, you must be careful. Whoever this man is, you must not give him the slightest hint that you have any suspicion he is guilty!''

''Oh, I'm being careful—you can be sure of that! We've had

more than our share of bad luck this year. Gatti was able to keep it out of the newspapers, but someone tried to blow up the Met stage last week.''

''Gerry!'' He was stunned into momentary silence. ''Was anyone hurt?''

''No, the bomb turned out to be a dud. And Scotti caught her before she was able to set it anyway.''

''She?! Her?!''

''Some political fanatic who'd gotten a job at the Met as a scrubwoman. It's a good thing Scotti caught her. Her next bomb might have worked.''

Belasco was visibly shaken, and Gerry immediately wished she hadn't said anything about it. ''But this is dreadful!'' he cried. ''What is happening in the world? How can you bring yourself to go into that place when there is so much danger?''

''Tell me a safe place in the world and I'll go there,'' she said dryly. She was glad she hadn't mentioned that the near-bombing took place during a performance of *Zazà;* that was the opera in which Belasco had directed her and he still had a proprietary interest in it. ''Actually, I think I'm pretty safe at the Met,'' she went on. ''The killer doesn't seem interested in anyone except choristers. It's the standing by and watching it happen without being able to do anything that's getting me down. As to the bombing—well, a bomb can be planted anywhere, can't it? The woman responsible is locked up. She won't be trying again.''

He shook his head. ''Gerry, I think you should get out of that opera house. Let me find a play for you. You'll be safe in my theatre.''

She forced a smile. ''Something like *Tiger Cats*?''

He dismissed *Tiger Cats* with a wave of his hand. ''No, I see you in a period piece. Elegant costumes with long trailing skirts, in a pre-war setting. That is your style.''

I hope not, she thought. Her headache banged away.

''I can promise you you'll never have to appear in one of these heavy-footed new plays,'' Belasco was saying. ''Graceless, clumsy things—where is the magic? Who wants to spend an eve-

"Are we going somewhere after we pick up Rico?" Emmy asked. "Why don't we just stay at his place?"

"Rico says Dorothy gets upset when we talk about the murders."

"She would," Emmy muttered. "Well, it will probably do him good to get out for a while."

"I hope so," Amato said worriedly. "He is ill, Emmy."

"I know."

"I mean he is truly ill, more than he admits. Do you not notice how he is changed?"

"In what way?"

"Think back. When is last time Rico plays a trick on you? When does he last nail one of your props to a table . . . or put flour in pockets of your costume?"

She stared at him. "You're right. It's been so long I can't even remember."

"He is changed."

They rode in silence for a while. Then Emmy said, "He is the one who called this team meeting, isn't he?"

"He says he now is sure Edward Ziegler is the killer."

"And you are just as sure Quaglia is."

Amato sighed. "I am less sure than ever. But Ziegler . . . eh, Emmy, I have to fight a temptation. I am tempted to dismiss Ziegler as suspect simply because he is *Rico's* suspect. I love Rico, but we both know what kind of detective he is."

She laughed shortly. "Unfortunately."

"Twice before he suspects wrong person. That is not good record. So when he says Ziegler is guilty, I think that means Ziegler is *not* guilty. But this is wrong! We must not think this way."

Emmy nodded. "Wouldn't it be ironic if this time he turns out to be right and all the rest of us are wrong?"

"Then you do not think Ziegler is guilty?"

"I don't know, Pasquale. I'm just here to listen to what the two of you have to say."

Caruso had been waiting in the lobby of the Vanderbilt and came bustling out when the limousine pulled up to the curb. His

ning listening to uninteresting, disputatious characters indulging i
class hatred or whatever disagreeable topic happens to be the sub
ject of debate that evening? No, we'll leave that sort of thing to the
Theatre Guild—they do love it so. Hatred and lust and treachery
and insanity, they can all find a home at the Guild. Not to mention
the polemics of that infernally talkative Irishman who has an opinion on everything in the world worth having an opinion about and
even a few that aren't! This is not theatre, this is animated political
tracts . . .'' He was off again.

Gerry concentrated on holding her throbbing head upright and
looking as if she were listening. *Adapt or die.* David Belasco
would never adapt. She'd misunderstood the nature of the schism
in the theatre; she'd thought Belasco had just been the target of
some envious newcomers. But clearly that wasn't the case at all.
Belasco was nearly seventy; it would be unrealistic to expect him
to reject the work of a lifetime in order to embrace the changes
brought about by a world still reeling from the effects of the big-
gest war it had ever fought. There would be no life-after-opera
with David Belasco for her. Not now.

It was too late.

The telephone rang, interrupting Belasco's diatribe. ''Ah, Mor-
ris—we have a problem,'' he said into the mouthpiece. ''We may
have to make some casting changes.''

Taking advantage of the distraction, Gerry picked up her coat
from the chair where Belasco had put it and blew him a goodbye
kiss. He smiled and waved a still-graceful hand.

When she left, he was deep into virtually the same telephone
conversation he'd been having when she arrived.

Pasquale Amato helped Emmy Destinn into the back seat of his
limousine and climbed in after her. The chauffeur closed the door
and went around to get into the driver's seat. ''The Vanderbilt
next, Mr. Amato?''

''*Sì*, the Vanderbilt.'' Amato cranked up the glass partition that
separated the front seat from the back.

eyes were bright and his cheeks had two red spots; he looked either feverish or excited or both. He told Amato's chauffeur to take them for a drive through Central Park and climbed into the back seat. The seat became uncomfortably crowded, since two of the three passengers were on the corpulent side.

Amato moved over to the jump seat and said, "Rico? Do you not feel well?"

"I feel *molto* well!" the tenor boomed. "Never do I feel better!"

Emmy laid a hand against his forehead. "No fever," she confirmed.

Caruso flapped both hands at them. "Do not fuss so! We have important decision to make! I think I now convince you Ziegler is the one who does these terrible things to chorus. But first, there is one little matter to be cleared up. Pasquale, I ask you to find out something. Ziegler, he tells me that at very time someone stabs Teresa Leone, he is talking to Quaglia about substitute musicians in orchestra. Right before *Carmen* begins. Eh, what does Quaglia say? Does it happen the way Ziegler says?"

"Yes and no," Amato replied. "Quaglia says it does happen— but it happens before *Forza,* not *Carmen.* He remembers because the orchestra substitutes have trouble playing the *Forza* 'fate' theme."

"Doesn't it also mean Quaglia has no alibi?" Emmy asked.

"*È vero,* but there is a difference," Amato said reluctantly. "If Ziegler is innocent, he makes simple mistake about which opera. But if Quaglia is guilty, would he not take advantage of Ziegler's mistake to provide himself with alibi? Would he not say yes, he and Ziegler are indeed talking together while poor Teresa Leone is being stabbed?"

"Not if he suspected a trap."

"No trap," Caruso said.

"He does not even stop to think, Emmy," Amato said. "He says, 'Eh, that is *Forza*—Ziegler mixes them up.' "

"He could have been afraid Ziegler would later remember it was

Forza and not *Carmen*," Emmy said stubbornly, "if indeed it was. Then where would he be—backing up a false story?"

Amato shook his head. "Then he could say he too mixes up the operas. No, Emmy, Quaglia is telling the truth. I know because I go into Ziegler's office when he is not there and check payroll records. It was *Forza* that has substitute orchestra members, not *Carmen*."

Caruso laughed delightedly. "Eh, what I tell you, Pasquale? You make good detective!" Then he shivered. "Your windows, Pasquale—are they not rolled all the way up?"

Amato checked. "All limousine windows, they leak a little," he apologized.

Caruso snuggled up closer to Emmy. "Now I have something to tell you." He paused dramatically. "Edward Ziegler is once singer in chorus himself!" He went on to tell his astonished fellow detectives the story he'd heard from his old chorister friend Tommaso. "Eh? What you say now?"

"I say there is more to Edward Ziegler than meets the eye," Emmy remarked. "None of us really knows that man. I wonder what other secrets he's been keeping to himself?"

"It is still not evidence, Rico," Amato complained. "We cannot call a man guilty because he once sang in chorus at another opera house!"

Caruso's eyes were sparkling. "But there is more! Attend. I talk to two choristers who sing with him at Manhattan Opera. They say he pretends not to remember them! One of the choristers, he knows Ziegler well. He says when they are at Manhattan, they eat together, they drink together—it is not possible that Ziegler forgets. Do you not see? *Per dio*, he is *ashamed* he is once chorister!"

Amato was having trouble accepting it. "To tell you true, I begin to think Gerry is right. I think it is maybe Setti."

"Gerry is not on our team!" Caruso cried, indignant that Amato would turn to an outside suspect. "Brr! I am cold. Do you not have rug for the lap, Pasquale?"

"Emmy is sitting on it." Amato held out a hand to steady her as she stood in the moving car to let Caruso pull the lap rug out from under her. While the tenor was wrapping himself up in the rug, Emmy asked Amato what had made him suspicious of Setti.

He shrugged. "He tries to make Quaglia look guilty. Setti tells me a lie. Remember the trouble Quaglia has with chorus at Covent Garden? Setti says Quaglia tries to strangle chorister. I am there at time of trouble and I know it does not happen—you are there too, Emmy, remember?"

She looked at him strangely. "But it did happen, Pasquale. Everyone knew about it."

He stared at her. "*I* do not know about it!"

"Oh, it was just a stupid fight, but Quaglia did get his hands around the other man's neck. Later Quaglia was mortified by the whole thing and apologized to the chorister. Don't you remember all that?"

"No!"

"I am not there," Caruso said apologetically.

Emmy was thinking. "Pasquale, could that have been the time you were gone for three or four days? Didn't you substitute for someone at the Paris Opéra at the last minute?"

Amato's mouth dropped open. "*Cielo!* I forget! *Sì*, I do go to Opéra then!"

"So you missed it," she nodded.

"Quaglia, he apologizes?" Caruso asked with interest.

"The only time I've ever heard him apologize," Emmy said. "That was even more startling than the fight."

"So Setti is not lying after all," Amato mused. "And Quaglia does fight with chorister. So perhaps he. . . ?"

"No, it is not Quaglia," Caruso said as if explaining things to a slow child. "It is Edward Ziegler. He hides things about himself . . . I think he hides a dark nature behind proper outside. He lies about alibi. He loses control for one little moment and wishes choristers dead. What happens when he loses control for longer period of time? He makes the wish come true. Ziegler is the killer."

Amato didn't say anything. Emmy leaned forward and touched

him on the knee. "It makes sense, Pasquale. You must agree it makes sense."

The baritone sighed heavily. "*Io sono contento.* I agree. It is Ziegler." He and Emmy exchanged a wry look while Caruso crowed a little. "Now what? The other team says Setti. So what do we do?"

"So we convince them they are wrong," Caruso said reasonably. "And then when we are all agreed, we go see Captain O'Halloran."

"And say what?" Emmy asked. "Do we say we have decided Edward Ziegler is guilty and will you go out and arrest him, please? Do you think he'll do it?"

"But he must!" Caruso exclaimed.

"On our command? Without evidence? He'll throw us out of the police station!"

"But, but, but—" Caruso sputtered.

"She is right, Rico," Amato said. "Do you say we do *not* go to the captain, Emmy?"

"No, we have to go to the police. But with more than we have now." She grunted. "If we haven't found any evidence by now, it's not likely we're ever going to. We need something else."

"*Non capisco.*"

"We need a plan."

They all fell silent. Only Amato's chauffeur was enjoying the wintry beauty of Central Park as the three singers in the back concentrated hard on thinking up a foolproof plan to catch a killer.

◻ **11** ◻ The name on the hotel register was Giovanni Fabbro—John Smith—and the hotel was the St. Regis. A room on the fourteenth floor had been rented for the afternoon; that was the only way three worried-looking men could be sure they'd not be interrupted by ringing telephones, threatening police, or snooping singers. They needed privacy.

The three of them shrugged out of their winter coats and looked for a place to sit down. There were only two chairs, so Giulio Setti sat on the side of the bed; the other two pulled the chairs around to face him.

"Are you sure no one followed you here?" Edward Ziegler asked. The other two said they didn't think so. "I know I was followed when I left the opera house, but I think I was able to lose him."

"I take roundabout route," Setti said. "I see no one when I enter hotel."

Alessandro Quaglia grunted agreement. "We are being watched, it is true. The police captain, he expects one of us to give himself away. This is why he tells *three* of us we are 'prime' suspect! *Cielo!* He knows nothing, that captain. He guesses."

The corners of Ziegler's mouth turned down. "He also seems to be laboring under the assumption that we'd all stop talking to one another once he'd pasted the label of 'suspect' on us. The first thing I did was tell Mr. Gatti."

Setti was shaking. "Is shameful! Shameful! Never in my life do I break the laws . . . and this captain says I *kill* my choristers!"

"He knows nothing, he guesses," Quaglia repeated impatiently. "He thinks he must do something, but he does not know what. So he picks three to bully—one, two, three, *we* three."

"You mean like drawing names out of a hat?" Ziegler asked. "I don't think he'd go that far, Maestro—I'm sure he thinks he has some reason to suspect us."

"He grasps at the straws. He even confronts me with foolish fight I have years ago. That is his reason? Pah!"

"Well, whether he has a reason or not, the point is what are we going to do about it?"

"*Is* there something to do?" Quaglia asked.

Setti smiled wryly. "Perhaps Mr. Ziegler means we should find real killer ourselves? Already enough detectives try, I think."

"That wasn't what I meant," Ziegler said. "I meant we should fine some way to protect ourselves. Frankly, I'm more worried about myself right now than I am about the choristers."

"I also," Setti agreed. "I do not wish to die in prison."

"How does one prove innocence?" Quaglia mused. "It is difficult, no? Perhaps impossible. I think about this ever since Captain O'Halloran points finger of accusation at me."

Ziegler nodded. "The only solution I could think of was that each of us should provide an alibi for one of the others—but it's too late for that now. We've already made our statements to the police, and nobody is going to believe it if all three of us suddenly remember we were with the others during the times the murders were committed."

"Yes, that only makes them more suspicious," Setti said. "Perhaps it is too late to protect ourselves against what is already done. But it is not too late to protect ourselves against what may still happen, *non è vero?*"

"What do you mean?"

"I mean I think we see more killings. The man who fires the gun backstage, he does not stop because he misses the last time. He tries again, do you not agree? And when he tries, if we have alibi for *that* time—then the captain must decide we are innocent men."

Quaglia raised two eyebrows at the chorus master. "Eh, Mr. Setti, I think you may have something there!"

Ziegler was staring at the other two in distaste. "What a *morbid* suggestion! We . . . sit back and wait for someone to die! Then within minutes after the killer strikes again, we three rush together and agree upon an alibi before we talk to the police? Bah!"

Quaglia looked annoyed. "We are in no position to be so particular, Mr. Ziegler. Or do you have other reason for objecting?"

"What are you implying?" Ziegler asked coldly.

"You say no too quickly. You do not even think about it."

"I don't have to think about it to know the suggestion is distasteful to me! And you were pretty quick with your insinuation, Maestro!"

"You make useless suggestion and then object when good one is—"

"*Cessiate!*" Setti commanded so sharply that the other two obeyed out of surprise. "Now is not time to quarrel! If we start the accusations among ourselves, we perhaps do exactly what the captain of police wants us to do, yes? Each must believe in innocence of other two! Without question!"

"He's right," Ziegler muttered. "My apologies, Maestro. I went too far."

"I too," Quaglia replied, pulling out a handkerchief and patting his forehead. "*Mi dispiace*—forgive me, I speak in haste."

"If Mr. Ziegler objects to arrangement of alibi after, uh, next killing," Setti suggested, "perhaps is other way. We do not *make up* alibi. We have true one!"

"Ever the diplomat, Mr. Setti," Ziegler murmured. "But how do we manage an alibi before the fact? We don't know when the next killing will take place."

Setti held his hands out, palms up. "We stay together from now on. Each is alibi for other two."

Quaglia snorted. "You both accompany me to podium when I conduct? *Impossibile.*"

"That is exception," Setti said. "You have entire orchestra for alibi then. And audience!"

But Ziegler was shaking his head. "Too many problems, Mr. Setti. We all have our jobs to do. You can't cancel your various rehearsals to sit in my office to watch me, and I can't let my work go to attend all your rehearsals. It's a good idea, but it's just not practical."

Setti sighed. "Then we lie?"

The other two were silent a moment. Then Ziegler said, "Very well, I consent. We lie."

"Momento." Quaglia was tapping a finger on the armrest of the chair to help him think better. "Why do we not hire bodyguards for ourselves?"

Setti frowned. "You think we are in danger?"

Ziegler said, "I suppose we could always see something that might make us a threat to the killer." Then his face lit up. "Ah! I see. The *bodyguard* would provide the alibi!"

"Precisamente," Quaglia nodded. "It is expense worth undertaking."

Setti looked dubious. "The bodyguard, he must be with us *all* the time?"

"I know, I don't much cherish the idea of a stranger looking over my shoulder twenty-four hours a day," Ziegler said. "But if it will get us out from under this cloud of suspicion, I don't see that there's any choice. Unless you have a better suggestion?"

"Perhaps a bodyguard for only the times we are in opera house?"

"No," Quaglia said. "It must be all the time or it will mean nothing. Alibi for only part of time is no alibi at all."

Setti shifted his weight on the bed. "I do not like it."

"Nobody *likes* it, Mr. Setti," Ziegler said with a touch of asperity. "You may do as you wish. I intend to hire a bodyguard as soon as we leave this hotel."

Quaglia agreed. "The sooner we tend to this business, the better."

Setti threw up his hands. "Eh, I too, then. I cannot be only one *without* alibi! But we must wait two days, no? Tomorrow is Christmas Eve!"

"Bodyguards work on holidays too," Ziegler said. "There's no need to wait. It won't be forever, Mr. Setti. As morbid as it sounds, all we have to do is prove ourselves innocent of *one* killing—and Captain O'Halloran will no longer be able to tell us we are his 'prime' suspects."

"I know nothing of this," Setti complained. "Where does one go to hire the bodyguard?"

"Pinkerton's, I suppose. That's where Mr. Gatti got the choristers' guards."

"Shall we go?" Quaglia asked. "I think it is better we leave separately."

"Yes," Ziegler agreed. "We still have to be careful."

Setti was the first to go. When the chorus master had wrapped up against the winter cold and departed, Quaglia said, "He does not want bodyguard with him."

"I noticed," Ziegler answered shortly. "I'll go next."

Quaglia waited ten minutes and then took the elevator down to the St. Regis lobby. He did not notice, as the other two had not noticed before him, when a police detective rose noiselessly from his chair in the lobby and followed him out.

Christmas Eve.

A working day for the Metropolitan Opera Company. The matinee performance was Puccini's *Madame Butterfly*, starring Geraldine Farrar and Antonio Scotti, conducted by Alessandro Quaglia. Scheduled for the evening was Halévy's *La Juive*, starring Enrico Caruso and conducted by Artur Bodanzky. More fun than waiting up for Santa.

But little of the Christmas spirit was in evidence backstage. Singers and crews alike had but one thought in mind: *He'll try again today*. Captain O'Halloran thought so too. He checked and rechecked the placement of his men, and noted with approval the way the private guards were never more than an arm's length away from the choristers they were protecting. Satisfied at last, O'Halloran went up to Geraldine Farrar's dressing room.

He barely recognized her. She'd immersed herself so completely in the costume, make-up, and physical mannerisms of the character she was singing that it would be easy to mistake her for a real Oriental woman. Already she was walking with Butterfly's mincing little steps, thinking herself into the proper frame of mind. "You look beautiful!" O'Halloran blurted out.

Gerry wasn't so far sunk into Butterfly's character that she couldn't acknowledge a compliment. "Thank you, Captain. Do you suppose you could ask your men and the guards to leave a path open by the stage exits? It's sometimes so crowded we can't get through!"

"I've already told them—Mr. Gatti explained the problem. I came up to tell you not to linger downstairs, Miss Farrar. Once you're off the stage, come straight back up here."

"Gladly." She shuddered. "I never thought I'd see the day when I'd be glad to get away from the opera stage, but . . ."

O'Halloran smiled sadly. "I know."

Just then Emmy Destinn stuck her head through the dressing-room doorway. "Captain O'Halloran? Is everything all right?"

"So far," he answered.

"Hello, Emmy," Gerry said resignedly. "Couldn't stay away?"

Emmy held up a handful of letters. "I came to pick up my mail, so I thought I'd stop back to wish you and Toto luck. It certainly is tense downstairs."

"Everyone's thinking the killer will try again today."

"Or tomorrow," Emmy said, sitting down and opening one of her letters, "when I sing." A double bill was scheduled for Christmas Day as well, *Mefistofele* in the afternoon and *Aïda* at night. "You might as well move into the opera house, Captain."

"I practically have," he groaned. "My wife's threatening to divorce me. Did you happen to see Mr. Gatti anywhere, Miss Destinnova?"

"I am here," said the general manager's voice behind him. "You wish to speak with me, Captain?"

"Ah, there you are. I just wanted to tell you I've repositioned some of my men and I think you should know where they are."

"The greenroom might be a good place to talk," Gerry said pointedly.

Gatti smiled. "We leave our Butterfly to prepare, yes? Come."

Emmy looked up from the letter she was reading. "Bad news, Gerry. Your frog died."

Gerry ignored her.

Out in the hallway, O'Halloran said, "Did I hear her correctly? Miss Farrar's *frog* died?"

Gatti sighed. "In her house in Prague, Emmy has big aquarium filled with frogs, all croaking in different keys. She names each one after different prima donna."

O'Halloran chuckled. "Must win her a lot of friends." He went on to explain the changes he'd made in the placement of his men. "I can't think of any place I've overlooked, can you?"

"No, you are very thorough, Captain. I can think of nothing more to be done," Gatti said gloomily.

"I shouldn't worry too much, Mr. Gatti," O'Halloran said cautiously. "If he tries anything today, we're bound to get him."

Gatti wanted to stop on the men's side a moment to calm any pre-performance jitters that might be in evidence, and then he and O'Halloran went back down to the stage level. Setti and Quaglia were there, with their newly hired bodyguards in tow.

"Is Mr. Ziegler here?" O'Halloran asked. "I haven't seen him."

"He is here somewhere," Gatti said. "I look for him too." He plodded off in search of his assistant.

"Do you think today is day you catch our killer, Captain?" a familiar baritone voice asked.

"May be, Mr. Amato." O'Halloran looked at the other man's street clothes. "Aren't you going to be late? You're not in costume."

"Today I do not sing—not until Monday. Today I try to stay home and not think of what happens here, but . . ." He spread his hands apologetically.

O'Halloran grunted. "Emmy Destinn's here for the same reason. Only she pretended to come in for her mail. You folks just don't listen, do you?"

"Too much is at stake, Captain," Amato replied soberly. "We cannot wait passively for someone to die."

O'Halloran could understand that. Amato went with him as he made one final round of the police. Upstage left was crowded, where the women's chorus gathered to make its entrance, all the singers made up to look like fragile porcelain dolls. A cordon of guards surrounded them.

"Toto, *do* stop telling me not to be nervous," Geraldine Farrar's voice floated nervously over the backstage hubbub. "Believe me, it doesn't help!"

"I say not one word more, *carissima*," Scotti said soothingly. "Now I must go." He blew her a kiss and made his way back to the other side of the stage.

Gerry took her place at the head of the women's chorus. "Remember, do not rush," she said to the choristers. "I want our first *Butterfly* to be right. Some of you got too close during rehearsal— if you step on my train, I'll fall! Stay back."

One of the women near the front said it was hard to stay back when the people behind you were pushing as hard as they could.

"Oh, I can't believe this!" Gerry cried. "Please, all of you— cooperate! Don't push—you'll all get on the stage. Go *slowly*."

"She *is* nervous, isn't she?" O'Halloran remarked to Amato.

"It is the entrance," Amato explained. "It makes all the women nervous, every time. They must glide on, you understand, with steps so small the audience is not supposed to see the feet move. And they have to enter over that bridge." He pointed to the narrow structure that began just offstage and arched to the center of the stage. "There is no room for mistake. If one woman slips, all the others are thrown off and the procession is ruined."

"Does that ever happen?"

"About half the time," Amato nodded.

Ziegler came up to them, followed by his bodyguard. "Have you seen Mr. Gatti?"

"I think he's off somewhere looking for you," O'Halloran said. Ziegler made a *tsk*ing sound and hurried away.

"Captain O'Halloran," Amato said, "that man who follows Mr. Ziegler—he is one of your policemen?"

"He's a private bodyguard. Mr. Ziegler hired him himself."

Amato inhaled quickly and then exchanged a long look with the police captain. But before he could say anything, someone called *"Silenzio!"*—it was time to begin.

The tenor and several singers playing servants opened the opera. Before long Scotti entered, and the men had the stage to themselves for a while. Then the moment for Butterfly's entrance arrived, an aria plus chorus that required much concentration aside from that devoted to the placement of feet. Fifty-one nervous women took deep breaths and began.

O'Halloran was enchanted. Never before had he seen or heard anything so *delicately* exciting; he promised himself that as soon as he could, he'd come back and see it all properly, from out front. He watched Geraldine Farrar turn herself into a different person as she successfully negotiated the bridge and stepped down on to the stage. About a dozen choristers stepped down behind her.

C-r-a-a-a-c-k.

"What is that?" Amato cried.

O'Halloran knew immediately. "Get off the bridge!" he yelled, elbowing his way through the guards. "Get off—now!"

Only a few of the choristers heard him. They glanced offstage uncertainly.

C-r-a-a-a-a-c-c-k. The bridge swayed.

"Jump!" O'Halloran roared to make himself heard above the music. "Keep them off!" he yelled to the men guarding the choristers at the end of the line who'd not yet stepped on the bridge. The guards obeyed instantly, pulling the women back out of the way. Now Amato and the other guards joined O'Halloran in yelling at the women onstage to jump off the bridge.

Five or six of them did. O'Halloran broke the fall of one woman and they tumbled unhurt to the floor. Amato jumped up and grabbed the ankle of a woman still on the bridge, forcing her to leap off. Then came the loudest *c-r-r-a-a-a-a-a-c-c-k-k* of them all, followed by the chilling sound of terrified women screaming as the bridge swayed one more time—and collapsed.

The splitting timbers made sounds like rifle shots as the bridge and its remaining passengers crashed to the stage floor. O'Halloran could hear the audience screaming and Gatti and Ziegler both yelling for someone to close the curtain. The captain jumped to his feet and started tossing aside the bridge debris to get to the women caught in it. The curtain closed.

The screaming stopped, to be replaced by the sobs and moans of the injured women. The debris was quickly cleared away and O'Halloran made a hasty count of the injured. "Call for an ambulance," he instructed one of his men. "Tell them we'll need more than one—we have at least fourteen injured here." The man nodded acknowledgment and hurried away. "But no deaths," O'Halloran added half to himself. Miracle of miracles.

Suddenly two fists grabbed his lapels and O'Halloran felt himself being shaken like a schoolboy. *"When do you stop this madman?"* The normally placid Antonio Scotti deafened O'Halloran with his rage. "Why do you not catch him? *Why do you permit this to happen?"*

"Easy, Mr. Scotti. We're all upset—"

"Upset? Do you say 'upset'? *Sì,* I think it is safe to say we are upset! Do your men not watch? Do they not see someone tampers with the bridge? Captain, *Gerry is first one across that bridge!"*

O'Halloran understood. "Mr. Scotti," he said quietly, "if you'll let go of me and let me do my job—"

Scotti released him with a shove. "Do your job? When do you ever do your job? All this time, and you do nothing! *Nothing!"*

The captain felt his face and neck turning red, but his anger died as quickly as it had arisen. All around him men and women were shouting instructions, checking on one another. O'Halloran turned away from Scotti without answering—because the baritone was right. All his time and all his effort, and he had accomplished exactly nothing.

Gatti-Casazza had quickly decided that when you fall off an opera, the best thing to do is climb right back on again; the performance would continue. He'd sent Ziegler out in front of the closed curtain to make the appropriate announcement to the worried and frightened audience and ordered the remains of the bridge cleared off the stage. The ambulances arrived and carried away the injured choristers. Quaglia decided at what point in the score the performance would resume and informed Setti and the soloists accordingly. Geraldine Farrar was strangely quiet throughout the uproar.

Setti gathered up those uninjured choristers whose costumes had not been ruined and gave them their instructions on how to finish the act. A few of the women protested at being expected to go on after what had just happened, but the majority of them were grimly determined to finish the performance. In fact, a new resolve was making itself evident on the stage. The bodyguards hired to protect the choristers sensed a change taking place in their charges: anger was replacing fear. The collapsing bridge had been the final straw.

That change in attitude was not limited to the chorus; it was as if the entire company united in a quiet determination not to let themselves be defeated by one man's madness. That new determination was reflected in the performance; Geraldine Farrar sang with a deliberation and a crispness that the audience had never heard from her in that particular role. This time the lushly romantic love duet that ended the act had an edge to it that didn't really belong there but that somehow satisfied all the same.

The Metropolitan Opera had had enough.

Backstage, O'Halloran and his men sifted through the bridge debris and found what looked like saw marks at the beginnings of the worst splits in the bridge's wooden underpinnings. With the help of the stagehands they reconstructed the bridge's layout and determined the sawing had been done high up on the braces, in spots that would be concealed by the bridge's side overhang. The wooden braces had not been sawed all the way through; they'd been left strong enough to support the weight of a few people but not the twenty or so who were on the bridge when it collapsed.

O'Halloran was at his wit's end. How in the world could anyone crawl under the bridge and saw away at the top of the braces without being seen or heard? The men assigned to watch the stage swore vehemently that no one had gone near the bridge since the time the stagehands had moved it into place that morning. So the damage was done *before* the bridge had been moved on to the stage?

It was Gatti-Casazza who solved that mystery for him. "It comes directly from the warehouse," he said in answer to O'Halloran's question. "This is first *Butterfly* of season, and the bridge is not used since last spring. *Sfortunatamente,* anyone could break into warehouse and saw up the scenery—at any time, I think."

O'Halloran rubbed his chin. "Because there are no police guarding the warehouse." It was the first he'd heard that the Metropolitan Opera House did not have the room to store scenery. "Did you have a break-in at your warehouse recently?"

"The warehouse is only leased," Gatti answered darkly. "The owner, he could simply replace lock or whatever is broken and never tell us. He lies to me before, about other things."

"What about the scenery for tonight's opera?"

"It is stacked outside on Seventh Avenue, waiting until *Butterfly* scenery is removed."

O'Halloran immediately teamed some of his men with a few of the stagehands and ordered them to check every inch of the scenery waiting outside in the snow. The captain was hoping the killer would be satisfied with the spectacular destruction he'd already caused that day and not go for a double-header, but he couldn't afford to gamble on it. And tomorrow was Christmas Day; he might just strike again then.

Madame Butterfly finished to strong applause. Emmy Destinn had meant to leave after the first act, but she was still there. Pasquale Amato was still there. Those two joined Antonio Scotti and Geraldine Farrar in the latter's private dressing room where they agreed to stay through the dinner hour. No one was hungry.

Quaglia, Gatti, and Ziegler left, the latter two to return within the hour. Setti stayed with the choristers. On stage, the world of the Orient gave way to fifteenth-century France as the carefully inspected first-act scenery for *La Juive* was moved into place. The cast for that night's opera began to arrive.

And immediately precipitated a new crisis. Enrico Caruso was ill.

He'd come in walking like an old man, holding his side and shuddering. He was accompanied by his wife, his physician, and two valets, all of them fussing over the tenor and none of them really helping. Caruso made the painful climb up the stairs to his dressing room, where he collapsed into a chair, breathing heavily.

Dorothy Caruso immediately went in search of any of her husband's friends who might be there and found four of them in Geraldine Farrar's dressing room. "You must talk to him!" she pleaded. "I didn't want him to come in tonight, but he wouldn't listen to me! You know how stubborn he is."

"But what is it?" Amato asked, alarmed. "What is wrong?"

"Oh, the doctor is still saying neuralgia, but it has to be something more serious than that! And on top of everything, he caught a chill when he went out motoring in Central Park with you and Emmy. He should be home in bed—or in a hospital!"

The four singers rushed to Caruso's dressing room and were shocked to find the tenor's face contorted with pain. But he simply refused to listen when they told him to go home.

"But this is foolishness, Rico!" Scotti protested. "No one expects you to sing when you are hurting so!"

"Eh, but they do, Toto, they do! All those people in audience, they choose to spend their Christmas Eve listening to me. I cannot disappoint them."

"They will understand," Gerry said.

"No, no—I sing, I sing."

"Is Gatti back yet?" Emmy asked. "He should know about this."

"Do not bother Mr. Gatti," Caruso gasped. "I sing."

Amato became angry. "Rico, you are killing yourself! What you do is not intelligent. *One* performance—it is not that important!"

"To me, it is important. The doctor, he tapes up my side so I can sing. *Mi faccia questo piacere*—go. All of you, please go. The make-up, it takes long time to put on. We must start."

Reluctantly, the others withdrew. Amato drew Dorothy outside with them. "You must call in consultant. A specialist. Do not listen to this doctor any longer."

She nodded. "I've already made up my mind to do just that. If we can get him through tonight, I'll call someone in tomorrow."

By the time Gatti-Casazza returned to the opera house, Caruso was feeling better. His step was firmer and he no longer kept pressing his hand against his side. Under the heavy make-up and curly beard of the elderly Jewish goldsmith he was playing that night, he didn't even look ill. The role of Eléazar in *La Juive* was one Caruso loved, even though he had to sing it in French. He'd hired an actor from the Lower East Side Yiddish theatre to coach him in the part. He was sure of himself in the role. It was Christmas Eve. He wanted to sing.

The Carusos had known nothing of the bridge that had collapsed during *Butterfly*. "Oh, this is dreadful, dreadful!" Dorothy cried to Geraldine Farrar when she heard. "Fourteen of them hurt? How seriously?"

"We've been told there was no permanent damage," Gerry said. "A few broken bones, some sprained ankles and knees, and a lot of scrapes and bruises. Quite painful for them—but nothing that won't heal in time."

"Thank heaven for that! I wondered why everyone was looking so grim when we came in. It just goes on and on, doesn't it? Will it never stop?"

"It will stop," Gerry promised her.

That evening's audience knew all about the bridge that had collapsed during the matinee performance—but they hadn't actually seen it happen, and that made all the difference. This was a different crowd tonight, one full of energy and holiday spirit and high expectations for the elaborate combination of stage spectacle, ballet, and great singing that had been promised them. Join your friends at the Metropolitan! Spend Christmas Eve with your favorite tenor! Happy holidays to everyone!

Maestro Artur Bodanzky took his place on the podium. The opera began, and within minutes Caruso entered. The listeners backstage were relieved to hear that the tenor's tone was firm and his articulation clear. He didn't *sound* like a sick man.

At first.

La Juive has five long acts and the role of Eléazar is an especially demanding one. From the orchestra pit Maestro Bodanzky scented danger and hurried backstage during the first intermission to suggest cuts in the lengthy opera. Caruso refused.

The performance resumed. Captain O'Halloran roamed the backstage area, frankly worried. This opera of which O'Halloran had never heard was a busy one in terms of the choristers' appearances. They were courtiers, servants, soldiers, Jews at the Feast of the Passover, Christian townspeople. There was some doubling, involving lightning-fast costume changes. O'Halloran was amazed at Giulio Setti, who was able to keep track of who was singing what in which scene without any kind of written list to help him. One hundred forty people, and Setti knew where every one of them was supposed to be! One hundred forty minus fourteen, O'Halloran reminded himself.

He paused for a moment to listen to Caruso. The man was a marvel; O'Halloran didn't know the music, but Caruso made him feel as if he did. The captain asked Edward Ziegler what *La Juive* was about and was told it was an opera about anti-Semitism, performed on this most Christian of holidays.

O'Halloran's men had checked the scenery for all six stage settings the opera called for and had found nothing. There was a platform that a few of the choristers and soloists would be standing on in the last act, but O'Halloran himself had made sure no one had sawed away at the platform's underpinnings. Not that it was likely, he thought; the maniac they were looking for didn't like to repeat himself.

He caught sight of that afternoon's stars peering anxiously out toward the stage. He walked quietly up behind Geraldine Farrar and Antonio Scotti and said, "Why are you still here? Why didn't you go home?"

Gerry waved her hands vaguely. "I'm not really sure, Captain. We just felt we ought to stay. And now Caruso is sick—"

"He is?" O'Halloran was surprised. "He sounds wonderful to me."

Scotti said, "But while he is sounding wonderful, he is feeling terrible. The doctor, he should not let him sing."

O'Halloran looked out on the stage and saw Caruso leaning heavily on one of the choristers. But although the body was suddenly weak, the voice was as strong and glorious as ever.

"What a tremendous effort he's putting into this performance," Gerry murmured softly. "Foolish, foolish . . . but heroic, too."

The performance proceeded without incident. Every time Caruso came off the stage he was bathed in sweat and his face twisted in pain. The stairs to the dressing-room level were too much for him, so he made a costume change in the wings—assisted by four friends, two valets, and one wife. Then they all stood agonizing while the tenor went back out to enchant his Christmas Eve audience; Gerry wondered if they knew what a generous gift he was giving them. His fourth-act aria *Rachel, quand du Seigneur* brought down the house. They knew.

"One more act," Amato said to O'Halloran. "Just one."

"Will he make it?"

The baritone's mouth twisted into a wry grin. "*Sì,* he will make it. The fool."

On stage for the last act, Caruso sang with an intensity and poignancy that had his backstage listeners all holding their breaths. The act was to end with Eléazar mounting the platform from which he would be hurled to a grisly death in a boiling cauldron. Gatti-Casazza arranged for the curtain to close just as Caruso made his way toward the platform so he wouldn't have to climb the steps. Timing was all-important.

It worked. The curtain closed just as the tenor reached the foot of the steps. The chorus sang its final phrases from behind the closed curtain; the orchestra played the chords that ended the opera.

And Caruso collapsed.

□ **12** □ The Christmas Day matinee performance of *Mefistofele* was marred by nothing more serious than a late lighting cue, but the police turned up something interesting right before the evening performance was about to begin. Fifty of the men choristers were scheduled to carry long poles to which brightly colored banners were attached. But eight of the poles had been booby-trapped; someone had driven carpet tacks through them, the sharp points sticking out just far enough to tear up the pole-carrier's hands. Emmy Destinn gazed calmly at the banner pole Captain O'Halloran was holding gingerly, said "Good for you," and marched out on the stage to sing a flawless *Aïda*. The Triumphal Scene was performed with slightly fewer banners than usual that night.

O'Halloran wondered if their elusive madman had crossed over into still another stage of his dementia; no one had died when the *Butterfly* bridge collapsed, and murder-by-carpet-tack was ridiculous. Did he, whoever he was, now want to maim instead of kill? O'Halloran decided it was more likely that he'd simply been prevented from killing by all the protection surrounding the choristers. The carpet tacks were just a mean-spirited gesture, a reminder that 'he' was still there.

When O'Halloran showed up backstage Monday night for *I Pagliacci,* he was disappointed to learn that Caruso had cancelled.

"He has pleurisy," Gatti-Casazza told him. "His wife calls in consulting physician who says Enrico's illness is misdiagnosed." Gatti pulled at his beard meditatively. "Dorothy is right all along . . . she says that Enrico's doctors do not know what is wrong."

"I'm surely sorry to hear that," O'Halloran said. "He'll be all right, won't he?"

"*Sì,* in time. When he collapses after *La Juive*—that frightens him, you understand. Now he listens. The new physician says rest, Dorothy says rest, I say rest—he rests. It is hard for Enrico to admit he is ill, but now he faces truth. He comes back in, eh, perhaps a month? It is better this way."

O'Halloran nodded. "Yeah, it won't hurt him to take it easy for a while. He'll be missed while he's gone, though."

Gatti made a sound halfway between a grunt and a groan. "Tonight much of audience demands the money back."

Pasquale Amato spotted them talking and hurried over; he was dressed and made up for the role of Tonio in the evening's production and looked as if he had something on his mind. He nodded to O'Halloran and said to Gatti, "Do you ask him?"

"I ask him now," Gatti answered. He cleared his throat. "Captain O'Halloran, a few of us wish to speak to you privately—away from the opera house and all its distractions. In your office, perhaps?"

Uh-huh, O'Halloran thought. "And just who, exactly, are 'a few of us'?"

"We two," Amato said. "Scotti. Gerry and Emmy."

"What a surprise. Look, I'm kind of busy now—"

"Please, Captain," Amato said urgently. "We do not ask unless it is important."

"I suppose you've got it all figured out who the killer is."

Amato hesitated, and then said, "We know it is one of two."

"Oh, you do, do you? Well, well—isn't that interesting! Are you going to tell me or do you want me to guess?"

"We tell you tomorrow morning," Gatti said firmly. "In your office. At ten-thirty." Then he remembered his authority did not extend to giving orders to the New York Police Department and added, "If that is satisfactory with you."

"And if it isn't you'll keep pestering me until I do listen to you," O'Halloran sighed. "All right, Mr. Gatti, Mr. Amato—ten-thirty tomorrow morning. My office."

"*Grazie,* Captain," Gatti said.

"*Bene!*" Amato smiled. "That is big relief. Now I sing better tonight because of you! Are you not happy to make contribution to opera?"

"I'm ecstatic," O'Halloran growled.

On Tuesday morning, December 28, heavy snow fell from a dark New York sky as if determined to bury the entire city before nightfall. All the overhead lights inside the police station had been turned on, but they weren't strong enough to disperse all the shadows. Faces looked jaundiced.

Captain O'Halloran had turned up the radiator in his office as far as it would go. Then he'd had to steal three extra chairs from other offices. Now five luminaries from the Metropolitan Opera sat in a semicircle facing his desk. There would have been six of them, O'Halloran was informed, but one of their number was still ill. Antonio Scotti was wearing an expensive-looking fur coat that he refused to take off in spite of the steam heat hissing behind him.

Geraldine Farrar said, "We've decided that the only way to catch this madman is to set a trap for him. There is no other way. We must create a situation in which he'll think he has a clear shot at one of the choristers and consequently reveal himself."

"Isn't that a trifle dangerous for the chorister?" O'Halloran muttered dryly. "I'll tell you right off, I'm not agreeing to any plan that uses a civilian as bait."

"We won't have to, Captain. All we have to do is make it *appear* as if the chorister is alone. We'll need the cooperation of one of the bodyguards—"

"Hold it. You've thought up your plan with somebody specific in mind, haven't you? What if you're wrong?"

"Then we'll know, won't we?" Emmy Destinn said complacently. "Besides, the plan isn't all that specific."

O'Halloran stared at them a moment. "Mr. Amato, last night you told me you knew the killer was one of two people. What two?"

"One of them is Edward Ziegler," Amato said slowly.

"And the other is Giulio Setti," Gerry Farrar added quickly.

O'Halloran felt a brief flash of amusement; the Great Detectives were not of one mind? "Why those two?"

Gatti-Casazza spoke for the first time. "Perhaps is best if we tell you what we do. We divide into two teams, and each team narrows list of suspects down to one person. But then is trouble—neither team convinces the other to change their minds. All along we plan to come to you when we think we know who killer is, but now . . ." He spread his hands apologetically. "Now we come with two names. One is my assistant, whom I trust. Other is friend of twenty years," he finished sadly.

"Which one do you suspect, Mr. Gatti?"

"Setti," he said heavily. "My old friend Setti."

O'Halloran was curious. "Who's Mr. Caruso's choice?"

"Ziegler," Scotti said, "but he is wrong. It is Setti."

"No, it *isn't*," Emmy said waspishly.

Eventually O'Halloran got it straightened out. Caruso, Destinn, and Amato suspected Edward Ziegler; Farrar, Scotti, and Gatti-Casazza suspected Giulio Setti. *And neither of them would be my choice,* the captain thought to himself. "Something puzzles me," he said aloud. "Miss Farrar, perhaps you could explain to me how a man of Giulio Setti's size and age could succeed in hanging a man who was bigger and younger and stronger than himself."

She took a deep breath. "I've given that a great deal of thought, and the only possible explanation is that Setti did *not* hang him."

"You mean we've got two murderers?"

"No, just one. I mean that poor man really did hang himself. It was exactly what everybody first thought it was—a suicide. Setti couldn't have done it, you're right. But we've been assuming all along that five deaths meant five murders. Couldn't only four of them be murders? And one a suicide?"

Emmy smirked. "Don't change your opinion, just explain away the fact."

"Emmy, stop that! Captain, it is possible, isn't it?"

"At this point I'm beginning to think anything is possible. As long as you're here," he added with a show of reluctance, "you might as well tell me about this trap you want to set up. How would it work?"

In outline it was simple, but the details would require a great deal of working out. One of the bodyguards would be primed to rush around in a state of near-panic, claiming he'd 'lost' the chorister he was supposed to be guarding. Then one of the Great Detectives would casually mention to another one—within earshot of the suspects—that he/she saw the chorister in question going into the wardrobe room or the properties room or some other semi-isolated spot to be selected later. Concealed inside said semi-isolated spot would be several of Captain O'Halloran's men, waiting to see who took the bait.

"Suppose someone did show up," O'Halloran objected. "He could just say he was helping to look for the missing chorister."

"Not if he carries gun or knife or bully club," Scotti said.

"Billy club," Gerry corrected. "Although 'bully' might be more accurate, come to think of it."

"But what if he's *not* carrying a weapon?" O'Halloran persisted.

"Then we'll have to think of something else," Emmy said. "But as long as there's a chance it might work, how will it hurt to try?"

"Seems awfully vague to me," the captain muttered. "He could even explain away the weapon—he could say he'd started carrying it back when the first murder was committed. Self-protection. It wouldn't prove anything."

The others were silent a moment. Then Gerry said, "You mean we have to catch him *in the act.*"

"Afraid so. And that means civilian bait, and that means no dice."

"No . . . dice?" Scotti repeated.

"He means we can't do it, Toto," Emmy sighed. "Captain, would you be willing to use one of your policemen as bait?"

"How?"

"He could take the place of the chorister."

"That won't work, Emmy," Gerry objected. "Setti knows every one of the choristers and knows them well. Ziegler probably knows most of them too," she added in belated acknowledgment of the other team's candidate.

"Can they identify them from the back?" Emmy asked. "When they're in costume and make-up?"

They all thought about that a while, and then the Metropolitan contingent was smiling broadly at the police captain. "Well, Captain?" Gatti asked. "What do you say?"

"It will take one whale of a lot of planning," he grumbled. "So many details to be taken care of!"

"I help you," Gatti offered. "Planning and details, that is my métier."

O'Halloran tried to make his voice casual as he asked when Quaglia was conducting next.

"Well, he's conducting *Tosca* on Thursday," Gerry said. "I don't know if he's scheduled before then."

"No, he is not," Gatti said. "*Tristan* and Bodanzky Wednesday, *Tosca* and Quaglia Thursday."

Then it hit Gerry. "Quaglia!" she cried excitedly, jumping out of her chair. "You suspect Quaglia!"

O'Halloran was annoyed. "Now, Miss Farrar, I didn't say that."

"Yes, you did! You wouldn't want to know when Quaglia was conducting if you didn't suspect him! You want him to be there when we spring the trap! Come on, Captain—admit it!"

"I just don't think he should be ruled out, that's all."

That satisfied her. She sat back down and said to Scotti, "He suspects Quaglia."

Amato rose and took a couple of steps toward O'Halloran's desk. "At one time I too suspect Quaglia," he told the captain in a tone of confidence-sharing, "but then I change my mind. Let me tell you why." He started on an involved explanation that the others were constantly interrupting and contradicting until O'Halloran finally yelled for quiet. "I want you to tell me exactly why you suspect these two men, but one at a time, please. Mr. Gatti, you start."

They all took turns telling him what they'd done and what they'd found out and why they had settled on the assistant manager and the chorus master. O'Halloran was surprised to learn that Ziegler had once sung in the chorus of another opera company; that was something his own investigation had not turned up. But on reflection he decided it meant little; Quaglia was still his candidate.

"Eh, I think of something," Scotti said. "If we try Thursday— *Tosca*, it is not big chorus opera."

"That's right," Gerry added, surprised she hadn't thought of it herself. "Only a limited chorus, and most of them go home after the first act."

"*Most* of them?" O'Halloran asked.

"A few appear in Act Two," Scotti explained. "And four or five men are needed to play prison guards in last act."

"That's good! The fewer people around, the better. But there'll still be four or five choristers around at the end of the opera?"

"Six, precisely," Gatti said.

O'Halloran leaned back in his chair and closed his eyes, thinking. He'd long since come to the conclusion on his own that the only way to stop the killer was to catch him in the process of attacking a victim; normal investigatory techniques weren't going to reveal the name of the killer in this case. But O'Halloran hadn't been able to think of how to go about it without using a chorister as bait; he couldn't endanger a civilian's life, even though doing so might save other lives. But the Met people's plan had possibilities. Spread the story that one of the choristers was separated from his bodyguard and then substitute one of his own men for the ostensibly missing singer—it just might work.

Emmy got tired of waiting and said, "Well, Captain? Are you with us?"

O'Halloran wished she hadn't put it just that way. "*If* we can work out a feasible plan, yes." He waited until the cheering had stopped and then went on, "I want the men who'll be taking the risks in on the planning. I want to make sure that every one of *you* knows exactly what you're doing. I want to see not only that the danger is minimal but also that the only ones exposed to it are police."

"You want a lot, Captain," Emmy complained. "But I for one don't mind letting someone else take all the risks."

"We understand the kind of man we hunt, Captain," Gatti said a little more tactfully. "I know you sometimes think we are crazy people—but we are not foolish."

Crazy but not foolish. *A man could do worse,* O'Halloran thought. "All right. Wait here until I get my men—and then we'll get to work on the plan. We've got a big job cut out for us."

"What is going on?" Beniamino Gigli demanded. "I know something is going on. I insist you tell me what is going on!"

"Why, whatever do you mean?" Geraldine Farrar said uneasily.

"You and Gatti-Casazza and Scotti, you whisper together and you exchange the *looks* that say you know something I do not know."

"Oh dear. We'll have to put a stop to *that.*"

"And Emmy Destinn and Pasquale Amato—why are they here? They do not sing tonight."

"They frequently listen from backstage."

"But not tonight," Gigli growled. "They too whisper and say I-know-something with the eyes. You tell me now what happens."

Gerry went *tsk-tsk.* "It's supposed to be a secret. If I tell you, will you promise not to repeat it to anyone?"

"What is it?"

"Do you give me your word?"

"*Sì, sì*—I promise. Now tell me."

"Well, we're planning a surprise party for Mr. Setti."

He blinked. "Oh, is that all." He turned on his heel and marched away.

Gerry let out a big breath. Gigli was singing the tenor role in *Tosca,* and he'd been in the opera house only fifteen minutes before he caught on to the fact that something was afoot. She'd have to warn the others.

She found Gatti-Casazza and Pasquale Amato on the stage level; their heads were together and they were whispering up a storm. "Oh, *there* you are!" Gerry trilled and sailed up to them with what she hoped was an open and honest demeanor. Quickly she related her little interchange with Gigli and warned them they were giving the game away. Then she laughed gaily. "Laugh!" she commanded between clenched teeth. Amato managed a convincing laugh, but the best Gatti could come up with was a *humph-humph* sound. Gerry glanced around, but no one seemed to be paying more attention than usual.

"Perhaps is best we do not talk at all," Amato said. "Or at least no more than necessary."

"Pasquale, will you tell the others?" Gerry asked. "I've got to start getting ready."

They separated. Amato found Emmy and Scotti and filled them in, and thereafter the five conspirators avoided one another with a determination that was, if anything, more obvious than their earlier huddling together.

A polite knock sounded on Gerry's dressing-room door. It was Alessandro Quaglia, up to his old trick of imposing last-minute instructions on the soloists. His bodyguard peeked over his shoulder. "Tonight we take your entrance a little faster—only *un poco*," Quaglia said. "The last *Tosca,* the entrance is too slow. It drags."

"There was nothing wrong with the entrance," she said sharply. Why was he always meddling with tempi? She suspected it was simply the easiest way he could think of to bedevil the singers.

"But you wish dynamic entrance, do you not? Last time is . . ." He waggled a hand to show lack of enchantment.

"Maestro Quaglia, could I persuade you to go over to the men's side and pester them instead of me? I'm really not up to this tonight."

Quaglia's face darkened; he left without a word. *Now that wasn't very gracious of me,* Gerry told herself. Quaglia might be O'Halloran's suspect, but he certainly wasn't *hers.* "Maestro!" she called after him. "Get him, please, will you?" she asked the bodyguard.

Quaglia came back. "Yes?"

"Very well, we'll do it your way, if you're convinced the entrance is draggy. Only not *too* fast—I want to be able to get the words out!"

He smiled at her. "Do not worry, Miss Farrar. We find tempo that pleases both of us."

Quaglia then followed Gerry's suggestion and went over to the men's side; he informed Gigli of Tosca's speeded-up entrance, since the tenor was on stage at the time. "Also, I feel we rush the first-act aria, do you not agree?"

"No, I do not agree. I sing it as I sing in rehearsal."

"Come now, Mr. Gigli, surely you have the breath to hold the notes a little longer?"

Gigli turned red. "I have breath enough to blow you out of dressing room!" he shouted. "Always you meddle—you speed Gerry up, you slow me down! Why you make these changes *now*?"

"Because first act is too much the same!" Quaglia shouted back. "We need to vary tempi! *She* agrees—why can you not be like her?"

Gigli laughed. "That is not what you say last week!"

Quaglia muttered something and left the tenor alone, both of them wondering exactly how fast or how slow the aria would be sung that evening. On the steps down to the stage level, the Maestro and his bodyguard ran into Edward Ziegler and *his* bodyguard. Ziegler took one look at Quaglia's face and asked what the matter was. "Eh, Gigli," Quaglia said. "He is worse prima donna than Farrar!"

"Impossible," Ziegler said, straight-faced.

"Tonight she is angel. *He* is devil."

Ziegler didn't offer to have a word with the tenor, knowing better than to get mixed up in musical disputes. "Is Mr. Scotti up here?"

Quaglia didn't know. He and his shadow continued on down while Ziegler made for Scotti's dressing room. The baritone was warming up while he applied his make-up.

"Mr. Scotti? Forgive me for interrupting," Ziegler said, "but there's been a change. The chorister you have some stage business with in the second act—it'll be a different man tonight, and he's never rehearsed the scene. He knows what to do, but you might have to do a little last-minute adjusting."

Scotti found this only mildly interesting. "What happens to regular chorister? Is he ill?"

"He showed up drunk. I fired him."

The baritone paused in the act of lining his left eye. "That seems drastic. Perhaps he sings better when he is drunk."

"Not likely," Ziegler said dryly.

Scotti turned from his mirror to face Ziegler directly. "Why do *you* fire this drunken chorister? Is that not Mr. Setti's job?"

"Not this time. Well, now that you know about it, I'll leave you to get on with your preparations." He left. The bodyguard gave Scotti a stern look and followed his employer.

Scotti turned back to his mirror, where one made-up eye and one natural one stared out at him. He sat thinking a moment about what Ziegler had just told him.

The other eye could wait. He got up and hurried down the stairs to the stage level. One of the stagehands pointed him toward where Setti stood talking to two of the choristers, their three bodyguards only a few feet away. Scotti motioned him aside.

"Yes, Mr. Scotti? Is something wrong?" the chorus master asked.

"Mr. Ziegler, he tells me of chorister who shows up drunk."

"Eh, sad business. He is no longer with us."

"But why does Mr. Ziegler fire him and not you?"

Setti shrugged. "We have trouble with this man before. I tell Mr. Ziegler, give him one more chance. If he comes in drunk again, you can fire him. Why you ask? He is friend of yours?"

Scotti grinned sheepishly. "I do not even know his name."

"Mr. Scotti, do you know you are wearing only one eye?"

"My eye!" Scotti slapped his hand over the wrong one and hurried away.

Setti was wondering what that was all about when he caught sight of Emmy Destinn peeking around a stage curtain. "Do you hear?" he asked her.

"I do not eavesdrop," she replied indignantly.

"Of course not," he said, "but I wonder why Mr. Scotti takes such interest in our departed chorister."

"He said he didn't even know his name."

"Yet he wants to know why he is fired."

That's not what he asked you, Emmy thought. "I suppose we're all concerned about anything that involves choristers these days," she said. "I shouldn't worry about it if I were you, Mr. Setti." She drifted away casually.

As soon as Setti turned back to the choristers, Emmy made a beeline for Gatti-Casazza. When she'd gotten his attention by poking a finger between his shoulder blades, he muttered, "We are not to talk together, do you not remember?"

"Do you know anything about the chorister who was just replaced?" she asked, ignoring his objection.

Quickly he grabbed her elbow and steered her five feet away, although no one was within hearing distance. "He is not really dismissed, but Setti and Ziegler do not know that. The chorister, he only pretends to be drunk."

"But why?"

"Because I ask him. It is Captain O'Halloran's idea. The chorister who replaces the 'drunk' one, he looks very much like Captain O'Halloran's man—the one who is 'bait'? The captain says substitution will be easier, with this other chorister."

"Ah! I see." Then she scowled. "Why did O'Halloran tell you and not the rest of us?"

Gatti made a what-can-I-say gesture. "Perhaps he thinks the fewer who know, the better? I do not know. Eh, it is almost time for curtain." He looked around; Gigli was in place. "Where is Gerry?"

"Here she is."

Gerry was just then coming down the stairs. She shot a dark look toward Gatti and Emmy when she saw them huddling together; they got the message and edged away from each other. Satisfied, Gerry moved to her place by the upstage entrance, passing Quaglia and his bodyguard on the way.

They were having an argument. "I've got to be in the orchestra pit," the bodyguard stated flatly. "How can I protect you from back here?"

"No, no—*impossibile*. You stay backstage."

"I don't like it, the way you'll be exposed out there—your back to the audience and all. Any one of 'em could take a shot at you!"

"It is not *audience* I worry about, *imbecille!*"

Gerry tuned them out; she tuned out everything except the opera that was about to start. The men did most of the work in the first act, which was fairly evenly divided between them. The tenor's idealism would gradually yield to the baritone's villainy, with the soprano acting as the bridge between them. But Act II—ah, Act II was *hers*.

The opera started. Before long Gigli launched into his aria, about half a beat ahead of the orchestra. But they got together after only a few more phrases and finished in fine style. Gigli sang a short scene with one of the supporting soloists and then her cue came. *Faster,* Gerry reminded herself and made her entrance— only to find that Quaglia was conducting at exactly the same tempo they'd rehearsed. *Blast the man.*

She'd been on stage only a few minutes when she looked into the orchestra pit and saw the back of somebody's head, not what one usually saw when looking down from the stage. A man was sitting in a chair pushed right up against the front of the stage, facing out toward the audience. He was not wearing evening attire nor was he holding a musical instrument. Gerry stared at the man's bald spot and realized Quaglia's bodyguard had gotten his own way.

She finished her duet with Gigli and left the stage. Scotti was standing there, waiting to make his entrance. She blew him a kiss and hurried over to where her maid was holding make-up and mir- ror; Gerry had to go back on again shortly. The choristers were gathering in place, with Setti fussing over them. Everything was normal.

And it stayed normal. They finished the act to thunderous ap- plause and the three principals hurried back upstairs to change their costumes. Quaglia came up and stuck his head in Gerry's dressing room long enough to ask if she didn't think the faster tempo made the entrance work better; she screeched at him to get out. Scotti changed quickly and hurried back down to find the stage manager and complain that the closing curtain had been slow. Gigli came down and snarled at Ziegler that the tenor didn't have enough to do in the second act, as if it were the assistant manager's fault. Everything was still normal.

The second act never lasted long enough to suit Gerry. She sang her big aria, killed Scotti (after whispering an apology first), and performed the pantomime action that ended the act. Backstage, there was more elbow room now; most of the choristers had left. Setti was riding herd on the few who would be needed in the last act.

Amato was waiting in Scotti's dressing room. "I do not see Captain O'Halloran anywhere, Toto! Mr. Gatti says he is here—but where?"

"He conceals himself deliberately, perhaps?" Scotti suggested. "Eh, my chest hurts." He rubbed the spot. "Gerry stabs hard tonight."

"The plan, it will not work," Amato worried. "It cannot work!"

"*Perchè non?* We think of everything, no?"

"The bodyguards! We do not think of Ziegler's and Setti's bodyguards when we make our plan! Quaglia's either. How can the killer walk into trap with someone watching his every move? How does he get rid of bodyguard?"

Scotti didn't know. He changed into street clothes and the two baritones went downstairs to listen to the final act. They stopped short when they spotted both their suspects and O'Halloran's as well with their heads together. What did the three of them have to say to one another? Amato and Scotti eased as close to the group as they could.

They were complaining about their bodyguards, who were all hovering nearby. "When we agree to this, I do not understand how bad it is,'' Quaglia was saying, mopping his forehead with a white handkerchief. "Mine is like *leech*."

"I know what you mean," Ziegler commiserated. "Mine keeps stepping on my heels."

"I try to tell you," Setti said placidly, "but you do not listen." The other two men glared at him.

"Are we not free of suspicion now?" Quaglia asked. "Our bodyguards are witnesses we do nothing to *Butterfly* bridge."

"Not precisely," Ziegler said. "I understand the police are saying the bridge could have been sabotaged long before the day of the performance."

Setti snorted. "They say that to excuse themselves, because they do not watch carefully enough."

"You could be right." Ziegler glanced over at his bodyguard. "They are there *all* the time, aren't they? I don't see how the choristers stand it."

"I think the choristers like them," Quaglia sighed. "Bodyguards make them feel important."

"Eh, do you have enough of this . . . protection?" Setti asked.

Ziegler and Quaglia exchanged a look. "Maybe it wasn't such a good idea," the former said. The conductor nodded.

"I am willing to discharge my bodyguard," Setti offered, "but only if you two do the same. At the same time?"

"Let's do it right now," Ziegler said through clenched teeth and strode purposefully toward the guards. The other two followed.

"*That* is how killer gets rid of bodyguard," Scotti said to Amato.

Amato watched the three suspects giving the bodyguards their walking papers. "One of those men," he said, "one of those three, he kills five people and injures others. It is hard to believe."

"*Sì.* Who would think Mr. Setti could do such terrible things?"

"No," Amato said. "Not Setti."

"Not Ziegler."

"Not *now,*" hissed Emmy Destinn, coming up behind them. "Keep your voices down."

Act III of *Tosca* was under way. Scotti made his way around to the back of the set and sat down on the mattress where Gerry would land when she leaped off the parapet to end the opera. He sat there half listening to the music and half thinking about Caruso. He was worried about his old friend and wished he could be there right then. That very night they were going to catch a killer, and Caruso would miss it. It didn't seem right.

At least he thought they were going to catch a killer. If all three suspects divested themselves of their bodyguards, what could go wrong? *A lot of things,* he thought glumly.

He looked up to see Gatti-Casazza picking his way through the backstage obstacle course. Gatti reached the mattress and bent over to say in a low voice, "Captain O'Halloran, he wishes us to stay in vicinity of stage once the plan is in operation. All five of us."

"Why?"

"For safety. Out in open, well-lighted place, you understand."

Scotti nodded. "Where is he? No one sees the captain but you."

Gatti waited until Gerry finished a high note she was holding. "He spends first two acts in my office. He says killer is more likely to take chances if he thinks head policeman is not here. But now the captain is in place. All is ready."

"Bene."

Gatti continued on to the left side of the stage, where Emmy stood watching and listening to Gerry's performance with an intensity that made him wary. Tosca had once been one of Emmy's best roles, but in later years Geraldine Farrar had pretty much made it her private property. Gerry's Tosca sold out the house; Emmy's did not. Gatti still scheduled Emmy in the role once in a while, just to keep her happy. But *Tosca* was Gerry's opera. "Emmy?"

She started, not having seen him come up. "Oh. I was caught up in the duet."

"It goes well tonight, do you not think?"

"I was just then thinking of what Maria Jeritza would do with the role when she gets here." Then Emmy gave him a smile of pure pleasure.

Gatti backed off. His decision that Geraldine Farrar would share the role with the new soprano from Vienna had not been without repercussions; even Antonio Scotti had bawled him out for it. But here was Emmy Destinn openly gloating . . .

The opera eventually drew to a close. Gerry leaped off the parapet, to be greeted with a congratulatory hug from Scotti. She ran around to the side of the stage and waited while Gigli milked his first curtain call, then went out and milked hers even longer. The gerryflappers in the audience were doing their part; even backstage the chant of *Ger-ee, Ger-ee* came through clearly. More curtain calls, with Gerry and Gigli clasping hands and beaming artificially at each other. Then it was over.

Gerry dashed upstairs and changed clothes faster than she'd ever changed before in her life. The auditorium was still emptying when the stage crew started striking the set. The scenery flats were stacked by the Seventh Avenue double doors, ready to be carted off to the warehouse the next morning. Quaglia was making a congratulatory round of the singers. The orchestra musicians had already left; they were always the first ones out.

Edward Ziegler wanted to go home himself, but Gatti-Casazza kept him there talking about one inconsequential detail after another. *Can't we take care of this tomorrow?* the assistant manager thought. But on Gatti talked—until he broke off in midsentence at the sight of a man still in the costume of a prison guard walking bent-over across the stage.

"Tony?" Gatti called. "Do you hurt your back?"

The man straightened up; and although he'd known what to expect, Gatti felt his stomach do a flip-flop when he looked into the face of the police detective who was replacing the chorister. "Oh, hello, Mr. Gatti," the false Tony said. "I lost my ring here tonight. I can't find it anywhere."

Gatti had met O'Halloran's man earlier in the day, and he'd been impressed by his resemblance to one of the choristers, a tenor named Tony Spinelli. With the addition of costume, bushy eyebrows, and drooping mustache, the police detective could fool almost anyone except Setti. The real chorister had been whisked out of the opera house the minute the performance had ended. "Your ring?" Gatti said. "Ask the stage manager if he finds it."

"I already did. That was my father's ring, Mr. Gatti," the man said worriedly.

"Perhaps the greenroom?"

"That was the first place I looked. But maybe I'd better look again." He smiled unhappily and moved away.

One more thing. "Where is your bodyguard?" Gatti called.

The false Tony looked around vaguely. "Oh, he's back there somewhere." He left the stage.

Ziegler was looking at Gatti curiously. "Do you know all the choristers by name?"

Gatti said no. "I try to remember as many as I can, but there are so many."

"Aren't there just," Ziegler remarked dryly.

Gatti asked Ziegler to find Tony's bodyguard before he left. Ziegler said he would.

Emmy Destinn was holding Giulio Setti in conversation, almost by force. She'd just about run out of things to say and was afraid she was going to lose him when a bodyguard started running across the stage toward them, his big feet hitting the floor noisily.

He skidded to a stop, breathing heavily. "Tony Spinelli," he gasped. "Have you seen him?"

"Not since end of performance," Setti said.

"Who?" Emmy asked innocently.

"One of the choristers," Setti explained. "Do you—"

"What about you, miss?" the bodyguard interrupted. "Bushy eyebrows, droopy mustache. Have you seen him?"

"I don't think so. Oh—you are supposed to be guarding him?" Emmy asked anxiously. "You haven't lost him, have you?" The bodyguard dashed away without answering. *Good performance,* Emmy thought. "Mr. Setti, you don't suppose—"

"Now, now, Miss Destinn, do not be alarmed," Setti said reassuringly. "It is probably nothing."

"Something is wrong?" Antonio Scotti asked, strolling up right on cue. "You look upset, Emmy."

"One of the bodyguards can't find the chorister he's assigned to protect!"

"*Cielo!* Who is missing?"

"Tony somebody," Emmy said.

"Spinelli," Setti added. "Tony Spinelli."

"Eh, Tony—that is all right, then," Scotti smiled. "I just see him go into greenroom. Nothing is wrong."

"Thank heavens," Emmy sighed.

"*Grazie a Dio,*" Setti nodded.

Scotti pulled out a pocket watch. "I wonder what takes Gerry so long. Come, Emmy—we go make her hurry. Good night, Mr. Setti."

"*Buona notte,*" the chorus master smiled.

I should never have taken the time to change, Geraldine Farrar thought as she locked the dressing-room door and told her maid to go home. She hurried down the stairs just in time to see Alessandro Quaglia, wearing his hat and coat, on his way out. "Maestro!" she called. "Have you seen Scotti?"

"I think he is on other side of stage," Quaglia said, strolling toward her. "Let me congratulate you again on an exquisite performance. Sometimes I think you are perfect Tosca!"

Only sometimes? "Thank you, Maestro. I think it went well tonight." She stood chatting easily about the evening's performance, keeping one eye on the stage. Before long she saw what she was waiting for. "Look—one of the choristers is still in costume."

Quaglia turned just in time to see the false Tony leaving the stage. "The wardrobe mistress will not like that."

"Yes—everybody else seems to have gone home. Maestro, there's something I'd like to try in the second act." She started explaining a complicated bit of stage business that would require a slower tempo from the orchestra if she was to work it all in.

Quaglia was dubious, as she'd hoped. They argued amiably about the new business, Gerry all the time thinking: *Where is Amato?*

There he was, hurrying toward them now. "Gerry, Maestro—do you hear? One of the choristers is missing!"

"Missing!" Gerry exclaimed. "What do you mean?"

"His bodyguard cannot find him. That means he is missing, no?"

"Oh dear! You don't think . . ."

"Something happens to him?" Quaglia finished for her.

"No one knows. He—wait, here is bodyguard now." The guard came running toward them, looking a question at Amato. "Not here," the baritone said.

"Did you try the chorus dressing room?" Gerry asked.

Fourth floor. The bodyguard dashed up the stairs.

"Which chorister is it?" Quaglia asked.

"Tony Spinelli," Amato said.

"Tony Spinelli," Gerry repeated. "I don't believe I know which one he is." Then she 'remembered'. "Maestro! That chorister still in costume we just saw—could that have been Tony Spinelli?"

Quaglia spread his hands. "I do not see his face."

"What did he look like?" Amato asked.

"Long droopy mustache," Gerry said. "Eyebrows that stick out a mile."

"That is Tony!" Amato cried jubilantly. "Where is he?"

"Why, when we saw him he was headed in the direction of the greenroom, wouldn't you say, Maestro?"

"In that direction, yes."

Amato laughed in well-simulated relief. "Then nothing is wrong." He looked up the stairway after the departed bodyguard. "Eh, they find each other eventually."

"Such carelessness!" Quaglia harrumphed. "Let the guard worry a while—perhaps he learns to pay better attention."

Amato offered his arm to Gerry. "Since we have no crisis to keep us here, let us find Toto and depart this place. You are ready?"

"I am ready." She took his arm and smiled at Quaglia. "We'll talk again later, Maestro."

His only answer was a smile and a bow.

"You don't suppose," Emmy Destinn asked, "that we are the only people left in this entire opera house, do you?"

She knew they weren't, but the other four understood what she meant. There was something depressing about an opera house after its audience had left. The work lights were on, illuminating the stage, but the wings and the auditorium were in shadow. The five of them stood obediently on the stage, just where Captain O'Halloran had told them to wait.

Scotti said, "Earlier I wish Rico can be here. Now I am not so sure." Gerry reached out and took his hand.

The tension was making Gatti-Casazza perspire. "What if he suspects a trap?" he asked, keeping his voice low. "What if he does not go to greenroom?"

But it was Amato who asked the question they were all really thinking. "Which one?" he said softly.

Which one.

They waited. Before long Gerry began to get the fidgets. "I don't imagine it would hurt if one of us went to take a look—"

"*No!*" four voices cried in unison.

"Well, it was just a suggestion," Gerry said.

They waited some more. What was in actuality only a few minutes seemed like an hour, so they all jumped when they heard a faint *pop!* from the direction of the greenroom. They looked at one another uncertainly.

"What do you suppose that was?" Emmy asked.

"It is not gunshot, surely?" Scotti murmured.

"No," Amato agreed. "Not loud enough."

"I am not so sure," Gatti worried. "At this distance . . . with greenroom door closed . . ."

The four singers exchanged a long look—and then as one dashed away toward the greenroom, leaving Gatti-Casazza standing alone in the middle of the stage. "The captain says wait here!" he called after them.

Amato reached the greenroom first, but hesitated when he saw the door was closed. "What do we do? Do we go in?"

"No, better not," Scotti cautioned. "We do not know what happens inside."

"Well, we can't just stand here wringing our hands," Gerry said. "We ought to do something!"

"Knock?" Emmy suggested. The other three stared at her.

"Something is wrong," a new voice said. "I know it—something is wrong!"

The singers turned to see Giulio Setti watching them anxiously. "Mr. Setti!" Gerry cried. "What are you doing here?"

His eyebrows shot up. "I am not supposed to be here?"

"You're supposed to be in—I mean, well, uh," she finished lamely.

"I hear something that could be pistol shot," the chorus master said. "Do you not hear it?"

"Yes, Mr. Setti, we hear it," Amato said. "We are wondering what to do."

Gerry and Scotti exchanged an embarrassed look. "We are wrong," the baritone said softly. She nodded and turned away, ashamed.

"Wrong about what?" Setti wanted to know.

"We are not sure it is gunshot," Amato interjected smoothly. "It is so faint, no?"

"True," Setti admitted.

"What else could it be?" Emmy asked.

Just then the greenroom door opened and one of O'Halloran's men stuck his head out. "Huh. The captain said it would be you folks making all that racket. He wants you to wait for him on the stage—he'll be with you shortly."

"For heaven's sake, tell us!" Gerry cried. "Did you get him?"

The man grinned sourly. "Yeah, we got 'im." He closed the door.

A cry of relief went up that startled Setti, who was still in the dark. "What is it? What happens?"

"You come back to the stage with us, Mr. Setti," Scotti said, "and we explain."

When they reached the stage, Gatti-Casazza was still standing there in dignified solitude. When he caught sight of Setti surrounded by his fellow detectives, he blanched. But then he realized that no policemen were holding the chorus master's arms. "Setti!" he cried. "What are you doing here?"

"That is second time someone asks me that," Setti complained—and was startled when his old friend of twenty years flung both arms around him in a giant bear hug.

Once it was explained to Setti that the police had just captured the chorus-killer, he became speechless. He couldn't even ask questions; his mouth just kept opening and shutting, opening and shutting. The rest of them, on the other hand, couldn't stop talking.

"I wonder why that shot was fired?" Emmy said. "Do you suppose that policeman was hurt—the one who was acting as bait?"

"Oh, I do not think of that!" Gatti gasped. "I hope he is all right!"

Amato said, "I think he is not hurt. The policeman in green-room who tells us to come back to stage, he would say, do you not think? Or they send for ambulance."

Scotti smiled wryly at Gerry. "Rico, he will not let us forget our mistake."

"I know," she groaned. "We'll never hear the end of it."

Then a voice spoke loudly out of the shadow at the side of the stage. "I would greatly appreciate it if someone would kindly explain to me what this is all about." Edward Ziegler stepped into the light and strode toward them. "Captain O'Halloran told me to wait here with you. Wait for what?"

There was a moment of stunned silence, and then Amato gasped, "Mr. Ziegler! You are here!"

Ziegler stopped, held his arms out, and looked down at himself. "As you say, I am here. Why is that so startling? From the expressions on your faces, I would judge that you expected me to be elsewhere? I repeat, will someone kindly explain to me what this is all about?"

"Quaglia," Emmy said breathlessly. "It's Quaglia."

"Qua-gli-a," Gatti repeated slowly, as if he had never heard the name before.

Scotti grimaced. "Captain O'Halloran was right."

"Right about what?" Ziegler asked testily. "And what's all this about Quaglia?"

Amato explained. "Maestro Quaglia, he . . . he is one who kills the choristers."

Ziegler was shocked. "What utter *balderdash*."

"No, it isn't," said Gerry. "Quaglia is the killer."

"But he can't be!"

Gerry sighed. "He can, and he is."

"I don't believe it!"

"Better listen to the lady," Captain O'Halloran said, walking out on to the stage. "It was Quaglia—he was the one we were looking for. And there's something more. I don't know how to tell you this, so I'll just say it straight out. He's dead."

On this night of shocks, that was perhaps the worst one. Setti was the first to recover his voice. "You shoot him?"

"No, sir, he shot himself," O'Halloran said. "With a Derringer only this big." He measured a distance with his thumb and forefinger. "When he saw he'd been caught in the act, he put a bullet in his brain. That's why I didn't want any of you coming into the greenroom. It's not a pretty sight."

Gerry shuddered. "I was so sure he couldn't have done it."

Gatti asked, "Your man, Captain—the one who pretends to be Tony Spinelli? He is unhurt?"

"Tony Spinelli?" Setti and Ziegler said together.

"The real Tony Spinelli is at home safe and sound," O'Halloran told the two ex-suspects. "One of my men, Sergeant Rossi, impersonated him. It was a set-up, to draw the killer to the green-room. And Sergeant Rossi is fine—not a scratch on him."

"He is a brave man," Emmy murmured.

"We were able to stop Quaglia in time," O'Halloran went on. "Two other men and I were hiding in the greenroom and we jumped him—just as he was going for Sergeant Rossi. With this." He reached into his pocket and pulled out a length of wire to which wooden handles had been attached at each end.

"A garrote?" Amato gasped.

O'Halloran nodded. "A garrote for the chorister and a Derringer for himself—if needed. The minute he knew we had him, he pulled out that little gun and held it to his head and shot himself." O'Halloran shook his head. "I've never seen anything like it. He didn't hesitate *one second*—as if he'd been prepared for this all along."

"Perhaps he wants to die," Scotti suggested.

"Maybe. I don't know. All I do know is that that man stopped thinking straight a long time ago. Lord knows when he went off the deep end, but somewhere along the line he made the chorus a scapegoat for everything he hated. He'd probably convinced him-self that he was just doling out punishment—punishment that was deserved, I mean."

Gerry's eyes were fixed on the garrote. "He . . . he was carry-ing that thing all the time I was talking to him?"

"I don't understand," Ziegler said plaintively. "It was *Quaglia's* idea that the three of us hire bodyguards—why would he want a bodyguard around? A guard would prevent his getting to any more of the choristers. It *was* Quaglia's idea, wasn't it, Mr. Setti?"

"*Sì,*" the chorus master agreed. "I remember clearly, in hotel room . . . and this is *before* bridge in *Butterfly* breaks down!"

"He'd already rigged the bridge to collapse by then," O'Hal-loran explained. "Mr. Gatti told me that bridge had been in the warehouse since last spring—he could have done it anytime. As for those bodyguards, well, you didn't hang on to them long, did you?''

Setti frowned. ''I think *I* am one who suggests we get rid of bodyguards—not Quaglia.''

''Doesn't matter. He knew you two would get sick of having them around sooner or later. Just as a matter of curiosity—when you did decide to get rid of the bodyguards, who brought the subject up?''

Setti and Ziegler exchanged a look. ''Quaglia,'' they said heavily.

O'Halloran nodded. ''There you are.''

Pasquale Amato suddenly whirled on Emmy Destinn. ''I *say* it is Quaglia—and you talk me out of it!'' She shrugged helplessly.

''I, too, think it is Quaglia,'' Setti announced to the stage at large. ''At one time.''

That was the signal for everyone to start talking at once. O'Halloran found himself bombarded not only with questions but with opinions as well. Ziegler was angry once he realized he'd been manipulated by a killer, but Setti was inclined to take a what's-done-is-done view.

Scotti watched the two of them talking and said to Gerry, ''We do those two decent men a great injustice, *carissima*.''

''I know,'' she said sadly. ''I've been thinking the same thing. I don't know about you, Toto, but I'm thoroughly ashamed of myself.'' She waited until the hubbub began to die down a little and then went over to the police captain. ''Well, O'Halloran, you win this one.'' She held out a hand. ''Congratulations.''

He took her hand, not knowing whether to shake it or kiss it; he compromised by just holding it. ''I have a nice little lecture prepared about amateur detectives who meddle in police matters.''

She shook her head. ''You won't have to deliver it—I've learned my lesson. I think we all have. We ended up accusing two innocent men, and that is unforgivable. You won't have to worry about us anymore, Captain. This was our swan song.''

O'Halloran was surprised by the note of finality in her voice. He released her hand and wished her a happy New Year.

"New Year's—yes, it's almost here, isn't it? Have a happy one yourself, Captain." She smiled and went back to Scotti.

Suddenly everyone was talked out. They would all have more to say about the night's events, repeatedly and at great length, but they would say it later. Now they wanted silence. As if on cue, they departed *en masse*—Geraldine Farrar, Antonio Scotti, Pasquale Amato, Emmy Destinn, Edward Ziegler, Giulio Setti.

Only Gatti-Casazza remained, waiting until the police had removed Alessandro Quaglia's body. He shook Captain O'Halloran's hand, telling him he had two lifetime seats at the Metropolitan Opera whenever he wanted them. The captain and his men left.

Gatti turned out the worklights in the now-empty opera house. Only the regular night watchman was there—no more police, no bodyguards. The bodyguards' salaries alone would guarantee that they'd finish the season in the red. And there was no way to measure the loss of five lives. The Metropolitan had paid a high price for survival.

But in two more days a new year begins, Gatti thought. A new year is starting, Jeritza is coming, a new season is waiting to be planned. New productions, new excitement.

"We survive," Gatti said aloud, and went home.

EPILOGUE

Caruso's appearance in *La Juive* on Christmas Eve of 1920 was his last performance; he died the following year. It was the beginning of the end of the Metropolitan Opera's "Golden Age".

Geraldine Farrar kept her word and retired at the end of the next season. She lived a full and active life, attaining *grande dame* status in her old age. She never remarried. Emmy Destinn left the Met at about the same time, even though her vocal powers were at their peak; she simply quit. She went back to Prague, married somebody, and never set foot on an opera stage again.

Pasquale Amato taught in New Orleans for a few years and then returned to New York as a vocal coach. Gatti-Casazza stayed on as the Met's general manager until 1935. Antonio Scotti put all his money into a touring opera company and went bankrupt; he spent his final years living on handouts from friends.

The Metropolitan continues.